The Turning Tides of Us

Lise Gold

Edited by Debbie McGowan

Cover design by Lise Gold Books

The heart has its reasons which reason knows not.

— Blaise Pascal

Prologue

Cormoran Island rises from the Mediterranean like a forgotten sentinel, its limestone cliffs carved by millennia of wind and waves. Time moves differently here. Days blend into years, years into centuries, marked only by the changing angles of sunlight on stone and the steady rhythm of tides.

Fishing boats drift past, yachts anchor before it, but they always depart, leaving the island to its solitude.

Only the goats remain. They appeared one day, carried perhaps by some long-forgotten shepherd or escaped from a passing vessel, and found their kingdom. They make paths where none existed, winding trails that spiral up steep slopes, and traverse impossible ledges. They understand what the island knows: that plans are fleeting things, as temporary as footprints in sand.

And so the island simply exists beyond the reach of progress and civilization. While cities of glass and steel climb ever higher into distant skies, the goats continue their sure-footed dance across its heights, and the sea will go on shaping its shores until the end of days.

Chapter 1

Evelyn

The taxi lurches forward, jolting me out of my jet-lagged haze. Palma de Mallorca unfolds outside the window—a postcard-perfect blend of historic architecture and sun-drenched modernity. It's warm, but with the sea breeze, it's a welcome respite from New York, where the stuffy summer heat has been clinging to the skyscrapers, turning the city into a concrete sauna.

"Primera vez en Mallorca?" the driver asks, his weathered face crinkling into a smile in the rearview mirror.

I blink, my brain sluggishly translating. "Sí," I manage, exhausting a good third of my Spanish vocabulary. I should have paid more attention in my Spanish classes. After covering The US, Italy, Hawaii, The Maldives, and Greece, it was only a matter of time before business would take me to a Spanish-speaking country.

He launches into what I assume is a well-rehearsed tour-guide spiel, and I nod politely, catching maybe one word in ten. He's rolled down his window, and although I prefer air con, I lack the energy to communicate, so I roll down my own window too.

3

The long-haul flight has left me feeling like a wrung-out dishrag. My tailored suit, usually a source of confidence, now feels constricting and slightly rumpled. I long for a hot shower to wash away the stale air of recycled cabin oxygen and the feeling of time zones blurring together. The thought of peeling off these clothes and slipping into something soft and comfortable is almost enough to make me groan out loud. Almost, but years of boardroom poker face prevent such displays, even in my exhausted state.

As we leave the city behind, the landscape transforms. Rolling hills blanketed in olive groves give way to craggy cliffs that plummet dramatically into the Mediterranean. The sea stretches out, a sheet of liquid sapphire that merges with the sky at the horizon. It's breathtaking, I'll give it that. But I'm not here for the view.

My phone buzzes. It's New York.

"Evelyn Rothschild," I say, my voice crisp and professional.

"Ms. Rothschild, it's Derek. Just wanted to confirm you landed safely."

I suppress a sigh. I'd left explicit instructions not to be bothered unless it was urgent. "I'm fine, Derek. Is there a problem?"

"No, not at all. It's just...well, with Jessica on maternity leave, we wanted to make sure you were okay. It's not too late to send over a temporary PA."

My jaw tightens. I'm surrounded by some of the most capable businesspeople in New York, and they're treating me like a lost child at summer camp. "I appreciate the concern, but I'm perfectly capable of handling this on my own," I say. "Unless the board has any objections?"

"No, of course not. It's just that your father always—"

"I'm not my father," I cut him off, perhaps more sharply

than necessary. I take a breath, soften my tone. "I don't trust temps, I already told you that. Now, the Mallorca plot is a significant opportunity for us. I need everyone focused on their roles, not worrying about whether I remembered to pack sunscreen, so let's just stick to our scheduled meetings. Understood?"

"Yes, Ms. Rothschild. Sorry for the interruption."

I end the call, catching the taxi driver's curious glance in the mirror. Great. Even with the language barrier, my irritation must be palpable.

My phone buzzes again, and Dad's smiling face lights up the screen. He's changed his profile picture to one that's totally ridiculous, his Hawaiian shirt screaming late mid-life crisis. I let it ring out; I'm not in the mood for another lecture on work-life balance or whatever wisdom he's peddling these days.

A moment later, a message notification pops up. It's a picture—Dad on a yacht, his arm around a much younger woman who could easily be my contemporary. They're both grinning into the camera, sun-kissed and carefree. The text reads: *Having a blast on Ibiza! Can't wait for you to meet Candy!*

Candy. Of course her name is Candy.

I stare at the image, a knot forming in my stomach. This man, beaming next to his child-bride—as I've taken to calling her in my head—is barely recognizable as the father I knew. The business titan who taught me everything, who was my mentor in the cutthroat world of luxury resort development. Now he's gallivanting around the Mediterranean while I'm left to uphold our legacy alone.

At least the company's safe now that it's under my control. I've made damn sure the gold digger can't sink her French-manicured claws into our assets.

I type out a response, my fingers stabbing at the screen with more force than necessary: *Looks lovely. Unfortunately, I'm quite busy with the Mallorca acquisition. Perhaps another time. Enjoy your trip.*

I've managed to dodge meeting Dad's latest squeeze for four months now, expertly maneuvering around family dinners and impromptu visits. If I have my way, I'll stretch that streak indefinitely. The last thing I need is to watch this Candy character bat her eyelashes at my father over some overpriced tapas.

I lean back, trying to relax, and my hand drifts to my necklace. It's a delicate gold chain with a small diamond pendant—a gift from my mother when I turned fourteen.

The taxi rounds a bend and suddenly, there it is. The Hotel Cala d'Or Royale rises from the coastline like a white mirage, its clean lines and expansive windows reflecting the sea. It's beautiful, objectively speaking. The kind of place that would feature in luxury travel magazines. The kind of place I've stayed in a hundred times before.

I always stay in the best hotels; they're a measure for the competition, a baseline we'll surpass. By the time I'm done here, the resort my company will build is going to be far better, prettier, and more luxurious than this one, quite frankly, putting it to shame.

The blast of air conditioning as I enter the lobby is a welcome relief from the heat. The space is a study in understated luxury—all soft lighting, gleaming marble, and strategically placed orchids. A massive crystal chandelier dominates the center of the room, casting prismatic patterns across the floor. It's nice. Professional. Exactly what I'd expect from a five-star resort.

I approach the reception desk, where a young woman

with a painfully bright smile greets me. "Bienvenida! Do you have a reservation?"

"Yes," I reply, sliding my passport across the polished desk. "Evelyn Rothschild."

Her eyes widen slightly at the name. Good. Reputation still counts for something.

"Of course, Ms. Rothschild. We've been expecting you. I hope your journey was pleasant?"

I nod, impatient to get to my room, have a shower, and start preparing for tomorrow's viewing. "It was fine, thank you."

She taps away at her computer, the clickety-clack of manicured nails on keys setting my teeth on edge. "I see you'll be staying with us for...oh my, two months? That's wonderful. We don't often have guests stay quite so long."

I force a smile. "I'm here on business."

"Ah, of course. Well, we have you in one of our premium ocean-view suites. I'm sure you'll find it most comfortable. Would you like an overview of our amenities? We have a world-class spa, three restaurants including a Michelin-starred—"

"That won't be necessary," I interrupt, holding out my hand for the key card. "I'm familiar with the property."

She blinks, momentarily thrown off her script. "Oh. Well, if there's anything you need during your stay, please don't hesitate to ask. We're here to make your time with us as pleasant as possible."

I take the key card, already turning toward the elevators. "Thank you. I'm sure it will be fine. Could you send a pot of strong, black coffee up to my room, please? A pot, not a cup."

Chapter 2

Val

The ice-cold cerveza slides down my throat, and I let out a contented sigh. After twenty-plus hours of travel from San Francisco, this feels like pure heaven.

I'm perched on a wooden stool at the edge of a small, open-air hotel bar. It's nothing fancy—just a rectangular platform built right into the rocky coastline. The bar has a thatched roof and is surrounded by a few dining tables that look out over the vast Mediterranean. Rough-hewn steps carved into the rock lead down to the water, and the whole setup is delightfully rustic.

"Otra?" the bartender asks, gesturing to my nearly empty glass.

I grin at him. "Por favor."

As he pours me another, I take in the view. The sun is setting, painting the sky in a riot of pinks and oranges that reflect off the water. A few small fishing boats bob in the distance. It's postcard-perfect, sure, but there's an authenticity here that you can't manufacture. This is the real Mallorca, not some sanitized tourist version. And best of all,

I can see Cormoran Island from here, a small, inhabited island that has recently been opened for commercial development through a government-initiated Request for Proposals. The local authorities have designated the island as a Special Economic Zone for tourism, inviting developers to submit plans for resort projects. The winning bid will be granted a long-term lease and various tax incentives, and I have my eyes on the prize.

"How long will you stay in Majorca?" the bartender asks as he slides my fresh beer across the bar top.

I shake my head. "I'm not sure yet. I'm here for work, actually. But when work looks like this..." I gesture to the stunning view, "it's hard to complain."

He laughs, a warm, rich sound. "I'm Mateo," he says, extending a hand.

"Val," I reply, shaking it.

"So, Val," he continues, leaning on the bar. It's a quiet evening, and he seems in the mood to chat. That's fine by me—talking to locals is half the reason I love what I do. "What kind of work brings you to our little corner of paradise?"

I take another sip of my beer, considering how to explain. "I'm in sustainable resort development," I start. "Basically, I create eco-friendly resorts that work with the environment instead of against it."

Mateo's eyebrows rise. "Interesting. We don't see many of those around here. We are one of a handful on the island. Are we going to be in competition?"

"Not quite," I say. "No offence, but our price points will be quite different. That is, if I manage to secure the plot. I'm here to pitch a project for that island over there."

Recognition dawns on Mateo's face as I point to it. "Ah, Illa Cormoran. Yes, there's been much talk about that. Some are excited for the jobs it might bring, others..." He trails off, shrugging.

I lean in, genuinely curious. "Others?"

Mateo glances around, then lowers his voice slightly. "Some worry about outsiders coming in, changing things. We've seen what big resorts can do to our coastline."

I nod, as it's a concern I've heard before. "That's exactly what I'm trying to avoid," I explain. "Although my resorts are high end with the emphasis on privacy, they're designed to blend in, to enhance what's already there instead of replacing it. We use local materials, employ local people, and most importantly, our resorts are sustainable. The goal is to create something that benefits everyone—visitors and residents alike."

"And this is your own business? You look so young to be doing such big things. More like a surfer girl than a businesswoman," he adds with a chuckle.

"I'm twenty-eight." I smile proudly. "I built my first resort with the help of crowdfunding in Hawaii six years ago. Then I opened my second resort on the Greek island of Santorini, and hopefully, Cormoran Island will be my third."

"And your resorts are turning a profit?" Mateo asks.

"They're doing very well. And not only that, but we've got a ninety-five percent average approval rating from the local community."

He whistles low. "That's not easy to achieve."

"Exactly," I agree. "I'm proud of it. But here in Mallorca, I'm up against some big resort chains, so it won't be easy. I can only hope the local authorities prefer my approach of preserving the island."

Mateo nods. "So you'll be staying with us?"

"Yes. I've booked a room here for a month, but who

knows? If things go my way, I could be here much longer." A gust of wind sweeps through the bar, carrying with it the scent of salt and sunbaked earth. I close my eyes for a moment, breathing it in. This. This is what I want to capture, to share. When I open my eyes, I catch Mateo watching me with an amused expression.

"You look like you belong here," he says.

"Sun, sea, nature... What's not to love?" I smile. "Do you know where I can rent a boat to check out the island tomorrow?"

"Sure." Mateo pours himself a small beer and takes a sip. "I can take you, if you want. I start work at midday, but I'm free in the morning. My parents have a small boat—my father uses it for fishing. Unless you're looking for something fancy?"

"No, that would be fantastic," I say, clinking my glass against his. "I'll pay you, of course."

"No need. I like being on the water. I don't do it often enough."

Sensing there's no point arguing with him, I shoot him a grateful smile. "Fine, then I'll pay you in tips. I have a feeling I'll be spending a lot of time on this barstool."

Mateo laughs and taps the piggy bank on the counter. "Tips are always welcome." He greets a Spanish-speaking family who take their seats at one of the tables by the water and heads over to bring them menus.

I'm tempted to get my laptop from my room and do some prep work for tomorrow, but I refrain. I've been traveling and I'm tired, so I deserve a break, and besides, there's not much I can add to my already polished business plan until I've seen the island firsthand. No, everything can wait, I decide. For now, I just want to soak up the atmosphere and work up the inspiration for what will be a challenging and exciting time ahead.

Mateo gestures in my direction as he chats to the family, no doubt passing on what I just told him, and they nod, smiling at me. There's curiosity in their looks but also a hint of wariness, and I don't blame them. They've probably seen their fair share of developers come through, making big promises and leaving even bigger scars on the island. I resist the urge to go over and introduce myself properly. It's best to wait until I win the pitch. Because I will win.

A group of young women takes up residence at a nearby table, and my gaze lingers on one of them, appreciating more than just the local scenery. When she meets my eyes, I quickly look away, reminding myself that I'm here to work, not to get distracted by beautiful women.

More patrons arrive and someone produces a guitar. Soon, the air is filled with the strains of Spanish music, mingling with the chatter and laughter of the crowd. Immensely pleased with my choice of accommodation, I hum along as I pick up a menu from the bar. The descriptions are in both Spanish and English, and I'm particularly drawn to the unfamiliar local dishes.

"What do you recommend?" I ask Mateo. "I'm looking for something typically Mallorcan."

He pauses, reading along. "For a true taste of Mallorca..." He taps the menu. "I'd suggest the Tumbet. It's a traditional vegetable dish—layers of potatoes, eggplant, and red peppers, all locally grown, topped with a rich tomato sauce."

"Sounds delicious," I say, already feeling my mouth water.

"Or," he continues, "if you're in the mood for seafood,

try the Llampuga amb Pebres. It's mahi-mahi fish with red peppers. It's a seasonal dish, and it's the perfect time for it."

I consider for a moment, torn between the options. "You know what? I think I'll have both."

Mateo grins. "Excellent choice. I'll let the kitchen know." He hesitates for a second, then adds, "And maybe a small plate of bread with olive oil, tomato, and a bit of salt? It's a staple here."

14

Chapter 3

Evelyn

The purr of the engine fades to a whisper as the luxury speedboat slows to a stop. I stand at the bow, my eyes fixed on the chunk of rock rising from the azure waters before us. Cormoran Island. My future masterpiece.

"This is as close as we can get, Ms. Rothschild," the captain calls out from behind the polished helm. He's a grizzled old sea dog, all leathery skin and salt-and-pepper beard, probably been navigating these waters since before I was born.

I nod, not taking my eyes off the island. It's smaller than I expected, a jagged silhouette against the cloudless sky. A handful of pine trees crown its peak, but apart from that, it looks quite bare from here. Bare is good, though. There will be less to remove.

"What can you tell me about it?" I ask, leaning on the boat's railing.

The captain joins me, squinting against the glare of the sun on water. "Not much to tell, really. It's uninhabited, except for the goats."

I turn to him, one eyebrow raised. "Goats?"

He nods, a hint of amusement in expression. "Yes, mountain goats. No one knows how they got here, but they've made the place their home. Hardy little buggers."

"How many?"

He shrugs. "No idea. Not many people visit the island because there's no beach or pier. It's a popular spot for yachts to anchor, though. It's great for snorkeling around here."

I file that information away. Snorkeling? Great. I already knew that, though. Goats? Not so much. I wonder how the local authorities would feel about us removing them, but there's no space for goats in a luxury resort.

"And how am I supposed to get onto the island?" I ask, eyeing the distance between our boat and the rocky shore.

The captain's lips twitch. "You'll have to wade a bit, I'm afraid. I can't get any closer without damaging the hull."

I look down at my outfit—crisp white palazzo pants and a sleeveless blouse. Not exactly wading attire. I'm not sure what I expected, but it wasn't this. Suppressing a sigh, I bend down to roll up my pants. The fabric resists, clearly not designed for such treatment, but I manage to get them just above my knees before giving up. It'll have to do.

"I don't suppose you have any water shoes on board?" I ask, already knowing the answer.

The captain shakes his head. "Afraid not, Ms. Rothschild. Would you like a life vest?"

"No, thank you. I'll be fine."

I slip off my sandals, hooking them onto my fingers along with my phone, and with as much dignity as I can muster, I climb down the retractable steps and into the water. It's cooler than I expected, sending a shock up my legs. The seabed is uneven, rocks and pebbles shifting under my feet with each step as the water reaches up to my thighs, soaking my pants despite my best efforts.

By the time I reach the shore, I'm wet and my feet are scraped and sore, but I've made it. I turn back to the boat, raising a hand in a brief wave to the captain. He returns the gesture, then settles back into his leather captain's chair and lights a cigarette, apparently content to wait out my exploration.

The climb up is steep and treacherous. Loose rocks skitter away under my feet, and holding my phone, I have to use my free hand to steady myself against larger boulders. My clothes, damp with seawater and now streaked with dust, cling uncomfortably to my skin. I can feel a blister forming on my heel where my wet foot is rubbing against my sandal.

This had better be worth it, I think grimly as I haul myself up over a particularly challenging outcrop. Building sites are never a walk in the park, but I can't say I've had a viewing quite like this before.

Finally, mercifully, the ground begins to level out. I straighten up, brush off my hands, and take stock of my surroundings. The vegetation is sparse up here, mostly scrubby bushes and the occasional stunted tree. But the view... The view is something else entirely.

I turn slowly, taking it all in. To the east, the coastline of Mallorca stretches out, a patchwork of sandy beaches and rocky cliffs. To the west, there's nothing but open sea, blue fading into deeper blue, and the morning sun bathes everything in a golden light.

A smile tugs at my lips. This is why I do what I do. This untamed beauty, this raw potential. I can already see it in my mind's eye—a series of luxury villas cascading down the hillside, each with its own infinity pool mirroring the sea. A discreet funicular to ferry guests up from a small, private marina, and maybe a helipad. It would be the ultimate getaway.

I snap a few photos to send back to the design team. They'll need to see this, to understand what we're working with. The terrain will be a challenge, but that's what makes it exciting. Anyone can build a resort on a flat, sandy surface, but this? This will be something else.

Lost in my vision, I don't notice the soft sound of hooves on stone until it's too late. A sudden chorus of bleating makes me whirl around, nearly losing my footing on the uneven ground.

There, not ten feet away, is a small herd of goats. They're shaggy, wild-looking things with curved horns. For a moment, we just stare at each other, equally startled by the unexpected encounter.

"Well," I say, trying to regain my composure. "I suppose you must be the mysterious inhabitants."

One of the goats—the largest, possibly the leader of the herd—takes a step forward, lowering its head slightly. Is it challenging me? Greeting me? Is it curious? I don't know anything about goats and find myself at a loss.

"Listen," I continue, feeling slightly ridiculous for talking to a goat but unable to stop myself. "I know this is your home, but things are going to be changing around here. Progress, you understand? It's nothing personal, so please don't look at me like that."

The goat bleats, a sound that seems almost dismissive. Then, as if on some silent signal, the whole herd begins to pick its way up the hill, leaving me alone.

I watch them go with a touch of amusement at the absurdity of the situation. But also, unexpectedly, a twinge of...something else. Guilt? Regret? I push the feeling aside.

I'm here to do a job, not to worry about the feelings of a bunch of feral goats.

Turning back to the view, I force myself to refocus. I need to survey the entire island, get a feel for the topography, the best sites, the potential challenges. Other developers will be circling like sharks, eager to snap up this prime piece of real estate.

I start to make my way along the ridge, my eyes scanning the landscape, my mind racing with plans and possibilities. Every so often, I catch a glimpse of movement out of the corner of my eye—a flash of fur, the glint of a horn in the sunlight. The goats are following me, I realize. Observing from a distance, silent and wary.

I ignore them and crest a small rise, struck anew by the beauty of this place. The way the sunlight glints off the water, the rugged charm of the unspoiled landscape. For a brief moment, I allow myself to see it through different eyes. Not as a developer sizing up a potential goldmine, but as... well, as a goat, I suppose. As a creature who calls this place home. I notice the way certain plants cling tenaciously to seemingly barren rock. The complex network of paths the goats have worn into the hillsides. The unexpected splash of color from hardy wildflowers pushing up through a crack in the stone.

A patch of lusher vegetation catches my attention, standing out against the scrubby bushes and stunted trees that dominate the landscape. Intrigued, I make my way toward it, carefully picking my path. As I get closer, I hear it before I see it—a faint trickling sound that grows louder with each step.

Pushing aside some dense foliage, I find a small, hidden grotto. There, emerging from a crack in the rocky face of a cliff is a spring. Clear water seeps out of the stone, forming a pool before trickling down in a narrow stream.

The area around the spring is vibrant green. Ferns and moss cover the damp rocks, and small, delicate flowers dot the surrounding area, adding color to the scene. The pool itself is no larger than a generous-size hot tub, its surface mirror-smooth except where the water bubbles up from the rock. It's deep enough that I can't see the bottom clearly, the water taking on a mysterious, dark-blue hue in its depths.

Excitement causes a flutter in my belly. I knew the island had a water source, but this is seriously charming. People with money like this kind of stuff. They want their luxuries, but they also want to feel like they're part of something special.

After snapping more pictures, I head back to the ridge, mentally running through the possibilities. A luxury spa built around the spring, perhaps? I'll have to ask my team to amend the plans in the next twenty-four hours. Or maybe we could bottle the water as an exclusive amenity for our guests. The marketing potential alone is enough to make me smile.

Another boat, smaller and less ostentatious than the one I arrived in, is heading toward the island. On board is a young couple, by the looks of it, and the woman is undressing, perhaps about to go for a swim.

Then, a familiar sound stops me in my tracks. Bleating. And it's close.

I turn slowly to find the herd of goats I saw before and some more, right behind me. I thought they were wary of me, but they don't seem intimidated at all anymore.

"Easy now," I say. I take a step back, and they take a step forward. One of the larger goats, a particularly shaggy creature with impressive horns, approaches me boldly. It stretches out its neck, sniffing at my clothes, then suddenly butts its head against my thigh. Is he attacking?

Panic overrides reason, and I clumsily start climbing down as fast as I can. It's madness, I know. These sure-footed creatures have a clear advantage on this treacherous terrain. My feet slip and slide on the loose rocks as I half stumble down the slope.

The sound of hooves on stone follows me, and I don't dare look back, focusing all my energy on not falling. *I'm almost down. Safety.* Without breaking stride, I plunge into the sea, fully clothed, and swim with desperate strokes toward the boat.

Only when the captain's helped me back in do I risk a glance back. The goats have stopped at the water's edge, watching me with what I swear looks like smug satisfaction.

"Everything all right, Ms. Rothschild?" the captain asks, poorly concealing his amusement.

I push my wet hair out of my face and muster what dignity I can. "Perfectly fine, thank you. I just..." I glance at my phone, clenched in my fist. "Fuck. My phone is wet."

"It will be okay. They're sturdy these days." He takes it from me, dries it off on a towel, then hands me a fresh one. "I'll leave it to dry in the sun."

"Hey, lady! Are you okay?" the woman in the other boat yells.

"Yes, thank you," I say, thoroughly embarrassed as I dry myself off. I don't feel like socializing, and I certainly don't need strangers worrying over me, but it's too late. They're already making their way over to us.

Chapter 4

Val

I was just getting undressed on the fishing boat when I spotted her. Despite the distance, I could hear her panicked yelps as she stumbled down the slope, chased by a herd of goats. Truth be told, the absurd sight was hilarious, but I still felt a little concerned as I watched her leap into the water and swim toward the boat anchored nearby.

"Mateo," I say, pointing to the vessel where the woman who mumbled she was fine is now drying herself off. "Can we get closer? I just want to check on her."

Mateo nods and chuckles as he steers us toward the other boat. Despite the woman's bedraggled appearance, there's something striking about her—an air of authority, perhaps, or just the way she holds herself even in this embarrassing situation.

"Hey!" I call out. "Are you sure you're all right? It looked pretty intense from here."

The woman looks up again, startled. For a moment, she seems torn between ignoring us and responding. Finally, she manages a tight smile. "Yes, I already told you I'm fine. Thank you."

Mateo waves at the captain and cuts the engine, letting us drift closer. They greet each other and strike up a conversation in Spanish.

"I'm Val," I say to the woman while the men are talking. She doesn't seem like the talkative type, but it would be weird to ignore her now that we're drifting so close. "This is Mateo," I continue. "We were just on our way to the island when we saw your, uh, escape."

The woman's eyes narrow slightly, assessing me. "Evelyn," she replies after a moment, her voice clipped. "If you're thinking of having a picnic or sunbathing, I wouldn't recommend going up there. Aside from the angry goats, there are no comfortable flat surfaces to sit on and there's very little shade."

I shake my head, still smiling. "I'm not here to sunbathe and I can handle a few goats. I just want to see the island."

"Handle them?" Evelyn scoffs. "They chased me off!"

"They tend to mimic behavior," I explain, remembering my encounters with mountain goats during hikes on my travels. "They only chase if you run away from them. If you stay calm, they usually just watch you."

Evelyn looks irritated. She clearly doesn't like to be lectured. "And why on earth do you want to view this godforsaken rock? There's nothing here."

Meeting her eyes, I decide to be honest. I suspect we're in the same business. That means we'll meet again at some point, so I might as well tell her. "I'm a developer. And I'm guessing you are too?"

The change in Evelyn's demeanor is immediate. Her back straightens, her chin lifts. "Evelyn Rothschild," she says coolly. "Rothschild Resorts."

"Oh?" I frown. Rothschild Resorts is one of the biggest players in luxury hotel development. They're known for their opulent, no-expenses-spared approach. The kind that involves butlers and helipads.

"Val Mendoza," I finally reply, matching her professional tone. "Eden Eco Escapes."

I'm surprised when recognition flickers in Evelyn's eyes. "Ah yes, the...eco-resort in Hawaii."

"We have two resorts now, actually," I say. "Hawaii and Santorini."

Evelyn raises an eyebrow. "Is that so? Well, congratulations, Ms. Mendoza, but I'm afraid you may have wasted a trip. Cormoran Island isn't exactly suited to your...rustic approach. There's no way the council will vote for a small developer over Rothschild Resorts."

Evelyn's dismissive attitude ignites a spark of irritation within me. I've faced this kind of condescension before from people who think sustainable means primitive, who can't see beyond their outdated notions of luxury.

"With all due respect, Ms. Rothschild," I counter, "I think you're underestimating me. This island perfectly lends itself for a truly sustainable, low-impact resort that could set a new standard for luxury eco-tourism. The world is changing. Wealthy tourists are becoming more conscious of their environmental impact. They want luxury that doesn't cost the earth, so perhaps you're the one who's wasting their time."

Evelyn laughs, a sound that's both melodious and infuriating. "Oh, honey," she says, rolling her eyes, "I've been in this business way longer than you. I know what our clients want."

Her patronizing tone makes my blood boil, but I force myself to stay calm. "Do you? Because from where I'm standing, companies like Rothschild Resorts are becoming dinosaurs. They might think they're big and impressive, but ultimately, they're headed for extinction."

I can see I've struck a nerve. Evelyn's smile falters for a moment before she regains her composure. "And your little eco-huts are the future, are they?"

"You've clearly never visited my resorts," I retort. "They offer all the luxury of a five-star hotel, without the waste and unnecessary bells and whistles. The beauty is in the architecture, in the way our buildings blend with the land-scape and offer outdoor living. They're powered by renew-able energy, use advanced water conservation systems, and have zero-waste policies. It's design and innovation at its best."

"That all sounds very...noble." Evelyn's tone is dripping with sarcasm. "But at the end of the day, luxury is about indulgence. People want to be spoiled, to forget about their everyday concerns. They don't want to be reminded about sustainability and conservation during their vacation. Next, you'll be telling me your guests enjoy composting toilets and cold showers." She rolls her eyes. "You have no idea what you're talking about. Our resorts are marvels of modern architecture and engineering."

"They're marvels of excess and waste," I argue. I shouldn't really lower myself to having an argument with her, but the truth is, I've secretly always wanted to meet Evelyn Rothschild, just to have this very conversation. "Do you have any idea how much energy it takes to air condition those massive lobbies? How much water is wasted on those golf courses? How much local culture is erased to make way for your standardized 'luxury' experience?"

A tense silence falls over both boats. I'm suddenly aware that Mateo and the other captain have stopped talking and they're listening to our exchange with mild discomfort.

Evelyn takes a deep breath, visibly trying to regain her composure. "Well, Ms. Mendoza, you certainly seem... passionate about your approach. But passion doesn't win bids. Experience, reputation, and financial backing do. And in those areas, Rothschild Resorts has you beat, so go home and play with your Barbies instead." She turns to the captain. "Let's head back. I'm dying for a coffee."

Her captain exchanges another few words with Mateo while Evelyn and I ignore each other.

"Go play with your Barbies," I mutter under my breath. She's wrong. Eden Eco Escapes may be younger and tiny compared to her company, but we're growing fast. Our Santorini resort was fully booked for its first year before we even broke ground, and we have a waiting list a mile long for our Hawaii property. Best of all, we've got investors lining up to be part of our next project. For the first time in my career, I don't have to crowdfund to build on my dreams. Backers are actually coming to me.

"Good luck with her," Mateo says when they're heading back. "She seems like a feisty one." He chuckles. "Any help you need, I'm your man. I'd love to see you beat her."

I nod, grateful for his support. "Thank you, I really appreciate that." I take off my shoes and attach the Velcro waterproof phone holder to my arm. "Wait here? I'll be back in about an hour." *Game on, Rothschild*, I think to myself as I dive into the water. *Game on.*

Chapter 5

Evelyn

Standing before the large screen in my hotel suite, I face the people who make up my top-tier team. Twenty of Rothschild Resorts' finest, all waiting for my direction. The suite has been transformed into a makeshift office, with plans taped to the wall, my laptop and the printer I ordered set up on the desk, and empty coffee mugs and water bottles are scattered across every available surface.

"All right," I begin. "We're T-minus three days from our presentation to the Mallorca Tourism Development Committee. I need everything to be perfect."

I pace in front of the screen, ticking off points on my fingers. "We'll need the revised three-D renderings of the resort layout, emphasizing how we're working with the island's natural topography. Make the natural spring one of the key focus points and move the spa there. Environmental impact assessments—I'm not happy with these yet. They need to look good, but realistic. We don't want to come off as naïve. And finally, we need the revised financial projections for the first five years, including projected job creation for locals and positive impact on the local economy."

"Who exactly will be at this presentation?" asks Derek, our director of operations.

I stop pacing and face the screen. "The committee consists of seven members. We've got the Mayor of Calviá, the Director of Sustainable Tourism for the Balearic Islands, representatives from the local chamber of commerce and environmental groups, and a few other bigwigs from the regional government. It's a tough crowd, but nothing we haven't handled before."

"And the competition?" Sarah, my marketing director, asks. "There's still no word of who else is running."

A smirk plays at my lips. "Well, I've already had the pleasure of meeting one of our rivals. Eden Eco Resorts, a tiny resort developer. Run by a girl who looks barely older than my daughter." I wave my hand dismissively. "They're not a threat. I'm more concerned about the Barton group—I spotted their business development director at the airport and I doubt he's here on vacation." I'm about to continue when my phone buzzes. "Speaking of my daughter... I need to take this call. Let's reconvene in ten minutes."

Without waiting for a response, I end the conference call and answer the video call. "Mia, sweetheart! How are you?"

My daughter's face fills the screen, and suddenly, the stress of the impending presentation fades away. "Mom! I'm good. How's Mallorca? Have you gotten a tan yet?"

I laugh, moving to the terrace to gaze out at the Mediterranean. "Hardly. I've been cooped up in my room most of the time, working on this presentation, and you know I don't sunbathe. I don't get it—it's such a useless pastime. But the view is beautiful." Focusing my attention back on Mia, I frown as I take in her appearance. Her once-sleek hair is now a mass of dreadlocks, and wearing an old, worn-out tank top and jersey shorts, she looks more like a bohemian backpacker than the daughter of a resort mogul. "Your hair..."

Mia cuts me off with a warning look. "Mom, please. Let's not go there again. I don't want another lecture about my 'lifestyle choices,'" she says, making air quotes with her fingers.

I swallow my comments, forcing a smile. "You're right, I'm sorry. So, what are you up to now?" She appears to be standing on a bustling street corner and behind her, the city thrums with life—honking scooters, chattering vendors, and the sizzle of street food carts. The buildings are a mishmash of old and new, faded French colonial architecture juxtaposed against gleaming modern storefronts, and strings of colorful lanterns crisscross the narrow street.

People weave around Mia, a constant flow of locals going about their day, interspersed with the occasional tourist. The humidity is evident even through the screen—I can see a faint sheen of sweat on Mia's forehead, and her tank top clings to her chest. Despite the apparent chaos, my daughter looks completely at ease.

"I just arrived in Hanoi," she says. "I'm going to travel around for a bit and next month I'm volunteering at an orphanage. It's in a really remote area, so I'll be sleeping on site with the other volunteers."

"Vietnam?" I perk up. "We have two beautiful resorts there. Wouldn't you prefer to stay in one of those? I could arrange—"

"No, Mom," Mia interrupts gently but firmly. "Thank you, but the resorts are nowhere near the orphanage. It's really remote. Besides, I'm not interested in luxury. This is about immersing myself in the local culture and helping others."

I can feel my frustration building, but I try to keep it in check. "Well, it sounds like you'll be away for quite some time. What about that marketing position that just opened up? Are you sure you're not interested? It would be perfect for you with your social media background and—"

"Mom." Mia's voice is tinged with exasperation. "I already told you, I'm not interested in that job. That's not the path I want to take."

I want to press on, to make her see reason. My daughter is brilliant, capable of so much more than traipsing around the globe, sleeping in hostels, and eating street food while blogging. But I know from experience that pushing too hard will only drive her further away.

"I just worry about you," I say softly. "You're so smart, so talented. Your food blog is doing well, I know, but..."

Mia's expression softens. "I know you worry, Mom. But I'm happy. My blog gives me enough income to travel, to experience the world on my own terms. It might be a world away from the high-end restaurants you're used to, but there's so much beauty in street food, in the stories of the people who make it. That's what I want to share with the world."

She holds up a dish she's just bought. It's a steaming bowl of what looks like noodle soup, the broth a rich, dark color. "Look at this. It's bún bò Huế, a specialty from central Vietnam. The woman who made this has been perfecting her recipe for over fifty years. Can you believe that? Fifty years of dedication to one single dish!"

Trying to show interest, I lean in closer to the screen. "It does look...interesting. What else are you planning to try while you're there?"

"Oh, there's so much! I want to try bánh mì from a street vendor in Saigon, and I've heard about this amazing place that makes cơm tấm, which is broken rice with grilled pork. And of course, I have to sample phở from different regions to compare the flavors. Oh, and there's this dessert called chè that comes in so many varieties..."

As she continues, I find myself torn between pride at her passion and lingering concern about her chosen path. But for now, I push those worries aside and simply listen, letting my daughter's excitement wash over me.

"That sounds amazing. Just...be safe, okay?" I finally say. "And call me if you need anything. Anything at all. And send me pictures. You know I love to get pictures from you."

"I will, Mom. I promise," Mia says with a smile. "I love you."

"I love you too, honey," I reply, wishing I could reach through the screen and hug her. As the call ends, I'm left staring at my reflection in the blank screen, wondering how my daughter and I ended up on such different paths. The contrast between her free-spirited adventurous life and my structured, ambitious world couldn't be starker, and on top of that, she doesn't even look like me. She looks like her father, a boy I briefly dated when I was seventeen. She has his big, dark eyes, his dark hair, and she's tall. Her father broke up with me when I told him I was pregnant. He's never been in the picture and Mia is okay with that. She's always been an easy child—again, much unlike me.

Remembering my team is waiting, I dial back in and apologize for the interruption. "Okay, let's nail this tagline," I say. "I'm not sold on the list you sent me. We need something that encapsulates everything Rothschild stands for. Opulence. Exclusivity. Unmatched luxury."

"We've discussed a few others," Sarah says. "How about 'Cormoran Island: A Rothschild Masterpiece'?"

"It's good, but not quite there," I reply. "We need to convey that this isn't just a resort. It's a destination for the elite. The culmination of luxury."

Sarah nods and scans a list in front of her. "You might like this one. 'Welcome to Cormoran: Where Only the Extraordinary Belong.'"

I pause, considering. "Now that's more like it. Build on this for the executive summary. Remember, we're not selling a vacation. We're selling an experience reserved for the pinnacle of society."

Chapter 6

Val

I stand before the Mallorca Tourism Development Committee, my heart racing but my exterior calm. The large screen behind me flickers to life, ready to showcase my vision for Cormoran Island. I've opted for a look that I hope strikes the perfect balance between professional and approachable—a white linen blazer over a navy T-shirt, paired with white linen trousers and leather sandals. My long dark hair is pulled back into a sleek ponytail, and as always, I've kept my makeup minimal, just a touch of mascara and tinted lip balm.

"Good morning," I begin, my voice steady despite the butterflies in my stomach. "Thank you for having me. I'm Val Mendoza, founder and CEO of Eden Eco Escapes. Today, I'm here to present our vision for Cormoran Island— Eco-Elegance Redefined."

With a click of my remote, the screen behind me comes to life, showing a sweeping aerial view of Cormoran Island. The image slowly zooms in, revealing the breathtaking integration of our proposed resort with the natural landscape.

"Ladies and gentlemen, what you're seeing is not just a

35

beautiful resort. It's a testament to what's possible when we work in harmony with nature instead of against it."

The rendering shows a structure that seems to grow organically from the island itself. The main building, crafted from local stone, embraces the front side of the island. Its design is a masterful blend of modern luxury and natural elements, with living walls of lush vegetation seamlessly integrated into the architecture.

"Our design philosophy is simple. We don't conquer the landscape, we become part of it," I explain, gesturing to the images. "Every aspect of this resort has been carefully considered to minimize our environmental impact while maximizing the guest experience."

The next slide showcases the interior of one of the suites. Floor-to-ceiling windows offer panoramic views of the Mediterranean, and walls that slide open completely blur the line between indoor and outdoor living.

"Now, let me draw your attention to the unique shape of our suites," I say, using my laser pointer to outline the distinctive dome structure. "Each suite is designed as a perfect hemisphere, reminiscent of a natural cave carved into the island's rock face."

The image zooms in, showing the curved walls and ceiling that seamlessly merge into one continuous surface.

"This dome shape isn't just aesthetically pleasing—it's a crucial part of our sustainable design. The curved structure naturally regulates temperature, reducing the need for artificial heating and cooling. It also provides incredible acoustics, allowing our guests to enjoy the soothing sounds of the sea while minimizing noise between suites."

I click to the next slide, which shows a cross-section of the dome suite.

"As you can see, the suite appears to be nestled right

into the island itself. This design not only provides a sense of intimacy and connection with the landscape but also helps to camouflage the structure, preserving the island's natural silhouette. Inside the dome is a spacious, open-plan living area. The curved walls give a sense of flow and continuity, leading the eye naturally toward the stunning sea view. We've used local materials wherever possible—you'll notice the floors are made from polished local stone, and the furniture is crafted from sustainable, native woods."

I pause, allowing the committee to absorb the details of the design. "Imagine waking up to the sound of waves, stepping out onto your private terrace, and feeling as though you're floating above the sea," I say. "Our suites are designed to provide unparalleled luxury while maintaining a deep connection to the natural world."

The next image shows a close-up view of a suite's private terrace.

"From your terrace, a short flight of natural stone steps leads down to your own private dock. This isn't just any dock—it's an extension of your living space, complete with comfortable lounge chairs, a saltwater pool, and a small bar area for those sunset cocktails. And when you're ready to fully immerse yourself in the Mediterranean, it's as simple as walking to the end of your dock and diving in. The crystal-clear waters are quite literally at your doorstep."

I can see the committee members leaning forward, clearly intrigued.

"For those who prefer a gentler entry, each dock is also equipped with a ladder for easy access in and out of the water. And for our guests who enjoy snorkeling or diving, we provide top-of-the-line equipment in each suite, so they can explore the marine life surrounding Cormoran Island at their leisure."

I click to the next image, which shows a sleek, eco-friendly boat docked at a beautifully designed pier.

"Transportation to and from the island is a crucial part of the guest experience. Our custom-designed boat, powered by a combination of solar and wind energy, will ferry guests to and from the mainland at their convenience. The journey itself becomes part of the luxury experience, offering stunning views and the opportunity to spot marine life."

I can see the Mayor of Calviá nodding appreciatively, while the Director of Sustainable Tourism is scribbling notes.

"Now, let's talk about energy," I continue, switching to an image that showcases the resort's innovative roof design. "The sloping roof you see here isn't just an architectural feature. It's covered in solar panels that are seamlessly integrated into the design. These panels, combined with our wind turbines and energy storage systems, will allow us to operate entirely off-grid." I smile as I regard my audience.

"But our commitment to sustainability goes beyond energy," I add, clicking to the next slide. "When I first visited Cormoran Island, I was charmed by its current inhabitants." The slide shows a group of mountain goats roaming peacefully near one of the resort's terraces. "As they were there first, they have the right to stay, don't you agree?"

This statement draws a few chuckles from the committee, but I think they like the idea.

"Rather than relocating these animals, we've designed our resort to coexist with them. The goats will be free to roam as they always have. We believe our guests will find their presence charming and authentic."

The next few slides showcase more details of the resort

—a restaurant with a roof garden where we'll grow our own herbs and vegetables, and a series of nature trails that wind through the less developed parts of the island.

"Now, let me share with you one of Cormoran Island's greatest treasures," I say, my voice filled with excitement. "As you may be aware, there's a natural spring hidden in the heart of the island." The image zooms in, showing the spring and the lush vegetation surrounding it.

"This spring isn't just a beautiful feature—it's a cornerstone of our sustainability efforts and guest experience. Our filtration system will allow us to bottle this pure, mineral-rich water for our guests, eliminating the need for imported bottled water and reducing plastic waste."

I click to the next slide, with architectural renderings of a beautiful, open-air structure built around the spring. "But we're not stopping there. We're transforming the area around the spring into an indulgent, natural spa experience. Imagine soaking in healing mineral pools fed directly by the spring, surrounded by the island's native flora. Our spa treatments will incorporate the spring water and locally sourced ingredients, offering our guests a truly immersive, rejuvenating experience that connects them deeply with the island's natural resources."

I can see the committee members are engaged, their eyes flickering between me and the images on the screen. Especially the representative from the local environmental group, who I expected to be my toughest critic, seems impressed.

"Now, let's talk about the economic impact," I say, switching to a slide filled with projections and graphs. "Eden Cormoran won't just be a boon for the environment —it will be a significant contributor to the local economy."

I walk them through our hiring plans, emphasizing our

commitment to employing local talent wherever possible. I outline our plans for partnering with local suppliers, from food producers to artisans who will create custom furnishings for the resort. "We believe that true sustainability isn't just about the environment—it's about creating a business that supports and enhances the local community."

As I near the end of my presentation, I can feel the energy in the room. The committee members ask thoughtful questions about our water conservation plans, our waste management strategies, and our approach to preserving the island's biodiversity.

I field each question confidently, drawing on my experience with our resorts in Hawaii and Santorini.

Finally, I come to my closing statement. The screen behind me fades to a simple image—our proposed logo for Eden Cormoran, a stylized tree whose branches form the shape of the island.

"Ladies and gentlemen, what we're proposing isn't just a resort. It's a new paradigm for luxury travel," I say. "Eden Cormoran will offer our guests the height of luxury, privacy, and comfort, while demonstrating that it's possible to do so in perfect harmony with nature."

I pause, making eye contact with each committee member in turn. There's a moment of silence and then, to my surprise and delight, the Mayor of Calviá starts to applaud. The rest of the committee joins in, and I feel a wave of relief and pride wash over me.

"Thank you, Ms. Mendoza," the mayor says, his voice warm. "That was certainly impressive. I'm sure we'll have plenty more questions, but we'll save those for the Q&A session."

"Of course," I reply, smiling. "I'm looking forward to our next meeting."

Stepping out of the conference room and into the bright hallway, I take a deep breath. The tension in my shoulders starts to dissipate, replaced by a growing sense of accomplishment. Whatever happens next, I know I've given it my all.

As I round the corner into the waiting area, my eyes lock with a familiar face. Evelyn Rothschild is sitting there, her posture perfect, her expression unreadable. She's dressed in an impeccable suit I suspect costs more than my entire wardrobe, her blonde hair styled in a way that screams control.

For a moment, we just stare at each other, the air thick with unspoken rivalry. I can feel her trying to read me, to gauge how my presentation went.

Walking past her, I can't resist the urge to say something, so I pause in my stride, a small smirk playing at the corners of my mouth. "Good luck in there," I say, my voice dripping with faux sweetness. "You're going to need it."

Chapter 7

Evelyn

I'm perched at a corner table on the hotel's rooftop restaurant, savoring the crisp bite of champagne and the briny freshness of locally sourced oysters. The sun is setting over the Mediterranean, and the view is nothing short of spectacular, with the coastline stretching out before me and the twinkling lights of the white mountain villages flickering to life in the distance.

The hotel's outdoor space is stunning, with modern furniture in muted tones of gray and white artfully arranged around a central bar area. Potted olive trees and fragrant herbs create natural dividers between seating areas, and soft lighting from strategically placed lanterns casts a warm glow over the space, complementing the fading natural light.

It's been a long day and it's one of those rare moments that I feel exhausted. I don't normally have to pitch. We simply buy the land, get our permissions, and start building, but that's not an option in this case. The past weeks have been hectic, keeping me going at full speed. But now that it's over, the fatigue crashes over me like a wave. Tonight, I can feel the weight of stress lingering in every muscle, in the slight tremor of my hand as I lift the champagne flute to my lips. It's a bone-deep weariness that I usually push aside, but I allow myself to acknowledge it, if only for a moment.

My phone buzzes and Dad's face lights up the screen, his new profile picture still jarring. I hesitate for a moment, then answer. He's probably calling to hear about the pitch.

"Hello, Dad," I say.

"Evelyn, sweetheart!" His voice is jubilant, almost manic. "I have the most wonderful news!"

I let out a sigh, expecting some ridiculous story about a sunset cruise or a wine tasting. "Oh?"

"Candy and I are engaged!"

The oyster I've just swallowed suddenly feels like a rock in my stomach. "I'm sorry, what?"

"We're getting married." He laughs and the sound grates on my nerves. "And there's more. We want to start a family. Can you believe it?"

For a moment, I'm speechless and down the champagne in one go. "Dad," I finally manage, "have you lost your mind?"

"Lost my mind? No, sweetheart, I've found it! I've never been happier. Candy is...she's everything I never knew I needed. She makes me feel young again."

I resist the urge to point out that he's not young, that the idea of him fathering children at his age is utterly absurd, unethical even. Instead, I take a deep breath, trying to center myself. "Dad, don't you think this is a bit...sudden? You've only known her for a few months."

"When you know, you know," he says, his voice dreamy. "Oh, Evelyn, I can't wait for you to meet her. You'll love her, I'm sure of it."

I highly doubt that, but I keep the thought to myself.

The idea of my father having babies makes me feel physically sick, and I need to change the subject before I say something I'll regret.

"That's...quite the news, Dad," I say, forcing a neutral tone. "Actually, I have some news of my own. Remember the pitch for Cormoran Island? It was today."

"Oh, was that today?" He sounds distracted. "I'm sure you did wonderfully. You always do."

I feel a pang of hurt at his lack of interest, quickly followed by irritation. "Yes, it was today. It went extremely well, actually. I have no doubt we've got this in the bag."

"That's great, honey," he says, but I can tell he's not really listening. "Candy wants to say hello. Here she is."

Before I can protest, a sickeningly sweet voice comes on the line. "Hi, Evelyn! It's so nice to finally talk to you. Your dad has told me so much about you!"

I grip my champagne glass so tightly I'm afraid it might shatter. "Hello, Candy," I manage to say. "Congratulations on your engagement."

"Thank you! Oh, I'm just so excited. Your father is such an amazing man. And I can't wait to be a mommy!"

Closing my eyes, I count to ten. "Listen, Candy, I'd love to chat, but I'm actually in the middle of a business dinner. Could you put my father back on?"

"Oh, of course! It was so nice talking to you. Bye-bye now!"

There's a shuffling sound, and then my father's voice returns. "Isn't she wonderful? So sweet."

"Dad," I say, "I really do need to go. But can we talk about this...engagement...when I'm back in New York? There's a lot to discuss."

"Of course. We'll have a big family dinner. You can

bring Mia. She just spoke to Candy and they're getting on like a house on fire."

Great. So my daughter has already been subjected to this circus. Mia has always been a lot more open-minded than me, though. I envy her for that. "Sure, Dad. I really do have to go now. Take care."

I end the call before he can say anything else, resisting the urge to throw my phone off the roof. Instead, I signal the waiter for a refill. As he pours, I try to push thoughts of my father's impending nuptials and potential offspring out of my mind. I need to focus on what's important: the project, the future of Rothschild Resorts.

The pitch went well—extremely well, in fact. I walked into that room exuding confidence and professionalism, and the committee was attentive from the moment I started speaking. To distract myself from my father's lunacy, I call Derek for a private catch-up.

"Evening, Evelyn," he says. "Quite a day, wasn't it?"

"Indeed it was. I think we can be very pleased with how the presentation went."

"That's great." Derek is silent for a beat. "About that... Have you heard anything about the other presentations?"

I raise an eyebrow. "Not specifically, no. But I'm not concerned. The Barton Group is our only real competition, and their last few projects have been uninspired at best."

Derek clears his throat—usually a sign of nothing good to come. "Well, there's been some talk... I spoke to a friend. He's a consultant who has connections with people involved in the decision-making process. Apparently, Eden Eco Resorts made quite an impression."

I can't help but laugh. "What, that Mendoza girl? Please. She may have a couple of quaint little resorts, but this is out of her league. The committee won't take her seriously."

"I wouldn't be so sure. Word is her presentation was innovative with cutting-edge sustainability features and she's got some serious financial backing now."

I feel a flicker of unease but ignore it. "Derek, relax. We're Rothschild Resorts. We have decades of experience, a stellar reputation, and the resources to create something truly spectacular. A few solar panels and wind turbines or whatever she's throwing at the committee aren't going to sway them."

"You're right, of course. I just thought you should know."

"Well, thank you for the information," I say. "We'll discuss the next steps in our meeting tomorrow. Assuming we get the green light, we'll start looking into securing reliable contractors."

As I end the call with Derek, I can feel the champagne going to my head, a pleasant warmth spreading through my body. I realize I need to eat something more substantial than oysters and signal the waiter for a menu.

Perusing the list of entrees, my mind drifts unbidden to Val Mendoza. I try to picture her presentation, imagine her standing before the committee in her cheap linen suit. I mean, who wears linen for a pitch?

I'm irritated with myself for even entertaining these thoughts. Why am I wasting mental energy on a young girl who looks more like a surfer than a serious resort developer? She may have made a splash with her trendy ideas and youthful enthusiasm, but at the end of the day, this is a ninety-million-dollar project. The committee will want experience, reliability, and a proven track record—all things that Rothschild Resorts has in spades.

Still, a nagging voice in the back of my mind whispers that I might be underestimating Val. I shake my head. I've worked too hard, come too far, to let some upstart with a few trendy ideas rattle me.

Let Val Mendoza have her eco-friendly pipe dreams. The future of Cormoran Island is in my hands, and I have no intention of letting it go.

Chapter 8

Val

I lean against the bar, a cold beer in hand, and let the warm evening breeze wash over my skin. It's a perfect night in Mallorca, and I intend to enjoy every moment of it.

After spending the day in a suit for the presentation, I couldn't wait to get back to my room and change. Now, dressed in nothing but a bikini top and denim shorts, I feel like myself again. The sand between my toes, the salt in my hair—this is where I'm most comfortable.

Now I have to prepare for the Q&A session with the committee, but that can wait until tomorrow. Work should be fun and balanced. If not, what's the point?

Mateo wipes down the bar. "Another cerveza?" he asks, eyeing my nearly empty glass.

"Please," I reply with a grin. "And a drink on me for that pretty lady over there. I nod in the direction of a blonde woman who has just taken a seat at the other side of the bar.

He stares at me for a moment, then says, "I hope you don't mind me saying, but I didn't realize you were...you know..."

49

"Gay?" I finish for him, chuckling. "Is that why you were so keen to take me out in your dad's boat? Dude, your gaydar is seriously off. Very few men actually peg me for straight."

Mateo laughs, shaking his head. "No, no! Nothing like that. I have a girlfriend. Teresa. We've been together for almost a year."

"Ah, young love," I tease, raising my fresh beer in a mock toast. "Well, now you know, and I'd like to buy her a drink."

Mateo's gaze drifts to the blonde woman. "But...what about her? Do you think she's...?"

I follow his gaze, taking her in. She's studying her manicured nails while waiting to order. "Pretty sure she's straight," I reply. "But she's on her own, and she's cute. So why not give it a go?"

"You really think that's going to work?" Mateo looks at me skeptically. "Hitting on a straight woman?"

"You'd be surprised. Sometimes people are more open to new experiences than they realize." I flash him a confident smile. "Besides, what's the harm in a little friendly conversation?"

"All right, all right," Mateo concedes and crosses the bar. I watch as he leans in, speaking to her quietly. She looks up, confusion evident on her face as he gestures in my direction. Her eyes meet mine, curiosity sparking in their depths.

To my slight surprise, she makes her way over to me and slides onto the stool next to mine.

"Hi," she says, her voice soft with a hint of an accent I can't quite place. "I'm Sophia. Mateo said you wanted to buy me a drink?"

I turn to face her, offering my most charming smile. "That's right. I'm Val."

Sophia tilts her head, studying me with a hint of wariness. "That's...kind of you. But why?"

I lean in slightly, keeping my body language open and non-threatening. "Well, to be honest, I think you're beautiful. And you looked like you could use someone to talk to."

A faint blush colors Sophia's cheeks. "Oh, I...thank you. That's very flattering." She pauses, seemingly to gather her thoughts. "I have to admit, I'm not used to getting this kind of attention from women."

I chuckle softly. "Is it making you uncomfortable? Because if it is, I'll back off. No hard feelings."

Sophia shakes her head. "No, no, it's not that. It's just... unexpected. But not in a bad way."

"Well, that's good to hear," I say, feeling a spark of hope. "So, Sophia, what can I get you?"

Sophia hesitates for a moment, then smiles. "I'll have a gin and tonic, please."

I signal to Mateo, who nods and starts preparing the drink. "Excellent choice. "Nothing beats a good G&T on a warm night like this."

Mateo hands Sophia the mixer, and I raise my beer. "Cheers."

Sophia clinks her glass against mine, her eyes narrowing with a mix of intrigue and amusement. "Cheers," she echoes.

We both take a sip, and I think she's relaxing a bit. "What brings you here?" I ask.

"I'm on holiday," she replies, running her finger along the rim of her glass. "My boyfriend and I were supposed to fly out together, but a work thing came up, so he's joining me tomorrow instead."

I nod, feeling a slight pang of disappointment. "Ah, I see. Well, I hope you're enjoying your solo time until he arrives." My interest is cooling a bit. While I'm always up for some casual fun, I'm not one to pursue women in relationships. It's not a big deal for me, but I know it can be a huge step for them, and I'd rather not be the cause of any complications or regrets. "So, what have you been up to in Mallorca so far?" I ask, shifting the conversation to safer, more neutral territory.

"I've just been hanging out here, mainly. And I went on a boat trip yesterday. I saw dolphins, that was amazing." She regards me. "What about you? I take it you're here by yourself?"

"Yeah. I'm here for business."

Sophia's eyebrows raise with interest. "Oh? What do you do?"

I give her a brief overview of my work, explaining how I'm here to pitch a project for Cormoran Island. I keep it concise, not wanting to bore her with the details.

"That sounds fascinating," Sophia says. "So, do you have a girlfriend?"

I shake my head, feeling a twinge of discomfort at the direction the conversation is taking. "No, I don't have a girlfriend. If I did, I wouldn't have offered to buy you a drink."

Sophia's eyes widen slightly, and I can see a flicker of something—interest? excitement?—in her gaze.

"Look," I say, deciding to be direct, "I'm sorry, but now that I know you're in a relationship, I want to be clear that I'm not trying to pursue anything here."

To my surprise, Sophia leans in closer, her voice lowering. "What if I told you *I* might be interested?"

Our conversation is interrupted by Mateo, who almost chokes on the water he's drinking. He's clearly been eavesdropping, and Sophia's bold statement has caught him off guard. I shoot him a warning look, silently communicating that he needs to mind his own business. Mateo, still coughing, takes the hint and quickly makes his way to a table of newly arrived guests, leaving Sophia and me to our increasingly complicated conversation.

I turn back to her, acutely aware of the tension that has suddenly sprung up between us.

"Sophia, I can't go there," I say. "I've been cheated on before, and it's not something I'd wish on anyone. Your boyfriend doesn't deserve that."

Sophia looks taken aback, perhaps not expecting such a firm response.

"Trust me." I offer her a small smile, trying to ease the tension. "It's better if we just have a friendly drink."

There's a moment of awkward silence before Sophia speaks again. "Okay, I get it. You seem like a decent person. Do you date at all?"

I shrug, relieved to move away from the more charged topic. "I have occasional meetups, but nothing serious. My main focus right now is growing my business. It doesn't leave much time for a committed relationship."

"And that's why you were hitting on me?" Sophia asks. "You just want something uncomplicated, far from home with no strings attached?"

"I guess you could say that." I shrug. "Sorry."

"No, it's fine," Sophia says. "It was flattering. It made me feel good about myself, so thank you." She blushes. "I love my boyfriend, but I've always been curious about women. I've never gone there, though. Do you think I should?"

I shake my head and blow out my cheeks. "Look, I don't know anything about your relationship, so I can't tell you what to do. Don't mess up something good, though, unless you genuinely think you might be gay, which I suspect you're not. You'll regret it. Or you could just talk to him about it. It might be something you could explore together."

Sophia nods. "Yeah... I'll keep that in mind." She sighs and glances at her watch. "I should probably head to my room and give him a call. He's been messaging me, but the Wi-Fi is bad here. Can I buy you a drink before I go?"

"I'm good, thank you." I smile and squeeze her arm. "Do you love him?"

"Yeah." She winces. "I feel bad now. I'm sorry if I made things weird earlier. I appreciate your honesty. It's refreshing, actually. I just thought...well, I guess I figured a woman doesn't count."

"Trust me, it does." I smile. "And don't worry about bumping into me at the bar when your boyfriend arrives. We've done nothing wrong, and I won't mention whatever this was."

"Okay." Sophia looks relieved. "I'll see you around then?" She gets off her stool and pauses. "For what it's worth, you're cute and attractive and super nice. You'll make some woman very happy one day."

Mateo whistles through his teeth as she disappears around the corner. "She's so into you. How did you do that?"

"Magic." I shoot him a wink.

He chuckles, reaching for the tap. "Well, Merlin, this magic show earns you a free beer."

"Hold up." Stopping him, I pull out a fifty. "I've got a better trick. Watch this disappear into your tip jar." Mateo's eyes bulge as I slip it in. "Val, no way, that's too much—"

"Abracadabra," I say with a flourish. "Have a good night, my friend. I'm turning in. I've got an early start."

Chapter 9

Evelyn

It's eerily quiet. No one speaks as we sit in uncomfortable chairs, waiting to be called in for the Q&A session following our pitches. I glance around the room, taking in my competition. There are two other developers besides me and Val Mendoza—a balding man in an ill-fitting suit from Barton, who keeps checking his watch, and a woman from a Spanish development company based in Madrid whose hair is pulled back so tightly it looks painful.

I'm not nervous. I know I've got this. The committee would be fools to choose anyone else but us.

My gaze lands on Val, and I can't help but smirk. She's trying to look composed, but I can see the tension in her shoulders, the way her foot taps restlessly against the carpeted floor. It's almost amusing how nervous she seems.

Taking the opportunity to really look at her, I have to admit, albeit grudgingly, that she is attractive. Her skin is a deep golden brown, the kind of tan that speaks of countless hours spent outdoors. It makes me wonder how she ever gets any work done. Does she run her so-called eco-resorts from a beach chair?

Her dark hair is pulled back, and even in a linen suit—an olive green one this time—there's something undeniably beachy about her. She looks like she'd be more at home with a surfboard under her arm than in a boardroom, and despite Derek's warning, it's hard to take her seriously as competition.

I'm not usually this desperate to secure a piece of land—or in this case, an island. Rothschild Resorts has its pick of prime locations around the world. But Cormoran Island is different. It's one of a kind, offering a level of privacy and exclusivity that could set us apart from the handful of competitors in our league. It's an opportunity I can't afford to let slip through my fingers.

The door to the meeting room opens, and a stern-faced woman calls out the names of the other two developers. They stand, straightening their clothes and plastering on confident smiles. Val and I watch them disappear into the room, the door closing behind them with a soft click. I wonder why they've been called in at the same time.

It's highly unusual for a committee to call in multiple candidates at once. Typically, these Q&A sessions are conducted individually to allow for focused discussion and to maintain confidentiality. The fact that they've brought in the other two developers together could mean several things, but my mind immediately jumps to the most promising possibility: they're out of the race.

I glance at Val, wondering if she's reached the same conclusion, and simultaneously, the fact that she's not in there with them worries me. Her brow is furrowed slightly as she types on her phone, and I can almost see the wheels turning in her head. Despite her apparent nervousness, there's a spark of intelligence in her eyes that tells me she's likely piecing together the implications of this unusual move.

If my suspicions are correct, it means the real competition is sitting right next to me. The thought both irritates and excites me. Val Mendoza might be more of a challenge than I initially gave her credit for, but I've never been one to back down from a fight.

Finally, after what feels like hours but is probably only ten minutes, the door opens again. The two developers emerge, their confident smiles replaced by tight-lipped frowns. The man's face is flushed, and the woman is clutching her laptop so tightly her knuckles have turned white.

A satisfied smile tugs at my lips. It's as good as confirmation that I've already won this pitch.

"Ms. Rothschild, Ms. Mendoza," the stern-faced woman calls out. "The committee will see you now."

I stand, smoothing down my suit and picking up my laptop. As I make my way to the door, I notice Val's puzzled expression. We exchange a quick glance. She's clearly as surprised as I am that we're being called in together.

We enter the room, and I take my seat, opening my laptop on the table in front of me, just in case I need specific numbers I can't remember. Val sits beside me, her confusion evident in the slight furrow of her brow. She hasn't brought her laptop; clearly, she's confident she'll be able to answer any questions off the top of her head.

The head of the committee, a distinguished-looking man with salt-and-pepper hair, clears his throat. "Thank you both for joining us," he begins. "We've decided to take a somewhat different approach to this final stage of the selection process."

I lean forward slightly, intrigued despite myself. What could they possibly have in mind?

"Both of your proposals have impressed us," he continues. "Ms. Rothschild, your plan showcases the level of luxury and attention to detail that Rothschild Resorts is known for. And Ms. Mendoza, your innovative approach to sustainable development is truly remarkable."

I feel a flicker of unease. Surely, they're not considering Val's proposal seriously?

"However," the committee head says, "we find ourselves at something of an impasse. Each of your proposals has strengths that the other lacks. Which is why we'd like to use this time while we're all together to discuss an unusual proposal."

He pauses, his gaze moving between Val and me. I can feel the tension in the room, thick enough to cut with a knife.

"We would like you to consider the possibility of a joint venture."

For a moment, I'm sure I've misheard. A joint venture? With Val Mendoza and her hippie company? It's absurd.

I glance at Val, expecting to see the same disbelief on her face. To my surprise, she looks intrigued, her head tilted slightly as she considers that.

"I'm not sure I understand," I say, fighting to keep my voice level. "Are you suggesting that Rothschild Resorts and Eden Eco Escapes work together on this project?"

The head of the committee nods, his expression serious. "That's correct, Ms. Rothschild. Let me elaborate on our thinking." He clasps his hands on the table. "Ms. Mendoza's proposal for Eden Eco Escapes truly captured our imagination. The innovative sustainability practices, the seamless integration with the natural environment, and the focus on preserving local ecosystems—these elements align seamlessly with our vision for Cormoran Island."

My stomach drops. *They preferred Val's plans?* I force myself to maintain a neutral expression, but inside, I'm reeling.

"However," he continues, and I perk up slightly at the word, "there's a significant issue with Ms. Mendoza's proposal. The lead time."

He turns to Val. "While your plans are impressive, Ms. Mendoza, your projected timeline of twenty-six months to complete the resort is longer than we'd like. We're eager to have the resort up and running within fifteen months, as it's crucial for us to start providing jobs for the local community as soon as possible."

Val nods, her brow furrowed in thought. "I'm afraid I'm unable to match your timeline," she says. "I don't want to make any false promises."

The committee head then turns to me. "This is where Rothschild Resorts comes in, Ms. Rothschild. Your company's extensive experience, resources, and proven track record in rapid, high-quality development could be invaluable. We believe that by combining Eden's innovative design and sustainability concepts with Rothschild's efficiency and expertise in luxury hospitality, we could create something truly remarkable—and do it within our desired timeframe."

I find myself at a loss for words. This is not at all how I expected this meeting to go. A joint venture with Eden Eco Escapes is out of the question. My company has always operated independently, maintaining complete control over our properties and our brand.

"We can't merge," I say. "It doesn't work like that."

"We're aware of that," he replies. "We would like Rothschild Resorts to take on the project in order to meet our timeline."

I feel a surge of satisfaction at this, but it's quickly tempered as he turns to Val.

"However, Ms. Mendoza, we want this project to stay true to the eco-friendly vision you presented. That's why we're proposing that you work as a consultant on the project, overseeing the implementation to ensure that the resort meets the sustainability standards you've outlined. Nothing will pass planning without your approval, should you both decide to go ahead with the collaboration."

Val's eyebrows raise slightly, a mix of surprise and interest crossing her face.

The committee head continues. "We believe this collaboration could result in a truly innovative and sustainable luxury resort, completed within our desired timeframe. He pauses, letting his words sink in before delivering the final piece of information. "I should add that if either of you disagree with this proposal, we'll have no choice but to award the project to a local company that's also still in the running."

The room falls silent as Val and I process this unexpected turn of events. I find myself in the unusual position of not knowing quite how to respond. This proposal is so far outside of our normal operating procedures, and yet...the alternative of losing the project entirely is unthinkable. *I won,* I remind myself. *Rothschild won the project. It will be our logo on the hotel, our operation. Our profit.*

I glance at Val, curious to see how she's taking this news. Her face is a mask of concentration as she considers this. There's no way she'll accept the proposal. She's not a consultant, she's a developer, like me. Why on earth would she agree to a collaboration on a project she's not in charge of?

As much as I hate to admit it, I can see the logic behind the committee's suggestion. Val's presentation must have been impressive if they're willing to drop Rothschild without her input. And the idea of combining our resources and expertise does have a certain appeal. It would certainly set this resort apart from anything else in the world.

I open my mouth, about to argue my case on revising my plans so Rothschild can do this solo, but Val beats me to it.

"That's an interesting proposition," she says. "I'd certainly be open to discussing it further."

I turn to stare at her, incredulous. Is she serious? I practically won, so what's in it for her?

"Ms. Rothschild?" another committee member prompts. "What are your thoughts?"

"I would need to discuss it with my board of directors before making any commitments. But I'm willing to consider the possibility," I say carefully, keeping my options open.

The committee head smiles, looking pleased. "Excellent. We'd like you both to take some time to think about it. Consider how you might work together."

He slides two identical folders across the table, one to me and one to Val. "These contain some specific questions we'd like you to address. We'll reconvene in one week to hear your thoughts."

I take the folder, my mind spinning with questions of my own. As we stand to leave, I feel like I've stepped into some sort of alternate reality. Val Mendoza as my consultant? It's almost laughable.

We exit the room in silence, both lost in our own thoughts. As we reach the waiting area, Val turns to me.

"So," she says, "I guess we have some talking to do."

Chapter 10

Val

Evelyn Rothschild, the polished heiress of the famous resort chain, is about to step into my world. When she insisted on meeting at her hotel on her schedule, I realized something crucial: she doesn't stand a chance without me. She needs me, and that means she'll have to play by my rules if she wants this contract.

I lean against the weathered wooden railing of the beachside restaurant, watching the waves crash against the shore. The salty breeze tugs at my loose hair, and I close my eyes for a moment, savoring the peaceful atmosphere. It's a stark contrast to the tension I know is coming.

I'd be lying if I said I wasn't disappointed about losing the pitch outright. But as I reflect on the committee's proposal, I still feel a surge of excitement. This isn't a total loss—far from it. My life's mission has always been to promote eco-friendly tourism, and while it may not be my company at the helm, this project presents a once-in-a-life-time opportunity. The chance to have Rothschild Resorts, a company I've long viewed as the antithesis of sustainable luxury, bow to my expertise. I can change things for the better, and that alone is worth its weight in gold.

That's why I wanted to meet here, at this humble eco-hotel. I suspect it drove Evelyn, accustomed to getting her way, up the wall, but if we're going to work together, she needs to understand that things will be different.

I spot her the moment she steps onto the concrete platform. Mateo, behind the bar, follows her with his eyes as she makes her way toward me. Wearing a designer suit, she's totally overdressed for the occasion, and perhaps I'm underdressed in the bikini and shorts I'm wearing.

"Ms. Mendoza," she greets me, her voice cool and professional. "May I call you Val?"

"Of course, Evelyn," I respond, gesturing to one of the tables. "Thank you for coming. Please, have a seat."

She sits down gracefully, her posture rigid. The atmosphere between us is thick with tension and awkwardness, and I decide to cut through it.

"Let's get to the point," I say, leaning forward slightly. "Do you want to do this or not?"

Evelyn's eyebrows raise at my directness. "Yes," she replies after a moment. "I want this project. I have a meeting with the board tomorrow to discuss the implications of taking on a consultant and running things...differently."

I nod, feeling a small thrill of victory. "Great. Then let's have a drink and talk details."

I signal to Mateo, who brings over a bottle of white wine in a cooler, water, and some tapas. It's not a wine the resort serves; I gave him a bottle I bought in Palma, suspecting Evelyn might have expensive taste.

"I wasn't planning on eating," Evelyn says, eyeing the food warily.

"Then don't," I reply cheerfully, pouring us each a glass of wine. "But we might as well enjoy ourselves while we talk, right?"

Evelyn takes a small sip of wine, and I see a flicker of surprise cross her face. "This is...quite good," she admits reluctantly.

"I'm glad you approve," I say, unable to keep a hint of smugness from my voice. "Now, let's discuss how this collaboration would work. Let's be practical."

Evelyn sets down her glass, her expression puzzled. "I don't understand why you're going along with this," she says. "You're essentially giving up control of your vision and surrendering to mine."

I chuckle. "Oh, Evelyn. You've got it all wrong. You think you've won, but in reality, I'm the one who's come out on top here."

"Right..." She shoots me a skeptical look. "And why is that?"

I lean back in my chair, feeling more relaxed now. "My life's mission is eco-friendly tourism. If I can get a company like Rothschild to swing that way, even on just one project? That's a massive win in my book. Think about it—your brand, your resources, all dedicated to creating a truly sustainable luxury resort. The impact that could have on the industry is huge. Plus," I add, reaching into my bag, "there's this." I slide a piece of paper across the table to her. "My hourly rate as a consultant."

Evelyn's eyes widen as she looks at the number. It's way too high, even making *me* a little uncomfortable, but I just love that look of sheer panic in her eyes. "This is...ridiculous," she says, her voice tight.

I shrug. "You need me for my expertise and my stamp of approval on the project. I'm losing out on potential profits and giving you my valuable time, so I'd say that's worth every penny."

Evelyn is quiet for a beat, sipping her wine as she considers. "All right," she says. "I think we can do this. But I have some conditions of my own."

"I'm listening." I smile politely as I meet her eyes, curious to hear what she has in mind. This is a stand-off and I'm not in the least intimidated.

"First," Evelyn begins, "while we'll certainly incorporate your eco-friendly practices, the overall aesthetic needs to align with the Rothschild brand. Our clients expect a certain level of luxury."

I nod. "Fair enough. I think you'll find that sustainability and luxury aren't mutually exclusive. We can create something truly unique that satisfies both our visions, but don't push it. If you're thinking of putting a helipad on the island, you can forget about it. I'll never agree to that. It's not just about the pollution, it will disturb the goats. And the goats are staying, by the way."

Evelyn's jaw tightens. "No helipad? That's a standard feature in all our resorts. Our high-profile clients expect private accessibility." She runs a hand through her hair, a rare gesture of discomfort breaking through her usual composed demeanor. "How are we supposed to cater to our VIP guests without helicopter access? Some of them won't even consider a resort without it."

"They can land in Palma and get a private charter from there," I say simply. "A beautiful charter, all part of the experience."

As the reality of the situation sinks in, Evelyn's expression shifts from shock to resignation. She lets out a long sigh, her shoulders slumping slightly. "And those fucking goats," she says, then takes a large sip of her wine, clearly needing a moment to process this new limitation. "We can't have the goats there. It's simply not an option."

"Fine. Then I won't be your consultant, and you won't get the contract," I reply, enjoying every moment. I came here with dreams of a resort on Cormoran Island and although those dreams are off the table, I'm getting something incredibly satisfying in return. Somewhere in the world, there will be another plot to build on my dreams, but I'll never get another chance to put a Rothschild in her place.

"This is going to be a harder sell to our usual clientele than I thought," she murmurs, more to herself than to me. "We'll need to completely rethink our transportation logistics, but we'll make it work somehow. Anyway," she continues, "I want weekly progress reports that I can forward to the board. You'll have to come up with solutions to every single obstacle involving sustainability. For this rate, I expect you to work your ass off."

"Of course. Communication is key in a partnership. I'm aware that my rate is significant, but you'll have me twenty-four seven." I slide a business card across the table that says, "Congratulations. You've just earned yourself Val's number!" They were a joke, a present from a friend. I never give these out to business contacts, but Evelyn doesn't need to know that, and tonight, I just want to mess with her a little. "Here's my personal number."

"Hmm...how professional." Evelyn slips the card into her purse, but she seems to relax a bit, perhaps realizing that I'm not going to fight her on every point. "And finally," she says, "I'll be in charge of the hiring process regarding the contractor."

I consider this for a moment. "I can agree to that, as long as we prioritize local hiring where possible."

Evelyn nods. "That's...reasonable. I think we can make that work."

"Good. And one more thing you need to know about me," I say with a grin.

Evelyn twirls her wine around in her glass as she regards me warily. "What's that?"

"I don't play with Barbies. I never have." I tilt my head and look her up and down, unable to hold back another comment I hope will make her uncomfortable. "I prefer real women."

Chapter 11

Evelyn

It's late by the time I settle into a comfortable chair on my hotel suite's terrace, and the evening breeze is cool and pleasant. My laptop sits open before me, and I'm holding my phone, waiting for Derek to join our video call. The sea breeze carries the faint scent of salt, a constant reminder that I'm far from my New York office.

As Derek's face appears on the screen, I straighten my posture, unconsciously smoothing down my silk blouse. "Evening, Derek," I greet him.

"Hi, Evelyn," he replies, his voice tinny through the phone's speaker. "How are you?"

"I'm fine." I allow myself a small smile of satisfaction. "I think we can be very pleased with how the board meeting went."

Derek nods. "Absolutely. Your idea for Rothschild Green Resorts was a stroke of genius."

"It was the logical solution," I say, trying not to sound too self-congratulatory. "It was the only way to make this proposal work around our current portfolio. And once I presented it that way, even the most skeptical board members could see the potential."

"True," Derek agrees. "The way you positioned it as a strategic move to stay ahead of our competitors was particularly effective. I could see the dollar signs in their eyes when you talked about the growing eco-friendly market." He drops a pause. "So, now that we have the green light, how do you think this is going to work out? Working with Ms. Mendoza, I mean. It's quite a departure from our usual way of doing things."

I wave a hand. "Oh, I'm not worried about that. Val is a silly young girl with dreams too big for her. I'll have her under my thumb in no time."

I open a new tab on my laptop and type "Val Mendoza Instagram" into the search bar. Her profile pops up immediately, filled with vibrant photos of tropical locations and smiling faces.

"Are you sure about that?" Derek's voice pulls me back to our conversation. "I know she impressed the committee with her presentation. And her ideas seem to have quite a following. She might be a challenge."

"Please," I scoff, scrolling through Val's Instagram feed. "She may have some good ideas, but she lacks the experience and business acumen to truly challenge us. We'll use her expertise where it's useful, but make no mistake, this is our project."

My eyes land on a photo of Val in a bikini, standing on a pristine beach with a surfboard tucked under her arm. *I knew it. She's such a cliché.* The sun glints off her tanned skin, and her smile is wide and genuine.

"If you say so," Derek replies. "Just don't underestimate her. That could be a costly mistake."

"I won't," I assure him, my eyes still fixed on the photo.

Why am I so drawn to this image? Is it professional curiosity or something else? I remember Val's comment from the other night—"I prefer real women." The words echo in my mind, stirring something I can't quite name.

Derek babbles on, but I don't register what he's saying until he calls my name. "Evelyn?" It snaps me back to attention. "Can you hear me?"

"Yes, I can now," I lie, refocusing my attention on him. "What were you saying?"

"I was asking if you're sure you don't want an assistant on site for this project. It's going to be a lot to manage, especially with the added complexity of working with a consultant."

I feel a flare of irritation at the suggestion. "For the last time, Derek, I don't need an assistant. I'm perfectly capable of handling this on my own. The wider team will join me once the contracts are signed but until then, stop treating me like I can't tie my own shoelaces."

"I apologize," he backtracks quickly. "It's just that with the time difference and the unique challenges of this project—"

"I said no," I cut him off, my tone leaving no room for argument. "I appreciate your concern, but I've got this under control. Is there anything else we need to discuss?"

Derek shakes his head, looking chastened. "No, that's all for now. I'll start working on the logistics for setting up the new sub-brand. We'll need to move quickly, as you'll need it for the final proposal."

"Good." I nod. "Keep me updated on the progress. I want daily updates."

"Of course," he agrees. "Good night, Evelyn. Try to get some rest."

I end the call without further pleasantries, setting my

phone aside with a sigh. The tension in my shoulders eases slightly as I lean back in my chair, my gaze drifting back to my laptop screen.

Almost without realizing it, I continue to scroll through Val's Instagram feed. There's something captivating about the way she moves through the world—so free, so unencumbered by the expectations and pressures that have defined my entire life.

I linger on a photo of her laughing with a group of locals in Santorini, her arm slung casually around an elderly woman's shoulders. The caption reads, "Learning traditional weaving techniques from the amazing women in Ekis village. Sustainability isn't just about the environment—it's about preserving cultural heritage too. #EcoLuxury #CulturalSustainability #EdenEcoEscapes"

Despite myself, I feel a twinge of admiration. Val's commitment to her ideals is evident in every post, every caption. It's not just a business strategy for her—it's a lifestyle.

I shake my head, closing the laptop with more force than necessary. What am I doing? This is ridiculous. Val Mendoza is a business associate. A consultant I could definitely do without.

And yet...as I stand up to head inside, I can't shake the image of Val in that bikini, her sun-kissed skin and easy smile. There's something about her that gets under my skin, something that both irritates and intrigues me.

I pour myself a glass of wine, wondering what she's doing right now. Is she out at that beach bar, charming the locals? Or is she hunched over her laptop, like me, preparing for our upcoming collaboration?

"Fuck," I mutter out loud. She's got me right where she wants. She knows she can pull out any moment and the project will be off. I know exactly what Val is doing. She's toying with me, and she probably finds it amusing. If I ever get the chance, I'll hit back hard.

Exchanging my glass for my phone once more, I pull Val's ridiculous business card from my purse and type: *Now you have my number. Let's discuss details tomorrow.*

My phone buzzes almost instantly with Val's reply. It's just an emoji—a thumbs-up. I roll my eyes, feeling a mixture of annoyance and something else I can't quite name. It's so childish, so unprofessional. Is this how she conducts all her business?

I remind myself that Val is practically the same age as my daughter. She's young, inexperienced. Whatever game she thinks she's playing, she'll get bored of it soon enough. Once the contracts are signed and the real work begins, she'll realize she's out of her depth and leave it to me to handle things.

As I'm contemplating this, another message from Val pops up: *Let's meet at La Taberna in the village. They have amazing paella. Does one p.m. work for you?*

I frown at the screen. The last thing I want to do is venture out into the village restaurant. It's a waste of time when we could easily meet here at the hotel. But I know I have to play along with Val's whims, at least until the contracts are signed.

I'll see you there, I type back, keeping my response curt. *Send me the address.*

Chapter 12

Val

La Taberna is a quaint little restaurant tucked away in the heart of the village. The rustic charm of the place, with its worn wooden tables and the scent of garlic and saffron wafting from the kitchen, feels wonderfully authentic.

Glancing at my watch, I note that I'm early. Perfect. I signal to the waiter, a young man with a friendly smile, and decide to take matters into my own hands.

"I'll have the seafood paella for two, please," I tell him in Spanish. "But not yet. Maybe in forty minutes? And a bottle of the house white wine."

As he nods and heads off to place the order, I smile smugly. I know I'm being childish, ordering for both of us without waiting for Evelyn. But after losing the pitch outright, these small victories are oddly satisfying. It's petty, sure, but it makes me feel more in control of the situation.

The waiter returns with the wine and two glasses, and I spot Evelyn entering the restaurant. I have to do a double-take—she's actually dressed down today. Instead of her usual suit, she's wearing a simple, fitted navy dress. It's clear she's made an effort to adapt to the local climate, probably realizing she'd be sweating all day if she didn't.

The casual outfit suits her. She looks more relaxed, more...human. Her legs are toned and the dress hugs her subtle curves beautifully. I realize with a start that I never noticed how attractive she is.

No. Don't even go there. She represents everything you've been fighting. Still, I can't deny there's a tiny spark of...something. I'm not sure what, but I file it away to examine later.

"Val," Evelyn greets me as she takes her seat. Her eyes dart around, taking in the rustic surroundings with a mix of curiosity and barely concealed disdain.

"Evelyn," I reply, offering her a smile. "The seafood paella here is to die for. I hope you don't mind, but I've taken the liberty of ordering for us."

Evelyn's eyebrows rise slightly, a flicker of irritation crossing her face. "Don't you always?" she says, her voice dripping with sarcasm.

I chuckle, pouring her a glass of wine. "Come on, live a little. You might actually enjoy not being in control for once."

She takes the glass, her fingers brushing against mine for a brief moment. "I doubt that," she mutters but takes a sip of the wine, nonetheless. "Did you go through the presentation I sent you?"

"I did. It's impressive, and I have some ideas I'd like to run by you."

Evelyn nods, seeming to relax a bit now that we're moving on to familiar territory.

As I launch into my ideas, I watch Evelyn carefully. She listens intently, her brow furrowed in concentration. Despite our differences, I have to admit she's sharp. She asks pointed questions, challenges some of my assumptions, and even offers a few suggestions that are pretty good.

The paella arrives, a steaming pan of fragrant rice studded with gambas, mussels, and chunks of fish. Evelyn eyes it warily at first, but after taking a tentative bite, she gives me an approving nod.

"This is...actually quite good," she admits, reaching for another forkful.

"Sometimes it pays to trust someone else," I say with a grin.

She gives me a cold stare but doesn't argue. As we continue our discussion between bites of paella, I'm oddly enjoying our back-and-forth. There's a kind of electricity to our interaction, a clash of worldviews and personalities that is both frustrating and interesting.

As Evelyn outlines her ideas for "Rothschild Green Resorts," I'm torn. On one hand, it's gratifying to see she's embracing the collaboration. On the other, I'm wary of how they might work around my vision just to tick boxes.

"Look," I say, setting down my fork, "I appreciate that you're incorporating sustainability into your brand. But we need to be careful not to turn this into just a marketing gimmick. The changes we make have to be substantial, not just surface level."

Evelyn's eyes narrow slightly. "I assure you, Val, we're taking this very seriously. Rothschild Resorts doesn't do anything halfway."

"I'm sure you don't," I reply, unable to keep a hint of challenge out of my voice. "But true sustainability often means sacrificing some of the excesses that your clients are used to. Are you prepared for that?"

She stares at me for a long moment, and it's impossible to read her mind. This woman has the best poker face I've ever come across. "I've been in this business for almost as long as you've been alive, Ms. Mendoza," she says. "I think I know a thing or two about adapting to new market demands, so don't waste my time with silly questions."

The tension rises between us, threatening to derail our meeting. This isn't productive, and if we're going to work together, we need to find some common ground. I take a moment, deciding to change tack.

"I apologize. I didn't mean to offend you in any way. Let's put the business talk aside while we eat," I suggest, my tone softening. "We'll be working closely together for quite a while. Maybe we should take this opportunity to get to know each other. That might make our collaboration easier moving forward."

Evelyn looks surprised by my sudden shift. She tilts her head, considering it, then nods. "I suppose that's not an unreasonable suggestion," she concedes, reaching for her wine glass.

"Great." I smile. "So, tell me, what made you want to get into the resort business in the first place?"

Evelyn takes a sip of wine before answering. "It's the family business," she says. "I grew up in Rothschild Resorts."

"And is it what you always wanted to do?"

Evelyn's expression shifts, a mix of nostalgia and something harder to read crossing her face. "Actually, no," she admits, surprising me with her candor. "When I was younger, I wanted nothing to do with it."

"Really? What changed?"

She prods a shrimp and studies it like the answer lies on her fork. "I started working in my father's company after I had my daughter."

I can't hide my surprise. "I had no idea you had a child," I say.

Evelyn's lips quirk into a half-smile. "Yes, her name is Mia. She's twenty-five now."

"What's she like?" I ask, genuinely curious.

"She's...nothing like me, actually. Free-spirited, always off on some new adventure. She runs a food blog, travels the world sampling street food in different countries."

I smile at that. "Sounds like she's doing pretty well."

Evelyn chuckles, a sound I've rarely heard from her. "Perhaps. Though I'd prefer if she showed a bit more interest in the family business."

"And her father?" I ask, then immediately regret it. "I'm sorry, that's probably too personal."

But Evelyn shakes her head. "It's fine. He's not in the picture. It's always just been Mia and me."

I nod. "That can't have been easy, balancing a child and working full time."

"It wasn't," she admits. "But in a way, it gave me focus. I had something to prove—to my father, to myself, and more importantly, to Mia. I wanted to show her that women could be successful, could run a business as well as any man."

As Evelyn talks about her daughter, I see a new side of her. There's a softness in her eyes, a hint of vulnerability that makes her more relatable. It's clear that despite their differences, she loves Mia deeply.

"Are you close?" I ask.

Evelyn nods, her smile widening. "We are. Even if I don't always understand her choices. She's a good person. I have no idea how she turned out like an angel." She meets my gaze. "And what's your angle?"

"I always wanted to work in the sustainable hospitality

business," I say. "My parents were environmental activists who instilled a deep respect for nature in me."

"Were?" Evelyn asks, stirring her fork through the remaining paella. "Are they no longer around?"

"They died in a boating accident while documenting ocean pollution for a documentary." I swallow hard and curse myself for letting the conversation go here. "I was fifteen."

"I'm so sorry." Evelyn puts a hand on my forearm, and for the first time, I believe she's actually being genuine. "I lost my mother when I was fourteen. It's always hard, of course, but when you're younger..."

I meet her eyes, and for a moment, the barriers between us seem to dissolve. We're no longer business rivals. We're just two women who have experienced loss at a young age.

"It shaped everything, didn't it?" I ask, surprised by the vulnerability in my own voice.

Evelyn nods, her hand still on my arm. It feels warm and comforting. "It did. For both of us, I imagine."

We sit in silence for a while. It's a strange feeling, this sudden connection with someone I've considered an adversary. But it's not unwelcome.

Finally, I clear my throat, trying to lighten the mood. "Well, I guess we both turned our pain into purpose, huh?"

Evelyn chuckles softly, withdrawing her hand. "Indeed we did." She locks her eyes with mine and I swear I see a little bit of empathy, perhaps understanding in them. "I'll do my best to keep this collaboration civil. I hope you'll do the same."

Chapter 13

Evelyn

The contract lies before me on the polished mahogany table, its pages filled with carefully negotiated clauses and conditions. This moment should feel triumphant. After all, I've secured the Cormoran Island project for Rothschild Resorts. Instead, an unfamiliar flutter of nerves dances in my stomach.

Across the table, Val Mendoza watches me with those infuriatingly perceptive eyes of hers. She's relaxed, leaning back in her chair with an easy confidence that both irritates and impresses me.

"Everything okay, Evelyn?" she asks. "You look like you're about to sign your life away."

I shoot her a look that would make most people cower. Val, annoyingly, just grins. "I'm fine," I say, my voice clipped. "Just...double-checking the details."

It's a lie and we both know it. My lawyers have gone over this contract so many times they could probably recite it from memory. What I'm really doing is stalling, trying to come to terms with the fact that for the first time in my career, I'm not in complete control.

This collaboration with Val—it's new territory for me. I'm used to calling all the shots, to having my vision executed precisely as I see fit. But now, with Val as our consultant, I'll have to...compromise. The word alone leaves a bitter taste in my mouth.

"It's okay to be nervous," Val says. "This is a big step for both of us. But I promise you can trust me."

I consider her words, turning them over in my mind. She's growing on me, but I don't trust her as far as I can throw her. Still, I pick up the pen and sign my name. The familiar motion calms me, reminding me of countless deals I've closed over the years. I'm still Evelyn Rothschild, and I can certainly handle this little challenge.

I slide the contract across to Val, who signs it without hesitation. It's done. We're officially working together.

"Well," Val says, shooting me a satisfied smile, "I think this calls for a celebration. How about a drink? We can plan the coming weeks in a more relaxed setting."

I glance at my watch—it's only four p.m. Then again, we are on a Mediterranean island. "I suppose there's no harm in a drink."

Val's eyebrows shoot up, clearly not expecting me to agree so readily. "Great! I know just the place—"

"Actually," I interrupt, seizing the opportunity, "It's my turn to pick the place. Let's go to my hotel. The rooftop bar has an excellent view."

Val laughs, a warm, genuine sound that I find strangely pleasant. "Okay. Fancy hotel bar it is."

Most people tend to find me intimidating, but Val seems unfazed, even amused by my attempts to assert control. As we step out of City Hall, I immediately flag down a station wagon taxi and point to the mountain bike she's unlocking. "Just throw it in the back. It will be safe at the hotel." I'm not about to let Val take decisions of our transportation or destination today.

"Hotel Cala d'Or Royale," I tell the driver as we settle into the back seat. Val raises an eyebrow but doesn't comment.

We've barely pulled away from the curb when my phone buzzes. It's a video call from Mia. I hesitate. There's no room here for a private conversation, but it's not always easy to get hold of her when she's traveling, and it might be important. "Hello, sweetheart," I say, picking up. "Everything okay?"

"Mom!" Mia's face fills the screen, her eyes sparkling with excitement. "Grandpa just called me about the wedding! Can you believe it?"

I force a smile, acutely aware of Val's presence beside me. Great. Now she's privy to the ins and outs on the Rothschild family dramas. "Yes, he told me." I let out a long sigh. "Apparently, they want children too. I mean, of course *she* does. She's clearly after his money."

"Maybe. But I've never seen him so happy. It's kind of cute." Mia grins. "You know what this means, right? I can call the baby aunt or uncle."

It's not funny, not really, but I can't help but laugh. Mia has always had a way with words. She's funnier than me, sharper. It's just another of the many ways we're different.

"You're terrible," I say, still chuckling. "I'll call you back later, okay? I'm in a taxi right now."

After I hang up, I notice Val staring at me. "Sorry," I say, straightening my blouse. "I had to take that."

"Was that your daughter?" she asks. "I didn't mean to eavesdrop, but there was no way to avoid hearing it."

I nod, feeling oddly exposed. "Yes, that was Mia."

Val continues to regard me with intense curiosity. "You're so different when you talk to her. You didn't seem like..."

"The maternal type?" I finish for her, my tone dry.

Val has the grace to look slightly embarrassed. "Honestly, yes. But just now...everything about your demeanor changed when you talked to her. It was really sweet."

"Thank you, I guess..." I feel a blush rise to my cheeks and look away. "And about my father," I continue. "He's getting married to some woman half his age. He's completely lost it. I'd appreciate it if you could keep this between us. I'm hoping I can talk some sense into him before the whole world finds out Donald Rothschild is an old pervert."

"How young are we talking?" Val asks, concern lacing her voice. "Because if the chairman of the company I'm working for is marrying a child bride...well, I don't want to be associated with that."

I shake my head and wave a hand. "She's not *that* young. Twenty-eight or something."

Val is silent for a beat, seemingly processing this information. When she finally speaks, her voice is tight with barely contained irritation. "I'm twenty-eight, and I'm not a child. I sincerely hope you're not ageist. Wait... Do you even take me seriously?"

Her words catch me off guard. I've never considered myself to be ageist, but Val's reaction makes me pause. "Of course I take you seriously," I say, acutely aware of the age difference between us. It hits me like a ton of bricks. Val is the same age as my father's fiancée, and she's younger than my daughter. "Your age has nothing to do with your professional capabilities." It's a lie, but it's the right answer.

"Doesn't it?" Val challenges. "Because you seem pretty quick to dismiss your father's fiancée based on her age alone, and don't think I've forgotten about that Barbie comment."

"I apologize for the Barbie dig," I say. "And about my father...that's different."

"How?" Val presses. "How is it different? Because he's your father? Because it makes you uncomfortable?"

I take a deep breath, trying to gather my thoughts. "It's just...complicated. There's a significant age gap between them, and I worry about her motivations."

Val shakes her head. "You know, I've dated women your age before, and I wasn't after their money."

"You've what?"

"Dated women your age," she repeats, her gaze steady. "Age doesn't define people. Maybe you should cut your father some slack if he's happy with his fiancée. And sure, she may have ulterior motives, but at least give her a chance before you make up your mind."

I feel something twist in my stomach. Is it discomfort? I'm not sure. "Well, frankly, it's none of your business, Val. My family affairs are private."

Val holds up her hands in a gesture of surrender and sits back. "You're right. It's none of my business."

We lapse into an uncomfortable silence, the air between us thick with unspoken tension. Val is young, yes, but there's a maturity and confidence about her that I can't deny.

As we near the hotel, I decide to break the silence. "Look, I'm sorry if I offended you. That wasn't my intention."

Val's expression softens slightly. "I appreciate that. And I'm sorry if I overstepped. I just... I've dealt with a lot of prejudice because of my age in this industry. It gets old."

"I can imagine," I say. "It's hard enough as it is for a woman." A strange mix of emotions lingers. Irritation at being called out, yes, but also a grudging respect for Val's boldness. And underneath it all, a curiosity I'm not quite ready to examine too closely.

Chapter 14

Val

Evelyn gestures to a waiter. "A bottle of Dom Pérignon, please," she says, then turns to me. "And how about some oysters? Val, do you eat oysters?"

"Yes, if they're locally and sustainably sourced, I'd love some." The waiter nods and I give him a smile. "And a tomato salad too, please," I add, glancing at the snack menu. "Oh, and some bread and olive oil."

Evelyn raises an eyebrow, a hint of amusement in her eyes. "I'm surprised you eat seafood. If I hadn't seen you wolf down that paella last week, I would have pegged you for a vegan."

"I used to be," I say. "But nowadays, I'm not so strict. I'm very mindful about what I eat, though. I love to experience local cuisines when I travel. It's part of immersing myself in different cultures."

"You love traveling?"

"Yes, don't you?" I'm pleasantly surprised how easy the small talk is after our frosty exchange in the car.

"It's work," Evelyn says with a shrug and moves back when the waiter arrives with our champagne. "I don't normally take time off unless I'm with Mia. I don't see the point. Anyway, let's talk about you. I think it's only fair after you've been privy to my family drama. I've read your CV, of course, and I noticed there weren't any universities listed."

I take a sip of the champagne, savoring the crisp, bubbly sensation on my tongue before answering. "That's correct. I've always preferred hands-on experience to formal education. Instead of applying to universities, I decided to work in my aunt and uncle's restaurant in San Francisco when I was seventeen."

"Did you live with them? After your..." Evelyn winces.

"Yes, I moved in with them after my parents died. They're both chefs and own a few upmarket vegan restaurants in San Francisco. They were early pioneers in vegan fine dining and it really paid off."

"Ah, so that's where your interest in high-end hospitality comes from," Evelyn muses.

"Exactly. Working there taught me so much about the industry. But I always had the travel bug, so I saved up and went backpacking. During my travels, I visited a lot of eco-friendly hotels and noticed a gap in the market. Back then, there wasn't much in the way of luxury sustainable travel, not like there is now." I shrug. "Not that I could afford to stay in high-end hotels. I just liked visiting, having a browse, you know?"

The oysters arrive, nestled in a bed of ice. Evelyn offers me first pick, and I choose one, inhaling the fresh, briny scent before tipping it into my mouth.

"So how did you go from noticing a gap in the market to actually starting your own company?" Evelyn asks, selecting an oyster for herself.

I smile, remembering those early days of excitement and uncertainty. "With my uncle's help, I put together a business plan and a presentation. Then I took a leap of faith and started crowdfunding. To my surprise, it went incredibly well."

"Crowdfunding for a luxury resort?" Evelyn looks skeptical. "That's...unconventional."

"It was," I agree. "But it caught the attention of some serious investors. They were intrigued by the concept and impressed by the initial response. I raised four million, not nearly enough, but to investors, that was a promising sign. They offered to provide the remainder of the capital I needed."

"So investors funded the project even though you had no track record in the industry?" Evelyn clarifies, her business acumen kicking in.

I nod. "Yes, they provided the bulk of the funding in exchange for equity. It was a whirlwind, going from this idea I had while backpacking to suddenly being responsible for twenty-five million in investment capital. I won't deny that I freaked out a little, but with the help of an amazing team, I got there in the end."

Evelyn frowns. "But that wasn't enough. You wanted to open another one."

"Seeing something thrive is addictive," I admit. "And what else was I going to do? Sit on my ass on a beach all day?"

Evelyn chuckles. "It's certainly addictive, and I'm impressed. Many people have ideas, but few have the drive and the talent to make them a reality."

Her compliment catches me off guard. It's probably the nicest thing she's said to me since we met. "Thank you. It wasn't easy, but I believed in the concept, and now, I can't imagine doing anything else. Besides, I needed something to focus on after I lost my parents. It's been my therapy, I suppose. Just knowing they'd be proud of me if they could see what I've achieved..." I feel a surge of emotion bubbling up and take a few deep breaths, fighting back tears. It happens every time I mention them, but the pain is more bearable than it used to be. Why am I telling her all of this? It makes no sense.

"They would be so incredibly proud of you," Evelyn says. "You must have been disappointed that you didn't win the pitch."

"I was." I help myself to another oyster. "But in the end, sustainability will always be at the forefront of what I do, in whatever shape or form. There will be more hotels in the future, they just won't be on Cormoran Island, and I can live with that as long as I know the island is treated with respect. Besides, working as a first consultant for the Rothschild Group will look great on my CV and the paycheck isn't bad either," I add with a wink, lightening the mood.

Evelyn laughs, and I'm glad she can see the humor of my ridiculous fee. I wouldn't have dared charge such a rate normally, but I guess I was pushing it just to annoy her.

"As I said, you'd better work your ass off." She regards me curiously the way she has since we met, like she's constantly trying to work me out. I'm doing the same and I have to admit, there are more layers to Evelyn Rothschild than I expected. The fading light softens her features, and I'm struck once again by how attractive she is when she's relaxed like this. Her dark eyes catch the golden light, and there's a hint of a smile playing at the corners of her mouth. It's a far cry from the ice queen I first encountered, and I'm genuinely enjoying her company, even feeling a little drawn to her. "But you can start working your ass off tomorrow," she continues. "The day is almost over, and I never work after a drink."

"You know I will," I shoot back at her. "I take it you've set up office in your room?"

"My suite," she corrects me. "How about eight a.m.?"

"That works for me." The bread arrives. It's still warm and I break off a piece and dip it in olive oil. It's delicious, but Evelyn doesn't seem interested. I bet she's one of those women who avoids carbs. "So which Ivy League school did you go to?" I ask. "I assume you had top-notch education?"

Evelyn hesitates for a moment, her fingers tracing the stem of her champagne glass. She looks at me, her eyes searching mine, as if weighing a decision. Finally, she lets out a soft sigh. "You know what? I might as well tell you. It's not a secret, after all." She takes a sip of champagne. "The truth is, I didn't have much of an education."

I can't hide my surprise. "Really? But I thought... I mean, you're Evelyn Rothschild. I just assumed..."

She gives me a wry smile. "Most people do. But life had other plans for me."

"Because you fell pregnant?" I ask.

Evelyn shakes her head, and for a moment, I see a flicker of something—vulnerability, perhaps?—before she looks away, her gaze drifting out over the darkening sea. She seems to be debating with herself, and I'm about to change the subject when she speaks.

"Not entirely," she says. "It started before Mia, and you were very young, so you won't remember, but I was often in the headlines back then. 'Heiress Rothschild Caught in Drug Scandal' or 'Rothschild Daughter Expelled Again.' That sort of thing. I was the wild child of New York's elite, always in some kind of trouble."

I frown and lean in. "I find that so hard to imagine."

She nods and takes a deep breath, and I hold mine,

sensing that I'm about to hear something important. "My life spiraled out of control after my mother passed away."

"I'm so sorry," I murmur, resisting the urge to reach out and touch her hand.

Evelyn nods. "I didn't know how to cope. My father didn't either. He poured all his energy into work, and I..." She trails off. "I became difficult. I started drinking, experimenting with drugs. I got expelled from two schools for misconduct and there was no place in an Ivy League school for me anymore. Not that I wanted to go. I didn't care about anything."

"I don't blame you. That must have been tough."

"Yeah. I was a different person then," Evelyn says, her voice soft. "A kid with too much money and too little supervision. And then..." She pauses, taking a sip of champagne. "I fell pregnant with Mia. It was like a wake-up call. Suddenly, there was this enormous responsibility, and I had to pull myself together somehow."

"So that's when you started working for your father?" I ask.

"Yes. At first, I considered an abortion, but I couldn't go through with it. It just... I don't know. It didn't feel right. My father paid for a nanny and gave me a job. He didn't expect much from me—he even told me so. But I did everything in my power to turn things around and managed to prove him wrong. Since then..."

"Since then, you've always been in control," I finish for her.

"Exactly. I've never had more than two drinks, never touched any illegal substances again. I like to think I've been a good mom. I did the best I could, anyway."

I lean back in my chair, processing this new information. The Evelyn sitting across from me now seems a world away from the rebellious teenager she's describing. Yet I can see how that girl became this woman—the drive, the determination, the need for control. It all makes sense now.

"Thank you for sharing that with me."

Evelyn seems to shake herself out of the moment. "Well," she says, her tone lighter, "now you know all my deep, dark secrets." She laughs. "How on earth did you manage to make me talk again?"

Chapter 15

Evelyn

I can't sleep. The silk sheets that cocooned me in comfort last night now feel suffocating. I toss and turn, my mind a whirlwind of thoughts I can't seem to quiet. For the first time in decades, doubt gnaws at the edges of my confidence.

Val's face keeps appearing in my mind's eye, her easy smile and piercing gaze unsettling me in ways I don't fully understand. Why do I care what she thinks of me? It shouldn't matter. She's just a consultant, a means to an end. And yet...

I sit up abruptly, running a hand through my disheveled hair. Did I say too much earlier? I've never been one to open up, to share personal details about my past. It's always been easier, safer, to keep people at arm's length. But something about Val made the words tumble out.

Will she see it as weakness? The thought makes my stomach churn. I've worked so hard to build this image of strength and control. What if I've undermined it all in one evening of vulnerability?

I swing my legs over the side of the bed, my bare feet

meeting the cool tiled floor. The clock on the bedside table glows an accusatory 2:17 a.m. In just a few hours, Val will be here, ready to start work on our project. *Our project.* I don't like the sound of that.

How are we supposed to work together? Val's business is so far removed from the Rothschild way of doing things. She'll want to change everything, interfere with plans I've spent weeks perfecting. I can already imagine the arguments, the compromises I'll be forced to make.

I pace the length of the bedroom, my silk nightgown swishing softly with each step. Normally, I'd be diving into the work headfirst, making decisions and moving forward at breakneck speed. But now, with Val involved, everything feels uncertain and off-balance.

I shake my head, trying to dislodge these thoughts. This isn't me. I don't dwell on people, don't let them get under my skin. So why can't I stop worrying?

The room suddenly feels too small, too confining, and I need air. I make my way to the terrace doors, slide them open, and step out into the warm night air.

The penthouse terrace is spacious and comfortable, but I haven't used it much. I sit on one of the sun loungers arranged around a small infinity pool, sinking into its plush cushions. The sky above is a blanket of stars, more than I've seen in years. Living in New York, it's easy to forget how vast and beautiful the night sky can be. The constellations spread out above me, a glittering map. It's beautiful, I realize with a start. When was the last time I noticed something for its beauty alone?

The sea stretches out before me, a dark expanse occasionally broken by the glimmer of starlight on waves. In the distance, I can make out the silhouette of Cormoran Island.

It looks so small and unassuming from here, it's hard to believe it's causing me so much turmoil.

I close my eyes, taking a deep breath of the salty air. The sound of waves lapping at the shore below is soothing, a constant rhythm that starts to calm my racing thoughts. For a moment, I allow myself to simply be. No plans, no strategies. Just me, lying under the stars, feeling small, uncertain, yet strangely alive. Is this what Val meant about connecting with nature? About finding beauty in simplicity?

I open my eyes, gazing back up at the star-studded sky. A shooting star streaks across the darkness, gone in a blink. *Make a wish*, a small voice in my head whispers. It's childish, I know, but in this moment of vulnerability, I allow myself the indulgence.

I wish... I pause, realizing I'm not sure what to wish for. Success? I've already achieved that. Money? I have more than I could ever spend. Love? The thought makes me uncomfortable. There's no place for love in my life, at least, not of the romantic kind. I've tried relationships but I never felt fulfilled.

Instead, I wish for health and happiness for Mia, then get up to grab my phone and settle back on the sunbed. Sleep seems impossible so I might as well keep myself busy, I reason, unlocking my phone and opening Google.

I type in "Valeria Mendoza." The results populate quickly, and I scroll through them.

Her business profiles appear first—LinkedIn, corporate websites, industry publications. I'm already familiar with most of the information from my earlier research. Val's professional accomplishments are impressive, especially for someone her age.

As I continue scrolling, I stumble upon her personal Instagram account again. I should stop snooping. I've already fallen down the Val rabbit hole a few times in the past week, and I keep going back to that picture of Val with her surfboard.

Another photo shows her atop a mountain, arms spread wide, embracing the view. The caption reads, "On top of the world! #AdventureAwaits" Her enthusiasm is palpable, even through the screen, and as I continue through her feed, I notice a pattern. Whether she's exploring a bustling street market in Thailand or lounging in a hammock in Bali, Val fully immerses herself in each moment. There's an authenticity to her posts that's refreshing in a world of staged social media perfection.

Lingering on a photo of her emerging from crystal-clear waters, droplets cascading down her toned body, I swallow hard. She's wearing a black triangle bikini, and the sight stirs something in me.

I quickly scroll past, and a group photo catches my attention. Val's arm is draped around a woman who looks to be older than me. They're both laughing, heads tilted toward each other in a way that suggests intimacy. The woman is striking—tall, with silver-streaked dark hair and laugh lines around her eyes. I wonder if this woman is an ex, or perhaps someone Val has been involved with.

Before I can stop it, my mind wanders to dangerous territory. I picture myself in that tropical setting, the warm sun on my skin, the sound of waves in the background, and Val's arm around me. The warmth I felt earlier intensifies, spreading through my body like wildfire.

In my mind's eye, Val pulls me closer, her hand coming to rest on my waist. I can almost feel the heat of her palm as she leans in. Then I'm picturing her lips meeting mine, soft and insistent.

Panic floods through me, and I sit up abruptly, nearly

dropping my phone. What am I doing? This is completely ridiculous and I've never thought about a woman like that before. Have I? No. My heart is racing, and I take a deep breath. It's just the lack of sleep, I reason. These thoughts don't mean anything. They can't.

And yet, as I try to push the images from my mind, I'm drawn back to Val's Instagram. I scroll further, hungrily taking in each new photo. There's one of her planting trees as part of a reforestation project. Like Mia, she's so free, so unencumbered by the expectations and pressures that have defined my entire life. Part of me wants to dismiss her as naïve or idealistic, but I can't.

I come across a video of Val giving a TEDx talk about sustainable tourism. Her passion is evident, her hands moving animatedly as she describes her vision for the future of the industry. I hang on her every word, impressed by her eloquence and conviction, and as I watch, I notice little details I hadn't picked up on before. The way she tucks her hair behind her ear when she's making a particularly important point. The slight frown that appears between her brows each time she pauses.

I realize with a start that I've been watching the video on repeat, and it's now well past three a.m. Closing my phone, I head back to bed, my mind still swirling with images of Val—surfing, laughing, changing the world.

Reaching for the strip of sleeping pills on my nightstand, I hesitate before I pop one out. I don't like to take them, but right now, I don't see another solution to quiet these strange, unsettling thoughts. With a sigh, I swallow a pill with a sip of water, hoping for a dreamless sleep to reset my mind before morning.

Chapter 16

Val

It's just past eight a.m. when I raise my hand to knock on Evelyn's door. I'm only a few minutes late, but I hate not being punctual, especially when it comes to work. My knuckles rap against the heavy wooden door, but there's no response. I check my watch again. 8:07 a.m. Surely Evelyn's in her suite? Or were we supposed to meet downstairs?

I wait another moment before knocking again, harder this time. Finally, I hear movement from inside the room. The lock clicks, and the door swings open.

"I told you, no room service in the mornings—" Evelyn's irritated voice cuts off abruptly as she realizes it's me standing there, not a member of the hotel staff.

I can't help but stare. This is not the perfectly put-together Evelyn Rothschild I'm used to seeing. Her hair is a mess, sticking up in all directions, and her eyes are bleary, unfocused, still heavy with sleep. She's wearing a silk night-gown that's slightly rumpled, and there's a faint imprint of a pillow crease on her cheek.

For a moment, we just stand there, both of us frozen in

surprise. Then I watch as the realization dawns on Evelyn's face. Her eyes widen, and a flush creeps up her neck, spreading across her cheeks. It's amusing, I have to admit.

"Val," she says, her voice hoarse from sleep. "I... I'm so sorry. I overslept. That never happens."

Something about seeing Evelyn Rothschild caught off guard like this is oddly satisfying. I can't help it—my gaze drops lower, taking in the way the silk clings to her body. Her breasts are full and firm, and I can see the faint outline of her nipples through the thin fabric. The sight is captivating, and for a second, I forget myself. Evelyn notices, her eyes narrowing slightly as she instinctively brings a hand up to cover her chest, and I curse myself internally. I quickly force my eyes back to her face.

"It's okay," I say, forcing a smile as I feel my own cheeks flush. "It happens to the best of us."

"Not to me." Evelyn runs a hand through her hair, looking mortified. "Please, come in," she says, stepping back from the door. "Make yourself comfortable. I'll just... I need to get ready. I won't be long."

I step inside, taking in the luxurious suite. There are papers scattered across a large desk, and a laptop sits open next to them.

"Take your time," I call out as Evelyn grabs a dry-cleaning bag from her wardrobe and disappears into what I assume is the bathroom. "I'll set up my laptop."

Thoroughly embarrassed that she caught me staring at her breasts, I set my bag down on the desk, trying push the image of her silk-clad figure from my mind. Opening my laptop, I take a deep breath, willing the heat in my cheeks to fade. This morning is not going as planned for either of us, and I'm surprised Evelyn overslept. She doesn't seem like the type to let anything interfere with her rigid schedule. Was she up late working?

About fifteen minutes later, the bathroom door opens. Evelyn emerges, looking much more like her usual self. Her hair is styled, her makeup flawless. She's wearing a white sleeveless blouse and tailored black pants, and she's barefoot, her toenails painted a soft shade of pink.

"I apologize again for the delay," she says, her voice now clear and controlled. "This is completely unacceptable. It won't happen again."

I wave off her apology. "Really, it's fine. We all have off days sometimes."

Evelyn's lips tighten slightly at that, as if the very idea of having an "off day" is offensive to her. She moves to the phone next to her bed, dials room service and barks something about two pots of black coffee, two cups, and breakfast. Then she's silent for a beat while she listens to whatever poor soul she's speaking to, finishing with, "No, no, no. Let me stop you right there. I don't have time to discuss the menu. Just bring up a bit of everything."

"So," she says, settling into an armchair across from me. "Shall we get started?"

I nod, pulling up the first set of plans on my laptop. "My team and I have been reviewing your designs for the resort, and I have some suggestions for how we can make them more sustainable without sacrificing luxury. How about we start with some easy fixes?"

Evelyn leans forward, her eyes sharp and focused. It's like watching a switch flip. The sleepy, somewhat disoriented woman from earlier is completely gone, replaced by the shrewd businesswoman I've come to know. "Shoot," she says.

I clear my throat and begin, "Let's start with some low-hanging fruit. First, we could implement a linen reuse program. Instead of automatically changing sheets and towels daily, we give guests the option to reuse them. This alone can significantly reduce water and energy consumption, and generally, guests are happy to do this. It's used in most luxury hotels nowadays, but not in Rothschild Resorts."

"Fine." Evelyn nods, her expression neutral. "Go on."

"Next, we should look at lighting. Switching to LED bulbs throughout the resort could cut energy use by up to seventy-five percent compared to traditional incandescent bulbs. We could also install motion sensors in less frequently used areas to ensure lights aren't left on unnecessarily."

I pause, gauging Evelyn's reaction. Her face remains impassive, but I notice a slight tightening around her eyes. "Our lighting is essential to the atmosphere in our hotels."

"I'm aware of that, but I'm confident we can get very close with the alternative." I continue without waiting for an answer. If she's not willing to give in on something as easy as lighting, we won't get anywhere. "Water conservation is another area. Salt-water pools are essential, and low-flow showerheads and dual-flush toilets can dramatically reduce water usage without impacting guest comfort. And for landscaping, we could use native, drought-resistant plants to minimize irrigation needs. We can—"

"And how much will all this cost?" Evelyn interrupts, her voice sharp.

I take a deep breath as I meet her eyes. "We're not talking huge costs on these points, Evelyn. As I said, these are the quick and easy fixes. The real costs will come in when we start talking about a water purifying system and solar power solutions. However, even these investments pay for themselves quite quickly through reduced utility costs."

"Our guests expect the best," Evelyn counters. "They're not going to be impressed by feeling like they're roughing it."

I can feel my frustration rising. "It's not about 'roughing it.' These are standard practices in modern luxury hotels. In fact, many of your competitors are already doing this and more. Maybe it's time you admit you're running behind when it comes to sustainable practices. It's the future of the industry. If you want to stay competitive—"

"We are competitive. We're so far ahead of the competition they can't even see us in the distance!"

The sound of Evelyn's hand hitting the side of her chair echoes through the room, and I'm startled by the sudden noise.

She looks as shocked as I feel at her outburst. "I... I'm sorry. I didn't mean to... I'm not good without coffee in the morning," she stammers and looks relieved when there's a knock on the door. She practically leaps up to answer it, eager for the interruption. "Fine. Let's go ahead with all that," she says, glancing at me over her shoulder. "Send my project manager the details."

I watch as Evelyn accepts the trolley from room service, tipping the attendant. The aroma of coffee fills the air as she pours us both a cup. She takes a long sip, closing her eyes briefly as if savoring the caffeine hit.

"Please," she gestures to the spread of pastries, fruit, and yogurt. "Help yourself."

"Thank you." I select a croissant, only to be polite. "Right. Well, another area you should consider is waste management. A comprehensive recycling and composting program could significantly reduce the resort's landfill contributions."

"And how would that work in practice? We can't expect our guests to sort their own trash."

"Of course not," I agree. "We'd implement a behind-the-scenes sorting system. Guests would dispose of waste as usual, but your staff would ensure it's properly sorted and recycled or composted. With bottled water from the natural spring, there shouldn't be that much plastic waste, and we can eliminate single-use plastics entirely by providing beautiful water dispensers and reusable glass bottles in the rooms. You will have to replace your mini toiletries with large refillable bottles, so that will also save on waste. Food waste will be returned to the kitchen through room service, so that's pretty straightforward. You'll need to employ a food and beverage director who has experience running zero-waste hotels or restaurants."

Evelyn nods slowly. She doesn't protest, and encouraged by her response, I press on.

"Other points easy to implement are installing key card systems that turn off lights and air conditioning when guests leave their rooms, the use of eco-friendly cleaning products, smart thermostats, and a paperless operating system."

"Okay. Forward it. I'll take a look." Evelyn blows out her cheeks as she refills her cup. "Any other 'easy fixes' as you call them?"

"Yes. The nightly entertainment—"

Evelyn interrupts, her eyes lighting up. "Ah yes, our signature fireworks display. It's truly spectacular, Val. Our guests love it."

I blink, sure I've misheard. "I'm sorry, did you say nightly fireworks? I thought they were weekly."

"No, nightly." Evelyn says, pride evident in her voice.

"It's become our trademark. Well, wherever it's legal, that is. Guests rave about it in their reviews. It's when marriage proposals take place, not to mention the fireworks display is our most popular feature on social media."

For a moment, I'm speechless. Then, I can't help it—a short, incredulous laugh escapes me. "You can't be serious."

Evelyn's expression hardens. "I assure you, I'm quite serious."

"Evelyn," I say, "there's no way we can keep a nightly fireworks display, or any fireworks display for that matter. Do you have any idea of the environmental impact?"

"It's what our guests expect," she argues. "It's part of the Rothschild experience."

I shake my head, my frustration mounting again. "It's completely unsustainable. The air pollution, the noise disrupting to local wildlife, not to mention the debris falling into the ocean."

"You're exaggerating," Evelyn dismisses with a wave of her hand. "It's just a bit of harmless fun."

"A bit of harmless fun?" I repeat, my voice rising. "It's ecological warfare! There's no way I'd ever approve such a thing."

Evelyn's jaw sets stubbornly. "The fireworks stay. End of discussion. It will be spectacular over the island."

I stand up, my patience finally snapping. "No, Evelyn. They don't. If you're not willing to give up something this obviously harmful, then I don't know what I'm doing here."

"How dare you!" Evelyn stands too, her eyes flashing. "I've agreed to all your other suggestions—"

"I was only just getting started!" I shoot back. "And as your locally appointed consultant, your plans will not go through without my approval, so keep that in mind. You need me on your side. If you don't want to do it properly, don't do it at all. Move on and leave Cormoran Island to someone who will treat it with respect."

We glare at each other across the coffee table, the tension palpable. It's clear we've reached an impasse, and I'm not sure where we go from here.

"Think about it," I finally say, gathering my things. "The island may not be the right fit for Rothschild Resorts. Let's reconvene tomorrow. That will give you time to go through what we've discussed so far in-depth."

Chapter 17

Evelyn

Making my way down to the beach restaurant of Val's hotel, I spot her immediately. Val is perched at the bar, chatting to the bartender—the same man who took her out to Cormoran Island in that rickety little fishing boat.

I stop and hang back, observing from a distance. The anger from our earlier argument still simmers beneath the surface, threatening to boil over at any moment. But I force myself to relax my posture. I need to keep my cool if I'm going to get through this.

Val has changed out of her linen pants and T-shirt, into a bikini top and shorts, her sun-kissed skin glowing in the late-afternoon light. She throws her head back in laughter at something the bartender says, and I feel a fresh wave of irritation wash over me.

How can she be so carefree? So utterly unbothered? While I've been agonizing over every detail of this project, losing sleep over logistics and financials, she gets to swan about in a bikini, sipping cocktails and basking in the adoration of everyone around her.

It's easy for her, I think bitterly. She's not the one taking all the risks here. She's not the one putting her reputation, her company's future, on the line. No, she just gets to waltz in with her eco-friendly ideas and her charm, dictating terms without any real stake in the outcome. For all I know, this could all be some sort of game to her—a way to toy with me, to exert power over Rothschild Resorts.

Unfortunately, without her approval, this resort will never become a reality, and that fact sits heavy in my stomach, a leaden weight of frustration.

I watch as Val leans across the bar, pointing at something behind it. The bartender nods, reaching for a bottle on a high shelf. The movement causes the muscles in Val's back to flex, drawing my eye to the smooth expanse of skin between her shoulder blades.

Despite my anger, despite my desire to march over there and give her a piece of my mind, I find myself oddly transfixed. There's a grace to her movements, a natural ease in the way she carries herself that I admire. It's infuriating, really, how attractive she is even when she's driving me to the brink of madness.

This strange attraction I feel toward Val is just another complication I don't need right now. It's confusing and silly and I have no idea what to do with it. Part of me wants to push her into the sea just to wipe that carefree smile off her face. But another part—a part I'm trying desperately to ignore—wants to join her at the bar, to bask in her presence and see if I can coax out one of those genuine laughs for myself.

Perhaps that's exactly what I need to do. Play nice and find a way to work with Val that doesn't involve us butting heads at every turn.

The memory of our argument makes me wince. I'm not sure why I reacted so strongly, why I dug my heels in over fireworks. It's not like me to lose control like that. Perhaps it was the lack of sleep, or the lingering embarrassment from oversleeping and being caught off guard. Or maybe it's just Val herself—something about her pushes all my buttons.

Whatever the reason, I know I need to do better. I can't let Val get under my skin like this, can't let her disarm me with her passionate arguments and her infuriatingly valid points. As I finally approach the bar, Val looks up, her eyes meeting mine. For a moment, I see surprise flicker across her face, quickly replaced by wariness. She straightens, her posture becoming more guarded. It's clear she's bracing herself for another confrontation.

"Evelyn," she says, her tone cautious. "I didn't expect to see you here."

I force a smile, trying to appear more relaxed than I feel. "Well, I thought we should talk. Clear the air after this morning."

Val's expression is still wary. "Okay. Would you like a drink?"

I hesitate for a moment, then nod. "Why not?"

Val turns to the bartender. "Mateo, can we get another of these, please?"

Mateo nods, already reaching for a bottle of local beer. It's a far cry from my usual champagne, and she's probably doing it to wind me up, but I accept it with a murmured thanks.

"So," Val says, turning back to me. "You wanted to talk?"

I take a sip of my drink and decide I don't mind the beer so much. I'm thirsty and it's nice and cold. "Yes. I wanted to apologize for my behavior this morning. It was unprofessional of me to lose my temper like that."

Val's eyebrows rise, clearly not expecting an apology. "I appreciate that," she says after a moment. "But I won't lie, I'm worried about the next steps. If this morning's meeting upset you, then..." She pauses. "Well, let's just say, that was only the beginning of a long list of points we need to address."

"I know," I say. "And I acknowledge that. As you've probably noticed, I don't like being told what to do, but I'll work on my attitude, I promise."

"Thank you, that would be most helpful." There's a hint of a smile playing around Val's lips, and the humorous sarcasm dripping from her voice tells me she's enjoying this.

Of course she is. Biting my tongue, I feel another outburst brewing. Why does this woman bring out the worst in me? Instead of replying, I sip my beer and focus on our surroundings. It's easier when I pretend she's not here.

A young woman approaches the bar. She's petite with wavy blonde hair, wearing a flowy sundress that accentuates her tan. Her eyes light up when she spots Val, and she waves.

Val returns the wave with a wink, and I feel an unexpected twinge in my chest. The woman's gaze lingers on Val a little too long, her smile a touch too intimate. *Why does this bother me?*

"I see you've made yourself quite popular among the women here," I remark, aiming for a casual tone but hearing a hint of something else in my voice. Annoyance? Jealousy? Surely not.

Val tilts her head as she regards me, then chuckles. "Oh, that's Sophia. She's actually here with her boyfriend." She nods toward a man who's just joined Sophia at the other end of the bar. "See? That's him."

I glance over, noting how Sophia's still stealing glances at Val even as her boyfriend puts an arm around her. I try not to let it irritate me, but I can feel a knot forming between my shoulder blades. "She certainly seems...friendly," I murmur.

"She's nice. Most people here are," Val says innocently.

I don't know what it is today. Everything about her infuriates me, but I'm here to make peace, so I clear my throat, searching for a way to redirect the conversation. "So, have you met any interesting women in Mallorca besides Sophia?"

Val grins, a mischievous glint in her eye. "What do you mean? I've met you, haven't I? You're certainly interesting." Her tone is playful, but there's a knowing look in her eyes that makes me uncomfortable. She leans in slightly, her voice lowering. "Why are you so curious about my love life?"

I feel heat rising to my cheeks and struggle to maintain my composure. Val's gaze is steady, challenging. She's deliberately trying to get a rise out of me.

"I'm not," I manage. "It's just a question. You didn't shy away from personal conversation yesterday."

Val's brows knit together, and she shakes her head. "You're right. I was just messing with you. I do find you interesting, though. That wasn't a lie." She drops her grin and sits back. "But no," she says, shaking her head. "I try not to get too distracted by women when I'm working. I mean, there's nothing wrong with a one-night stand, but if it became more than that, I wouldn't get anything done." Her gaze lingers on mine a moment too long for comfort, and I feel a flutter in my stomach.

"What about you?" Val asks. "Are you dating anyone?"

"No, I don't date." In fact, I haven't in years. "It's...a waste of time."

"A waste of time? That's an interesting perspective. Care to elaborate?"

I shift on my barstool, suddenly very aware of how close we are. I can smell the faint scent of coconut sunscreen on her skin, see the light dusting of freckles across her nose. "What I mean is exactly that," I say, straightening myself and squaring my shoulders in an attempt to regain composure. "I don't have time for romantic entanglements. They're messy, complicated. Inefficient. And quite frankly, boring."

Val frowns. "But what about sex?"

"Sex is not a priority for me." I feel my cheeks warming again. "It never has been."

"I see..." Val's knee brushes against mine. I doubt it's deliberate and it's crazy that I even notice it, but somehow even the tiniest touch coming from her has way more impact than it should. "So you don't like sex?"

Although I should have seen it coming, the question catches me off guard. "I...I think it's overrated."

"Hmm..." Val stretches her arms above her head. The movement draws my attention to the toned lines of her body. "Well," she says, her voice taking on a playful lilt, "if you ever decide you want to make romance a priority, I'm sure you'd have no shortage of admirers. You're quite the catch."

I nearly choke on my beer. "I... That's..." I stammer, struggling to form a coherent response.

Val just smiles, then turns to signal Mateo for another round of drinks, and I take the moment to collect myself.

"I'd rather not discuss my nonexistent love life." I glance

at the second beer Mateo puts in front of me, contemplating if I should refuse.

"Then let's discuss the local cuisine," Val says. "We need to address food and beverage, and I think it's something we can talk about without butting heads."

Chapter 18

Val

"Last call, ladies," Mateo announces, his voice cutting through the hum of our conversation. "I'm closing up shop in ten minutes."

I blink, surprised by the interruption, and glancing at my watch, I do a double-take. It's nearly midnight. We've been talking for hours.

Evelyn seems equally taken aback. Her eyebrows arch as she checks her own watch. "My goodness," she murmurs. "Where has the time gone?"

As the night wore on, she gradually unwound, like a tightly coiled spring slowly releasing its tension. Her hair, perfectly coiffed at the start of the evening, now has a few strands escaping, framing her face in a way that makes her look younger. The setting sun has long since faded, replaced by the glow of the bar's lanterns that accentuate the strong lines of her cheekbones and the depth of her dark eyes.

I catch myself staring and quickly look away, finishing my drink to cover my momentary lapse. I've been fighting the urge to flirt with her all night, reminding myself repeatedly that this is a professional relationship. Not that I want anything from her; we'd never work. But something about the atmosphere, the sea breeze, and the way Evelyn's laugh has become more frequent and genuine as the hours have passed, makes it hard to maintain that professional distance when I'm so used to flirting in situations like this.

"You know," I say, unable to resist, "you're much nicer when you're not trying to control everything around you."

I brace myself for a sharp retort, but to my surprise, Evelyn laughs. "I suppose I deserved that," she admits. "I'm aware I'm not the easiest person to work with."

"Oh? I hadn't noticed," I tease, earning another chuckle.

Evelyn shakes her head. "At least now that I'm at the head of the company, it's much simpler. My team doesn't have to agree with me on everything." She pauses, taking a sip of her drink. "I've got the board members, of course, but they trust me to manage things, so I rarely have someone to butt heads with. Until now," she adds. "But I'll try harder."

"Well, look at you, finally embracing collaboration," I say, raising my glass in a mock toast. "There's hope for you yet, Rothschild."

"Perhaps," she concedes. Then, to my astonishment, she says, "And you're not so bad yourself, Mendoza. We've come a long way tonight."

I nod. "Who knew we could be so civilized?"

There's a pause, a moment where we just look at each other until Mateo starts cleaning the tables around us. All the other patrons have left and he's turned off the music, leaving only the sound of the sea crashing against the rocky shore.

We both stand, and suddenly there's an awkwardness that wasn't there before. Evelyn smooths down her blouse. "I should get going," she says, glancing away. "I'll catch a taxi on the main road."

"Right," I nod, a little disappointed that the evening is ending. "Same time tomorrow morning? Eight o'clock?"

"Eight o'clock," she confirms. She hesitates, as if she wants to say something more, but then she simply nods and turns to leave.

I watch her go, her silhouette elegant even in the darkness.

"You're staring." Mateo's voice startles me out of my reverie. "If you're not leaving, help me stack these chairs. We can have a nightcap together when we're done. Or are you just going to stand there lusting after lady boss?" He knows I've been hired as a consultant but I almost wish I hadn't told him.

"That's ridiculous." I scoff, turning to help him gather the scattered tables and chairs. "We were discussing business, that's all."

Mateo narrows his eyes, a knowing smirk on his face. "Uh-huh. Must have been some fascinating business."

I silently curse my complexion for betraying me. "I was just being polite."

"Val, I've seen you flirt with women at this bar. I know what it looks like."

"I wasn't flirting," I protest weakly. "Besides, she's not even gay."

"Didn't think that usually stopped you," he quips.

I shake my head, trying to dislodge an arsenal of contradicting thoughts. This is dangerous territory. Evelyn is my client, and whatever I might be feeling—attraction, curiosity, or just the allure of the forbidden—I can't afford to indulge.

"Earth to Val," Mateo says. "You're doing it again. Staring off into space with that dopey look on your face. But for what it's worth, I think she likes you too."

"Evelyn Rothschild doesn't 'like' people. She tolerates them at best."

"Sure." Mateo shrugs, turning to wipe down the bar.

I open my mouth to argue, then stop myself and start stacking the chairs instead. Evelyn's almost impossible to work with, at least from what I've witnessed so far, and tomorrow will be no different. We might have had a pleasant night, fun even, but that doesn't mean this consultancy deal won't be a nightmare.

"One last drink on the house," Mateo says after we've finished.

He disappears behind the bar and returns with two beers. "Come on. I know a great spot."

We make our way down to the shore, where a large, flat rock juts out over the water. Mateo leads the way, his feet finding familiar holds in the uneven surface. I follow, careful not to slip on the damp stone.

I settle on the edge beside him, our feet dangling into the cool water. The moon is high now, casting a silvery path across the sea, and I savor the crisp taste of my beer and the peaceful moment.

"You're really lucky to live here," I say. "It's beautiful."

He nods, his eyes fixed on the horizon. "I know. I'm blessed, truly. Wouldn't want it any other way." He pauses, swirling the beer in his bottle. "I just hope it stays this way. I worry about big hotel chains coming in, changing everything. Before you know it, we'll have fast-food joints on every corner, souvenir shops pushing out local businesses, and cruise ships dumping thousands of tourists on our side of the island. Sure, we need tourism. Our economy is built on it, but there's a fine line between development and overdevelopment."

I feel a pang of guilt. Isn't that exactly what I'm helping

to bring about? "What else?" I ask, genuinely curious. "What other changes do you fear?"

Mateo sighs, his brow furrowing. "Traffic, for one. Our roads aren't built for heavy traffic. And then there's the strain on our resources—water, electricity. Not to mention the impact on local wildlife and ecosystems." He shakes his head. "Don't get me wrong, I'm not against progress. But I've seen what unchecked development can do to places like this."

I nod, understanding his concerns all too well. "I can't control everything that happens here," I admit. "But I promise you, Mateo, I'll do everything in my power to make sure the Rothschild resort has a positive impact. It's why I agreed to be a consultant in the first place."

"You really think you can make a difference?" He looks at me skeptically.

"It's why I do what I do. Sustainable tourism isn't just a buzzword for me. It's a mission. If I can get a company like Rothschild to embrace eco-friendly practices, to respect the local community and environment...well, that could set a precedent for future developments."

"I hope you're right," he says. "Because this island isn't just a pretty place for tourists. It's my home, the home of many."

"I know." I turn to him with a sweet smile. "Look, no one can stop development. But we can use development to change the world in a positive way, one step at the time."

Chapter 19

Evelyn

"Absolutely not, Val. We are not letting wild goats roam freely around a luxury resort!" I exclaim, my voice rising despite my resolve to stay calm. I was hoping we could start on a better note today, but there's no reasoning with Val.

Val's eyes flash with frustration. "They're an integral part of the island's ecosystem. We can't just remove them from their natural habitat."

"I'm not suggesting we remove them entirely," I counter, pinching the bridge of my nose. "Just...relocate them to a designated area. A sort of nature reserve, if you will."

"You mean an enclosed petting zoo," Val says flatly, crossing her arms.

I bristle at her tone. "It's not a petting zoo. It's a controlled environment where guests can appreciate the local wildlife without the risk of...incidents."

"Incidents?" Val repeats, incredulous. "What, are you afraid a goat might eat someone's Gucci loafers?"

"That's the least of my concerns," I snap. "You can't

deny that having goats wandering around poses certain... logistical challenges. Not to mention safety and hygiene concerns."

Val leans forward, her voice intense. "Those goats have been on that island for generations. Cordoning them off in some artificial enclosure defeats the entire purpose of an eco-friendly resort."

"And what would you suggest?" I ask, exasperated. "Let them run amok? Have guests dodging goat droppings on their way to the spa?"

"We work around them," Val insists. "Design pathways and structures that allow for coexistence. Educate guests about them. Make it part of the experience, not an inconvenience to be tucked away."

I'm about to argue further when the shrill ring of the hotel room phone cuts through our debate. I hold up a hand to silence Val, grateful for the interruption. "Yes?"

"Ms. Rothschild, you have a visitor in the lobby," the receptionist informs me. "Mr. Donald Rothschild and his companion."

I feel the color drain from my face. *Dad? Here? Now?* "I...thank you. Please send them up."

As I hang up, I turn to find Val watching me curiously. "Everything okay?" she asks, her anger seemingly forgotten.

I smooth down my blouse and clear my throat. "My father's here," I explain, trying to keep my voice neutral. "With his...fiancée."

Val's eyebrows shoot up. "Oh? I can leave, give you some privacy..."

"No, it's fine. If he sees we're in the middle of a meeting, maybe he'll leave us alone for a few hours. That'll give me time to mentally prepare for the Candy circus."

A knock at the door prevents Val from responding, and I take a deep breath, steeling myself as I open it.

"Evelyn, sweetheart!" My father's voice fills the room as he sweeps in, pulling me into a bear hug before I can protest. He smells of expensive cologne and cigars and I wince. He's never called me "sweetheart" to my face before.

"Dad," I manage, extricating myself from his embrace. "What a...surprise."

"Surprise indeed!" He beams, ignoring my obvious discomfort. "We docked in Palma last night, so we thought we'd pop in and see you."

As if on cue, a young woman bounces into the room. She's wearing a beaded white bikini top and a matching sarong that leaves little to the imagination. Her bleach-blonde hair is piled high on her head, and her smile is so bright it's almost blinding.

"Hi, Evelyn!" she chirps, hugging me like we're old friends. "It's so amazing to finally meet you in person!"

I stand there, frozen, as the scent of sweet perfume and bubblegum assaults my senses. "Candy," I manage to choke out. "How...nice."

It's then that my father notices we're not alone. His eyes land on Val, who's been watching us with poorly concealed amusement. "And who's this lovely young lady?"

"This is Val Mendoza," I explain, trying to regain some semblance of control over the situation. "She's a sustainability consultant we're working with on the Mallorca project."

"Sustainability?" my father repeats, shaking her hand. "I'm all for it, but I had no idea we hired consultants for that."

"The local authorities made it a requirement," I say. "I

would have told you about it, but you don't seem to have much interest in the company these days."

My father has the grace to look slightly abashed, but Candy jumps in before he can respond. "Oh, that's so cool!" she gushes, turning to Val. "So like, do you save the turtles and stuff?"

Val, to her credit, manages to keep a straight face. "Among other things," she says diplomatically. "It's more about ensuring the resort has a positive impact on the local environment and community."

"Totally cool." Candy nods sagely, as if Val has just imparted the wisdom of the ages.

My father claps his hands together. "Well, why don't we all go down to the beach for an iced coffee? Candy got me hooked on matcha lattes." He raises his brows. "Val? Are you in? I'm sure the business talk can wait."

"Actually, Dad," I start, but he's already heading for the door, Candy in tow.

"Come on, ladies," he calls over his shoulder. "Who wants to work in a place like this? Live a little!"

I turn to Val, who's amused grin only heightens my irritation. "I'm sorry. I don't think I have a choice, but you don't have to come. We can continue this later today or tomorrow."

"Tempting, but I think I'd rather see how this plays out," she teases. "Your father invited me, after all."

I shoot her a warning glare, but she still follows. She's punishing me for wanting to get rid of the goats. She's taking pleasure in my discomfort. I feel like I'm walking into some sort of bizarre nightmare. I'm reduced to playing referee between my father's midlife crisis, his Barbie side-kick, and an eco-warrior with a vendetta against petting zoos.

We settle at the hotel's beachside bar, my father immediately ordering hipster matchas for him and Candy while she's kicking off her flip-flops and digging her toes into the sand with the enthusiasm of a toddler. Val and I both order a black coffee, and I sincerely hope she'll excuse herself after. I don't want her to judge me for my father's madness, yet I have no doubt she will. I bet she'll be on a call to her team tonight, making fun of our family and cracking up about how uncomfortable I was.

I watch as my father fawns over Candy, his eyes practically sparkling while she regales us with some story about her latest Instagram post. I force a smile, nodding at appropriate intervals, while internally I'm screaming. Val, to her credit, seems genuinely interested—or maybe she's just a better actor than I am.

"And then, like, the flamingo float just totally flipped over! Didn't it, babe?" Candy giggles and nudges my father. "It was totally embarrassing, but it got so many likes!"

My father chuckles, patting her hand affectionately. "You're so adorable. Isn't she adorable, Evelyn?"

I thank the waiter who brings over our coffees. "Absolutely charming," I manage, wincing as I sip the strong brew that's still too hot to drink.

Val catches my eye, a hint of sympathy in her gaze. She clears her throat. "So, Mr. Rothschild, Evelyn tells me you've been traveling a lot lately?"

I silently thank her for the change of subject.

"Oh, please, call me Donald," my father insists. "And yes, Candy and I have been having the most fantastic adventures. We just came from Ibiza, isn't that right, sugar plum?"

Candy nods enthusiastically. "It was beyond! We did

this couples' yoga retreat, and Donald was, like, totally Zen by the end of it."

I choke on my coffee, trying to banish the mental image of my father attempting downward dog. Val pats my back, poorly concealing a smirk.

"I didn't realize you were into yoga, Dad."

"Oh, you know me, always up for trying new things. Candy's opened my eyes to so many experiences. Just last month, we went skydiving! Didn't you see the videos I sent you?"

This time, it's Val's turn to choke on her drink. "Skydiving?" she repeats, her eyes wide.

"Oh yeah," Candy chimes in. "It was Donald's idea. I chickened out at the last minute, but he jumped."

"How...adventurous of you, Dad. I'm sorry, I must have missed that," I say, resisting the urge to point out that at his age, simply waking up each morning should be enough to feel alive.

"What can I say? Life's too short to play it safe, princess." He reaches across the table to pat my hand. "That's why we're getting married next month."

"Next month?" I feel a headache coming on and stare at my father, struggling to process this. "You can't be serious."

"As serious as a heart attack." He beams. "We've found the perfect spot on Ibiza. It's absolutely beautiful, and we expect you to be there, of course."

I open my mouth to protest, but no words come out. I'm saved from responding when Candy suddenly jumps up, tugging on my father's arm.

"Babe, let's go for a swim! The water looks amazing."

To my horror, my father stands up and takes of his shirt. "Great idea, sugar plum. Evelyn, Val, care to join us?"

"We're good," I say mutely, watching as they dash

toward the water. A wave of nausea washes over me. "I don't understand," I mutter, more to myself than to Val. "He's gone completely crazy. How can he not see how ridiculous this is?"

Val, who's been quiet, speaks up. "They seem happy, though. Look at them."

I scoff, turning to her. "Happy? They're not compatible at all! The age difference alone—"

"It's not about age," she interrupts. "It's about mindset."

"Oh, and my father's mindset has suddenly tumbled to that of a naïve twenty-eight-year-old?" I snap. "I have to stop him before he makes the biggest mistake of his life."

"Do what you need to do, but I doubt you'll be able to change his mind," Val says, standing up. "I'm heading back to my hotel to work so you can spend some quality time with your father." She smiles. "Give Candy a chance. You might be surprised."

I roll my eyes and let out a huff. "I doubt it. I'll call you later and again, apologies for the interruption."

My father lifts Candy onto his shoulders, both of them laughing uproariously. My world is spinning out of control. The resort, the goats, and now this impending wedding—it's all too much. I signal the waiter to order something stronger than coffee. I'm going to need it.

Chapter 20

Val

As my feet touch the rocky shore of Cormoran Island, I'm greeted by a chorus of bleats. I look up to see a small herd of goats watching me from the nearby cliffs. I'm glad I found a rental boat for my extended stay. It gives me the freedom to zip around the coastline and make these impromptu visits to the island whenever I need to.

"Well, hello there," I call out as I drop the anchor. "Nice to see you again!"

To my amusement, several of the goats bleat back.

"Aww, you guys are too cute. I'm sorry for the interruption. I just need to check on a few things around the island —is that okay with you?"

The goats stare at me silently for a moment before a few of them start meandering. As I begin hiking up the trail, I notice they're following me at a distance, and I smile to myself, already charmed by these shaggy island residents.

I pull out my phone to snap a quick photo to send to Marcus, my right-hand man at Eden Eco Escapes. "Sorry,

Evelyn," I mutter under my breath, "but the goats really are staying."

When I round a bend, I spot three kid goats frolicking nearby. They're bouncing and headbutting each other playfully, their little hooves kicking up dust. I pause to watch their antics, chuckling as one particularly enthusiastic kid does an impressive midair twist.

"Show-offs," I call out teasingly. The kids pause their play, then scamper off to join the adult goats.

Continuing up the winding path, I take in the rugged beauty of the island. The sun warms my skin and the sea breeze rustles through the scrubby vegetation. It's peaceful here in a wild, untamed way that I find invigorating.

I sit down to voice record a few observations. The terrain is challenging, with lots of loose rocks and steep inclines. We'll need to be strategic about pathway placement to minimize erosion. As I'm recording, I feel a gentle nudge against my back, and look behind me to see one of the kid goats headbutting me.

"Hey, little guy," I say, petting him. "How do you feel about the hotel, huh?" The kid bleats and prances in a circle, and then something to my other side tugs at my hair. It's one of the adult goats attempting to eat my ponytail. "Hey now, I'm not on the menu, buddy." I chuckle as I extract my hair from its mouth and straighten myself.

My thoughts turn to Evelyn, and I wonder how she's faring with her father and his young fiancée. Maybe I shouldn't have bailed; she was pretty distraught, but it really did seem like a family matter. Plus, I couldn't pass up the chance to explore the island further without Evelyn hovering and fretting about liability issues.

Hearing a splash, I shield my eyes from the sun and stare out over the sea while I try to spot where the noise came from. A dolphin leaps up, and another one follows. I smile in delight as they dive and resurface, and then I spot more. Three, four, five. It's a mesmerizing sight I feel lucky to witness. One dolphin clicks and whistles, and it sounds like it's laughing.

For the next few minutes, I'm treated to an impromptu dolphin show as they leap and spin through the air. Their joy is infectious, and I find myself whooping and cheering them on, much to the goats' confusion. I'm just about to take a picture of them when my phone rings. It's Marcus, and I answer quickly, surprised there's network out here.

"Hey, Marcus, what's up?" I ask, watching as the dolphins continue their acrobatic display in the distance.

"Just checking in," he says. "How's it going with Evelyn and the Rothschild crew?"

I sigh, running a hand through my windswept hair. "It's...challenging. Evelyn's not exactly easy to work with, but we're making progress. Slowly."

"Still, a shame we didn't get the gig." There's a hint of disappointment in Marcus's voice.

"Yeah, I know," I say. "But in the end, it's all about making a positive change. It's not ideal, but we're still influencing a major player in the industry."

"True," Marcus concedes. "Speaking of which, it sounds like there's going to be a lot of work coming our way. Evelyn's architectural plans need to be reinterpreted, right?"

"Exactly," I nod, even though he can't see me. "We need to research building materials that can replace some of the ones Rothschild is planning on using. Let's try utilizing our own list of suppliers first. Evelyn is going to throw a tantrum when I tell her I can't approve her current ones. I'm working on her, though, I think she's starting to come around...slowly."

Marcus laughs. "Well, if anyone can melt the ice queen, it's you, Val."

I shrug and laugh along. "She can be infuriating, but deep down, she's not that bad. Just...set in her ways. Anyway, what's new on your end?"

"Actually, something interesting has come up," Marcus says. "And since you're in the area, I thought you might want to check it out for yourself. A significant plot of coastal land has come onto the market on Ibiza, which is only a short flight from where you are."

"Oh? Tell me more."

"Well, it's not a conservation area, so we could potentially buy the land outright. The island of Ibiza seems like a good fit for us, and from what I can see in the pictures, this strip of coastline looks stunning."

I smile, already intrigued. "What's the catch? Why is it not gone already?"

"It doesn't come with permission for high build, so I doubt it will be snapped up by big developers, and it's too pricey for private developers. But for our low-impact approach? It could be perfect."

"That does sound interesting," I say. "Send me the details. How soon would I need to view it?"

"No immediate rush, but the sooner the better. Think you could squeeze in a quick trip in the next couple of weeks or so?"

"Yeah, I think I could make that work. Evelyn has a wedding there, so that might be good timing."

"Great," Marcus says. "I'll email you the details. Oh, and Val?"

"Yeah?"

"Try not to adopt any goats while you're there, okay? We don't have space for them in the office."

"I can't believe that picture sent. I'm literally in the middle of nowhere." I laugh, glancing at my furry entourage. "No promises. Talk to you later, Marcus."

The Ibiza property sounds promising, a potential new project that's all our own. It's a reminder that while the Cormoran Island collaboration is important, it's not the be-all and end-all.

I tuck my phone away and continue my hike, my mind now split between the challenges of working with Evelyn and the possibilities of this new opportunity. The goats trail behind me, seemingly content to follow wherever I lead.

As I reach the top of a steep incline, I pause to catch my breath and take in the view. The Mediterranean is gorgeous, shifting from turquoise to cobalt, its colors as changeable as my thoughts. In the distance is the coastline of Mallorca where limestone cliffs rise jagged and pale against the sky, their faces dotted with clusters of wild pine. Red-roofed villas nestle into the hillsides, and white-walled villages perch precariously near the edges, daring gravity. Between the cliffs, crescents of golden sand curve into coves where fishing boats bob in the waters.

A flash of silver catches my eye as the dolphins return, breaking through the surface in graceful arcs. These are the moments I live for—raw beauty, untamed and perfect. I wonder if Evelyn ever allows herself this kind of stillness, if she's ever felt the wild pulse of a place seep into her bones. Somehow, I doubt it.

Chapter 21

Evelyn

"**D**ad, can we talk?" I ask, glancing down at the beach where Candy is sunbathing. She's finally out of earshot.

My father looks up from his phone, his brow furrowing. "Of course, princess. What's on your mind?"

"It's about the wedding," I begin. "Don't you think you're rushing into it?"

He sighs, a familiar look of exasperation crossing his face. "Evelyn, you won't understand this as you've never been in a loving, committed relationship, but when you know, you know. Candy and I are in love."

His words hit me like a slap in the face. Not because I'm a jealous daddy's girl, but because he's right. I've never been in what most people would call a loving, committed relationship. But the way he says it, as if I'm incapable of understanding love, stings more than I care to admit. Is he implying that I don't even know what love is?

"I'm so happy for you, Dad. Really, I am," I lie. "But you've only known Candy for four months. Surely, you can see why I'm worried."

"I appreciate your concern, but I'm a grown man. I know what I'm doing," he says, his tone sharpening.

I decide to change tack. "Have you at least considered a prenuptial agreement? It would be common sense, right, in your situation?"

His eyes narrow, and I can see I've struck a nerve. "A prenup? For heaven's sake, Evelyn. Is that all you can think about? Money?"

"You should protect yourself," I argue, feeling frustration building in my chest.

"Candy doesn't need my money. She has her own," Dad says. "Did you know she has over five million followers on Instagram? Cosmetics companies are falling over themselves to have her promote their products. She's doing just fine on her own."

I blink, taken aback by this information. It's somewhat reassuring to hear that Candy isn't entirely dependent on my father financially, but it doesn't change the fact that there's still a significant disparity in their wealth.

"That's...good to hear," I say carefully. "I just want to make sure you're thinking this through."

He shakes his head. "You know, Evelyn, I wish you'd find love too. After your mother died, I closed myself off. I threw myself into work, but now..." He pauses, his gaze drifting to where Candy lies on the beach. "Now I realize there are more important things in life. Everything else seems so contrived, everything apart from love."

I take a deep breath, fighting back the emotions his mention of Mom has stirred up. We never talk about her; it's the first time he's mentioned her in a long time. "Dad, I have no interest in relationships. How about this. I promise not to complain about your love life if you stay out of mine."

He turns back to me, his eyes hardening. "That's not

good enough, Evelyn. Candy is important to me, and she's going to be a part of my life whether you like it or not. You need to accept that."

I open my mouth to argue, but he holds up a hand, silencing me. "There's something else. We're going to stick around until the wedding, and I've invited Mia to come stay with us. I've already booked her room."

"Mia?" I repeat, caught off guard. "But she was supposed to start a volunteering project—"

"She's postponed it," he explains. "I thought it would be nice for us all to spend some quality time together before the big day."

A mix of emotions hit me at this news. On one hand, I'm delighted to have Mia here. On the other, the thought of playing happy family with Candy...

"That's...thoughtful of you," I say. "But you know I'm very busy with work. I won't have much time to—"

"Make time," my father says firmly. "This is important, Evelyn. Family is important."

I bite back a retort about how he didn't seem to think family was so important when he was busy empire building all those years ago. Instead, I nod stiffly. "I'll do my best."

"That's all I ask." His expression softens. "Give her a chance. You might be surprised."

He sounds like Val. I doubt I'll ever warm to Candy. "Anything else I should know about?" I ask, hoping to wrap up this conversation.

He shakes his head. "No. No more surprises. Why don't you join us on the beach? The water's lovely."

"Maybe later," I say, already backing away. "I have some work to catch up on."

Walking back to the hotel, I'm mentally rearranging my

calendar. Mia's arrival changes things, and of course I want to spend time with her. Candy, not so much.

I pull out my phone and call Val. She picks up on the first ring.

"Evelyn? Everything okay?"

"Yes. I'm just calling to discuss some changes to the project timeline. With the wedding and Mia's arrival—"

"Your daughter is coming? How lovely!"

I smile. "Yes, but that also means we might have to work around her stay. Would you be okay with that?"

"Sure, I'm flexible." Val chuckles. "It doesn't have to be a problem. If you stop fighting me on every single point, we could save a lot of time. We both have great teams. All we have to do is agree so we can delegate and move things forward."

Clenching my jaw, I sigh. "You can forget about that. If you had everything your way, our VIP guests would be washing themselves in the spring and shitting in an outdoor compost toilet."

Val chuckles. "Come on, Evelyn. You know that's not true. If you'd ever visited one of my resorts, you'd know I never skimp on comfort for our guests. We offer luxury with a conscience, not a primitive camping experience."

"Sure, one of your *two* resorts," I reply pointedly. "I have over five hundred to my name, so I think I'll decide what advice to take from a start-up."

There's a pause, and I'm worried I've gone too far. She sighs. "Look, just because you're having a bad day with your new stepmom arriving doesn't give you the right to take it out on me. And as far as my advice is concerned, take it or leave it, but without me, there will be no Rothschild Resort on Cormoran Island."

Her stepmom comment makes my blood boil, but I refuse to take the bait. "Fine, let's meet as soon as possible."

"I can be there in an hour," Val replies. Her voice sounds distant, and I can hear the faint sound of waves in the background. There's also another sound, one I recognize all too well.

"Do I hear goats? Where are you?" I ask, already knowing the answer.

"I'm on the island," she responds casually.

"You went to Cormoran without me?"

"I did. Is that a crime?"

"No, it's not a crime," I mutter, grinding my teeth. "But I would have appreciated being informed."

"Relax, Evelyn," Val replies, her tone maddeningly casual. "I'm just doing some on-site research. I'll fill you in when I get back."

"Fine. I'll see you in an hour at my hotel." I hang up before she can respond. I hate feeling like I'm losing my grip. Val is taking liberties, my father has lost the plot, and now Mia's coming into this chaos. I need to regain some semblance of order, and fast.

Chapter 22

Val

Evelyn seems distracted. She's more docile than usual, giving in to my suggestions without much of a fight. While this is positive for me, I can't shake the feeling that something's seriously wrong. Despite her composed exterior, there's an underlying tension in her movements, a tightness around her eyes that betrays her stress.

"Evelyn," I say, setting aside the report we've been reviewing, "is everything okay? You seem...off."

She blinks, as if surprised by the question. "I'm fine," she says automatically, but her voice lacks its usual conviction.

I raise an eyebrow, not buying it for a second. "Come on, you can talk to me. Is it your father?"

Evelyn hesitates, her fingers drumming an anxious rhythm on the desk. Finally, she sighs. "Of course his upcoming wedding bothers me. I wouldn't be human if it didn't. It's just...everything feels like a mess right now. Work, personal matters...it's all piling up and I can't seem to think clearly."

"But we're doing so well," I say, almost feeling sorry for her. Almost. "I know you prefer to have things your way, but collaboration doesn't have to be stressful. It can be insightful and speed things up rather than stalling them."

"I know that. I'm not an idiot, and I'm trying here." She huffs. "I'm sorry. I'm just in a bad mood. I can't even find something decent to wear. I need my dry-cleaning done—this was all I had left." She brushes her sleeveless blouse that looks perfectly fine to me, then strides to her closet and yanks open the door. Before I can react, an avalanche of clothes tumbles out, scattering across the floor in a chaotic heap of designer labels. "See? Everything's a mess."

I watch, fascinated, as Evelyn's composure crumbles. Her hands are shaking as she tries to gather the fallen garments.

"Hey, hey," I say, moving to help her. "It's okay. This is an easy fix."

Evelyn looks at me, her eyes wild. "Easy fix? How? This is a disaster! I asked the cleaner to take care of it before you arrived, but she didn't speak English."

I can't help but chuckle, which earns me a glare. "Evelyn, you know your hotel has a dry-cleaning service, right?"

She blinks at me, confusion replacing panic for a moment. "What?"

"There's a bag in your closet," I explain, reaching past her to pull out a large, white laundry bag. "Just put your clothes in here, hang it on your door, and the hotel will take care of it. You'll have everything back, fresh and pressed, by tomorrow."

Evelyn picks up the bag, turning it over in her hands like it's some alien artifact. "Oh...of course. I should have thought of that."

I tilt my head and study her. For an intelligent woman,

she seems utterly clueless. "Is this the first time you've been away for an extended period?"

"No," she says. "But My PA usually travels with me and takes care of all these...details. She's on maternity leave."

"Ah, I see," I say, helping her gather clothes into the bag. "Are you recruiting for a new PA?"

"Absolutely not. Vera is staying. I don't know what I'd do without her long term."

I pause, a silk blouse in my hands. "Wait, you expect her to come back full time after having a baby?"

"Of course. I worked after I had Mia. It's doable, and besides, I don't trust anyone else."

I frown. "Evelyn, you travel constantly. There's no way your PA is going to be jetting around the world with an infant in tow. It's more likely she'll quit once her paid leave is over."

The color drains from Evelyn's face as the reality of my words sink in. For a moment, she just stands there, frozen. Then, to my utter shock, she bursts into tears.

"Oh God," she sobs, sinking onto the bed. "I can't do this. I can't do any of this! And now I'm crying. I swear, I never cry."

I stand there, clutching the laundry bag, completely out of my depth. Evelyn Rothschild, the ice queen of luxury resorts, is having a full-blown meltdown over laundry and a PA.

"Hey, it's okay," I say, awkwardly patting her shoulder. "We'll figure it out."

As I watch Evelyn cry, I'm struck by the absurdity of the situation. This woman, who can negotiate multi-million-dollar deals without breaking a sweat, is undone by the prospect of sorting out her own dry cleaning. It's almost comical, but I can't bring myself to laugh at her distress.

"I'm sorry." Evelyn takes a deep breath and tries to regain her composure. "This is ridiculous. I don't know what's come over me. Perhaps I'm hormonal."

I sit next to her, offering a box of tissues from her nightstand. "It's not ridiculous. You're stressed and overwhelmed. It happens to everyone."

She takes a tissue, dabbing at her eyes. "Not to me. I don't... I don't do this."

"Break down?" I ask gently. "Or do your own laundry?"

That earns me a watery chuckle. "Both, I suppose."

It's clear that there are stark differences in our upbringing. While I was taking care of the household because my parents were always busy, Evelyn was surrounded by nannies and housekeepers who tended her every beck and call.

As I watch Evelyn dab at her eyes some more, I decide to lighten the mood. With the risk of overstepping, I pick up a delicate champagne-colored lace bra from the pile of clothes and hold it up with a mischievous grin.

"Well, well, Ms. Rothschild. Do you wear these to board meetings?"

Evelyn's eyes widen, and a deep blush spreads across her cheeks. She seems more taken aback by my comment than I intended, and I immediately regret my attempt at humor.

"I'm sorry," I say sheepishly, lowering the bra. "That was inappropriate. I was just trying to make you laugh."

To my surprise, Evelyn's shock morphs into a smirk. "Ms. Mendoza, if you must know, I save those for my clandestine meetings with eco-warriors."

I laugh at her unexpected retort. "Touché, Evelyn. I didn't know you had it in you."

She raises an eyebrow, a glint of challenge in her eyes.

"There's a lot you don't know about me. What about you? What does Val Mendoza wear under her sustainable attire?"

"Oh, I don't bother with bras," I say casually, shrugging. "Too constricting. Plus, the ladies love it that way. Less clothing to remove."

Evelyn's blush deepens, and she averts her gaze. I suspect my offhand comment might have made her uncomfortable. "Oops." I cover my mouth with my hand. "Was that too much?"

She chuckles and shakes her head. At least she's smiling again, so that's a win. "Do you talk like this in board meetings?"

"I try not to."

Evelyn playfully snatches the bra from my hands and adds it to the bag. "Admittedly, it's refreshing. Apart from Mia, everyone's always so formal around me. It's nice to have someone who doesn't treat me like I'm made of glass." Finally meeting my eyes again, she adds, "How would you like to add 'PA' to your résumé?"

I burst out laughing at Evelyn's mock job offer. "Me, your PA? Can you imagine? I'd probably mix up your complicated coffee orders—was it a half-caf, double-shot, oat milk latte with a sprinkle of gold dust, or a triple-shot, almond milk cappuccino with a dash of unicorn tears? And don't get me started on tracking down your impossible-to-find hairbrushes made from yeti fur or that shampoo infused with moon rocks."

Evelyn raises an eyebrow, a mix of amusement and indignation on her face. "As you well know, I drink my coffee black, thank you very much. And I'm not that high maintenance." She pauses, then adds with a hint of a smile, "I only use horsehair brushes sourced from outer Mongolia, and my shampoo is made with a modest blend of caviar and truffles. See? Perfectly reasonable." She nudges me. "But seriously, how do you manage without someone handling all these things for you?"

"Well, I do have a PA," I say, folding the last blouse and adding it to the laundry bag. "She doesn't travel with me, but she handles a lot of the administrative stuff I don't have time for. Scheduling, emails, research, that kind of thing. And yes, admittedly, she also takes care of my dry cleaning," I add with a sheepish grin. "I bring it into the office every Friday."

Chapter 23

Evelyn

I smooth down my dress for the hundredth time, stealing another glance at the mirror. My reflection stares back at me, an uncertainty in my eyes I haven't seen since my teenage years. I've been fussing over my appearance for an hour, unable to settle on the right look for today's meeting with Val.

It's ridiculous, really. I've never been this indecisive about my wardrobe before. Normally, I'd throw on one of my tailored suits without a second thought. But lately, I find myself caring more about what Val thinks of me, and I can't figure out why.

I run my fingers through my hair, debating whether to pull it back or let it hang loose. After a moment's hesitation, I decide to let it fall around my shoulders. The natural waves frame my face, softening my features. I haven't bothered with heels either; it seems pointless when working in a suite, so I'm still barefoot. It feels nice, comforting and grounding. Perhaps it will help me relax.

My gaze drifts to the clock on the nightstand. Val should be here any minute, and anticipation flutters in my stomach. Against all odds, these morning meetings have become a bright spot in my day, a refreshing change from the awkward dinners with my father and Candy since they arrived.

I still cringe inwardly, remembering my embarrassing outburst last week. Losing control like that in front of Val was mortifying, but surprisingly, it seems to have melted some of the tension between us. Working with her has become easier, more fluid. I'm even starting to trust her a little, which is unexpected and somewhat unsettling.

There's a knock on the door and I give myself one last once-over in the mirror. My knee-length white cotton dress is casual, more suitable for the beach, but Val never dresses up, so why should I?

I pad toward the door, my bare feet silent on the plush carpet. I reach for the handle, a small smile tugging at my lips. But when I swing the door open, it's not Val standing there. It's Mia.

"Surprise!" she exclaims, her face breaking into a wide grin.

I'm frozen in shock for a beat. Then joy surges through me, and I pull her into a tight hug. "Mia! What are you doing here? You weren't supposed to arrive until tomorrow!"

She laughs, squeezing me back. "I managed to catch an earlier flight. I hope that's okay?"

"Of course it's okay," I say, stepping back to look at her properly. Her hair—still in dreads—is longer than when I last saw her, and she's wearing ripped denim shorts and a faded T-shirt from some band I've never heard of. She looks happy and healthy.

"Come in, come in," I urge, ushering her inside. Mia steps into the suite, her eyes roaming over the opulent décor. "Nice place, Mom. But isn't it a bit much for one person?"

I chuckle, shaking my head. That's my Mia—always unimpressed by luxury. She grew up surrounded by the best of everything, staying in our finest resorts, but she never needed any of it.

"Yeah. It's big enough for a family," I say. "You can stay with me, if you don't mind me working here."

"It's fine. Grandpa already booked me a room." Mia looks me up and down curiously. "What happened? Did you meet a man or something?"

"What?" I frown. "No. Why would you say that?"

Mia shrugs. "I don't know. You just look...different. Younger, more girlie or something. It's so unlike you, Mom, but it's nice to see you dress a bit more chilled."

Her words make me feel even more insecure about my appearance, and I glance down at my dress, once again second-guessing my choice. "Do you think I look weird?" I ask, unable to keep the worry from my voice.

"No, no!" Mia quickly reassures me, rubbing my arm. "You look great, really. Are you expecting someone?"

"No, just my consultant I'm working with while I'm here."

"Oh, yes." Mia nods. "Grandpa told me about that. The sustainability expert, right? I'm glad you're finally tackling the issue. It's been bugging me."

"Her name is Val Mendoza," I say, watching as Mia makes her way to the mini-bar and pulls out a can of Coke. "Isn't it a bit early for that? I have a fresh pot of coffee if you want."

Mia sighs as she cracks open the can. "Mom, I'm thirty-two. I'm perfectly capable of making decisions on my choice of morning beverage." She takes a long sip before adding,

"Besides, I've just traveled across the world. I'm still in a different time zone."

"Of course you are." I hold up my hands in surrender, knowing when to pick my battles. "Fair enough. Do you want to do something today? I can cancel my meeting."

But Mia shakes her head. "No, don't change your plans for me. I need to sleep anyway. I'll probably just relax by the pool or take a dip in the sea. I doubt I'll be able to stay awake for much else."

"Sure. That sounds like a good plan. You should rest and adjust to the time difference. We'll have plenty of time to catch up later. Let me know if you need anything, though."

Mia smiles, taking another sip of her Coke. "Don't worry about me, Mom."

"I know, I know. It's just...it's good to have you here."

She steps forward and gives me another quick hug. "It's good to be here. Have you met Candy? I'm so curious about her, but I didn't want to wake them up and—"

There's another knock on the door, saving me from answering the question. "That must be Val."

Val stands there, looking fresh and relaxed in denim shorts and a loose, white T-shirt that says "Queen of Hearts." Her eyes flick over me, and I feel a flush creeping up my neck.

"Good morning, Evelyn, you look nice," she says, her gaze lingering on my dress before Mia joins me at the door. "Oh, I didn't realize you had company."

"Val, this is my daughter, Mia," I say, gesturing between them. "She arrived a day early. Mia, this is Val, our sustainability consultant."

Val's face lights up with recognition. "Mia! I've heard so much about you. It's great to finally meet you in person."

Mia steps forward and pulls her into a hug. She does that, even with strangers, and it never ceases to puzzle me. "Likewise. I hope my mom hasn't been too much trouble."

"Not at all. Your mom's been great to work with," Val says. Although I know it's an outright lie, I still appreciate it.

I suddenly feel out of place in my own suite as she turns back to Mia. "By the way, you are such an amazing food blogger. I looked you up last night—those street food reviews are incredible."

I blink in surprise. "You looked up Mia's blog?"

"Of course! I'm a total foodie so I was curious."

Mia beams at the compliment. "Thanks! I'm actually planning to write about some traditional Mallorcan dishes while I'm here."

"Oh, you have to try the sobrassada," Val says eagerly. "There's this little place in the old town that makes the best I've ever had."

As they launch into a discussion about local cuisine, I increasingly feel like a third wheel, so I clear my throat, trying to regain some control over the situation. "Val, would you like a coffee?" I ask, pouring myself a second.

"Yes, please. I'd love one." Val, who has been standing in the doorway all along, finally steps inside.

"We'll continue this later," Mia says, grabbing her can of Coke. "I'll leave you guys to it. It was great to meet you, Val. Maybe we can all have dinner together sometime?"

"I'd love that," Val says, and we wave Mia out.

This is awkward. Val and Mia weren't supposed to meet. Why that bothers me so much, I'm not entirely sure. After all, Val has already met my father and Candy. But Mia is different. I've always preferred to keep her to myself, separate from my professional life.

"Your daughter seems lovely," she says. "You must be so proud of her."

"I am. She's very independent."

"That's clear from her blog. The way she immerses herself in different cultures through their food is fascinating. Have you ever done a foodie trip with her?"

The question catches me off guard. The idea of traipsing around street food stalls with Mia and sleeping in basic accommodation seems so far removed from my usual world. "No, I haven't. Perhaps I will sometime," I say noncommittally, reaching for the report we're supposed to review. I don't want to have this conversation; it makes me feel guilty. Should I show more interest in Mia's world? Should I have joined her on one of her trips? She has asked me a few times. "Anyway, let's talk about solar panels..."

"Of course. Let's get to work." Val clearly senses my mood.

As we dive into work, I try to focus on the task at hand, but my mind keeps drifting. I'm hyper-aware of Val's presence—the way she tucks her hair behind her ear when she's concentrating, the enthusiasm in her voice when she tries to convince me. Her lips when she speaks. There's a nagging feeling that something has shifted, that the careful boundaries I've fought to maintain are starting to blur. One thing is clear, though—working with Val is becoming increasingly complicated, and I'm not entirely sure I'm prepared for what that might mean.

Chapter 24

Val

"I think that covers everything for today," I say, stretching my arms above my head. The movement causes my T-shirt to ride up slightly, and I notice Evelyn's eyes flick down before quickly darting away. *Interesting.*

"There is one more thing I need to discuss with you," I add, leaning forward. "On a more private basis."

Evelyn's posture stiffens slightly. "Oh? What is it?"

"I need to take a few days off to view a plot of land on Ibiza." I pause, gauging her reaction. "I was thinking I could do it while you're there for the wedding. That way, it won't eat into your time."

Evelyn's shoulders relax. "Oh, is that all? That's absolutely fine, Val. And I need to apologize in advance for not being available twenty-four seven now that Mia is here. I want to spend some quality time with her."

"Of course. Family comes first."

"I'm glad you understand." A mischievous glint appears in her eyes. "You could always come to the wedding with me as my plus-one. Join the party while you're there."

"I'm sure you can find a better chaperone than me," I tease. "Who wouldn't want to be Evelyn Rothschild's plus-one? Eligible men must be queuing up for you."

She smiles but averts her gaze. It's in moments like these that she almost seems shy, and I'm struck by how far we've come. Just a few weeks ago, I couldn't imagine having this kind of easy rapport with Evelyn. Now, here we are, joking and teasing.

"Trust me, there's no one I want to bring," Evelyn says with a wry smile. "I'll be going solo. I haven't brought a plus-one to an event in decades."

I lean back in my chair, studying her face. There's a hint of resignation in her eyes, a touch of loneliness perhaps. "Really? That long?"

Evelyn shakes her head, her fingers toying with the pen on her desk. "No, not for a very long time. Well, apart from Mia, of course. But she's my daughter, not exactly a date."

"So you haven't dated at all?" I ask, curiosity getting the better of me. She's told me she has no interest in relationships but it's still hard to imagine someone like Evelyn Rothschild being single for so long.

She hesitates, her gaze drifting to the window. "Not much," she admits softly. "There were a few...flings, I suppose. But nothing substantial."

I nod. "I get it. I don't date much either these days. Too busy." I pause, a grin tugging at my lips. "But I'd miss sex if I didn't have it occasionally."

Evelyn's eyes widen slightly. She opens her mouth to speak, then closes it again, seemingly at a loss for words. I watch as she swallows hard, her fingers now drumming an anxious rhythm on the desk.

"I...well..." she stammers, clearly flustered. Finally, she

takes a deep breath and meets my eyes. "As I already told you, I don't need sex," she says. "It was never that good, to be honest, and I prefer to have my bed to myself."

I lean forward, genuinely intrigued. "So you're telling me that Evelyn Rothschild, one of the most beautiful and powerful women I've met, hasn't had a good roll in the hay in over three decades?"

Evelyn laughs and shakes her head. "When you put it like that, it does sound rather pathetic, doesn't it?"

"Not pathetic," I say quickly. "Just...surprising. I mean, look at you."

She raises an eyebrow, and there's that blush again. "Look at me?"

I wince, realizing I might have said too much. "I just mean...you're an attractive woman, Evelyn."

Evelyn fidgets with the hem of her dress. There's a vulnerability in her posture, as if she's not sure how to handle the compliment. She seems to shrink into herself for a moment, her shoulders hunching. When she finally meets my gaze again, there's uncertainty in her eyes.

"Thank you." She tilts her head, studying me. "And how long has it been for you, Ms. Mendoza?" There's a challenge in her voice that makes my heart beat a little faster.

"Too long," I admit with a chuckle. "A few months, maybe? That's an eternity in Val-time."

Evelyn laughs again, and I'm captivated by the way her eyes crinkle at the corners when she's genuinely amused. "Val-time? Is that an official measurement?"

"Totally," I say, grinning. "It's right up there with island time and New York minutes."

She shakes her head in amusement. A quiet moment

falls between us, but it's not entirely uncomfortable. I've noticed that Evelyn has a way with silences. She seems to know how to use them to her advantage, letting them stretch out in a way that might make others squirm. But not me. I'm content to sit here, watching the play of emotions across her face.

Her gaze drifts to the terrace doors, where the late-afternoon sun is streaming in. Her profile is striking in this light —all elegant lines and sharp angles softened by the golden glow of the low sun.

"May I ask you a personal question?" she says.

"Aren't we already having a highly personal conversation?" I shoot her a humorous grin. "I mean, we've covered your decades-long dry spell and my 'Val-time' measurement of sexual frequency."

A smile tugs at the corners of her mouth. "I suppose you're right," she concedes. "Have you ever been with a man?"

I'm surprised. Not by the question itself, but by the fact that Evelyn is the one asking it.

"No," I answer. "I haven't."

Evelyn frowns. "Never? Not even...?"

I shake my head. "Not even a kiss. I've known I was gay since I was a teenager."

She nods slowly, processing this information. "And you've never been curious?"

"About men?" I shrug. "Not really. I mean, there's no attraction there, so why would I?"

"Right. Of course." Her gaze is intense, as if she's trying to see into my mind. "And women...they provide that spark for you?"

"Oh yeah. Definitely," I say, playfully drawing out the words.

There's another beat of silence, and I decide to turn the tables on her.

"What about you, Evelyn? Ever been curious about women?"

"No!" She throws her head back and laughs. "I...well, I..." she stammers, clearly uncomfortable with the question.

I hold up a hand and laugh along. "It's okay. You don't have to answer that. I was just teasing."

"No, it's all right," she says. "I suppose turnabout is fair play." She pauses, considering her words carefully. "To be honest, I've never really thought about it. But..." She hesitates. "I suppose I can appreciate the beauty of women. Aesthetically speaking, of course."

"Of course," I echo, trying to keep the amusement out of my voice. There's something endearing about watching Evelyn navigate this conversation, her usual confidence giving way to a more vulnerable side.

"I mean, you're very attractive," she continues. "You have this young, eternal glow about you. Sometimes I wish I could be ten years younger again."

"Really?"

"Only physically," Evelyn clarifies. Then her expression grows more serious. "Sometimes I feel like life is passing by too quickly. Before I know it, I'll be retiring, and what will I do then? That worries me."

"Age is just a number. It's how you feel that matters," I say, aware I've just thrown two of the biggest clichés at her. "It's what makes you feel alive. That's how I try to live my life. Every day, I do something that matters."

"What exactly do you mean by that?" she asks.

I pause, considering how to put my philosophy into words. "I mean making every day count. Finding beauty or meaning in every day. For instance, yesterday I sat on the island and watched dolphins play in the waves. Their joy was so pure, so contagious, it brought tears to my eyes." I smile, meeting her gaze. "And today? Today I'm having this conversation with you. It's unexpected and meaningful. For me, these are the moments that make life rich."

Chapter 25

Evelyn

I stab at my salad with more force than necessary, spearing a cherry tomato and popping it into my mouth. The burst of sweetness does little to counteract the sour taste this conversation is leaving.

"We're having the ceremony on the beach at sunset," my father says, his eyes twinkling as he gazes at Candy. "Barefoot in the sand, with just our closest friends and family."

"It's going to be magical," Candy gushes, clasping her hands together. Her engagement ring catches the light, its massive diamond winking at me mockingly. Tonight, she's wearing a flowy, off-the-shoulder sundress in a vibrant tropical print that barely skims her mid-thighs, and her feet are adorned with strappy sandals that lace up her calves and show off her endless, toned legs. She looks like a model; of course my father's into her. The question is, what does she see in him? She can't possibly have any other motive than money.

"Magical," he repeats. "Just like you, honey."

I take a sip of my wine to hide my grimace. My father,

the man who used to call backpackers "fucking hippies" and wouldn't be caught dead without a pressed suit, is now waxing poetic about a bohemian beach wedding. The cognitive dissonance is giving me whiplash.

"We want it to be really laid-back and organic," Candy continues, twirling a strand of her sun-bleached hair around her finger. "Like, instead of formal centerpieces, we're thinking of using dried seaweed and seashells."

"That's so cool," Mia chimes in. "It's way more personal than some stuffy ballroom affair."

I glance at my daughter, trying to gauge if her excitement is genuine or if she's just being polite. To my dismay, she seems utterly sincere.

"What do you think, princess?" My father turns to me, his smile expectant. "Doesn't it sound wonderful?"

I force a smile onto my face, hoping it doesn't look as strained as it feels. "Yes, it sounds wonderful. Who doesn't love a beach wedding?"

My father doesn't seem to notice my lack of enthusiasm. He's too busy staring at Candy, who's now scrolling through her phone, showing Mia pictures of boho wedding inspiration on Pinterest.

I take the moment to really look at my father. He's wearing a linen shirt, unbuttoned far too low for a man his age, revealing a swath of graying chest hair. His legs, slightly knobby, stick out from a pair of floral shorts that look like they were stolen from a surfer. There's a leather cord around his neck with some sort of shell pendant. The whole ensemble is so far removed from the man I grew up with that I half expect him to pull out a doobie.

"And after the ceremony we're having a bonfire," Candy continues. "We'll roast marshmallows, and hopefully, I'll be able to find a good acoustic guitarist."

"I can play guitar!" Mia volunteers. "I don't have my guitar with me, but I can come a day early to buy one on Ibiza and help you with preparations."

I bite back a groan. *Great. Now my daughter is going to serenade my father and his child bride.*

"That would be amazing, sweetie," my father says, reaching across the table to squeeze Mia's hand. "We'd love to have you perform."

The genuine affection in his voice catches me off guard. Despite my reservations about this whole situation, I can't deny that my father seems happier, lighter, somehow. The perpetual furrow between his brows is gone, replaced by laugh lines that crinkle when he smiles.

"And we'd love for you to propose a toast, Evelyn," Candy says, turning those earnest blue eyes on me. "Something about love and new beginnings?"

I nearly choke on my wine. The idea of me toasting to love in front of a crowd is almost as absurd as my father's new bohemian persona.

"I wouldn't be very good at that," I demur, dabbing at my mouth with my napkin.

"Oh, come on, Mom." Mia nudges me. "You give speeches all the time for work."

"That's different," I protest. "Those are presentations, not...talks about feelings."

My father chuckles. "Some things never change. My Evelyn was always more comfortable with spreadsheets than sonnets."

Muttering that I'll think about it, I focus on my salad.

"Don't worry, whatever you're comfortable with," Candy says sweetly, peeling one of the grilled gambas in front of her. "By the way, we're going to see this amazing crystal healer in Palma tomorrow night." She licks her fingers. "He's going to align our energies before the wedding."

My father smiles widely, wrapping an arm around Candy's shoulders. "It's all part of our spiritual journey toward the wedding."

I bite my tongue, swallowing the sarcastic comment that threatens to escape. "So you'll be gone all evening?"

"Oh, yes," Candy says. "It's a lengthy process. We probably won't be back until quite late. Sorry about that."

It's the best thing that's come out of her mouth all night, and I'm suddenly feeling more upbeat as I turn to Mia. "In that case, why don't you and I go out for dinner tomorrow night? I know you wanted to try some local cuisine for your blog." I gesture to our surroundings. "I know fancy hotels aren't really your thing, so we'll go wherever you want."

"Yes, let's do that." Mia leans in and kisses my cheek, and I smile, genuinely this time. The prospect of spending an evening alone with my daughter, away from all this wedding madness, fills me with a warmth I haven't felt in days. "So," she says, "tell me more about Val. She seemed super nice when we met earlier."

At the mention of Val's name, I feel an unexpected jolt, as if someone's hooked a live wire to my spine. "She's... competent," I say.

"Oh, she's lovely," Candy chimes in, and my father, as always with her, nods in agreement.

"Indeed. If she's here on her own, she's always welcome to join us for dinner."

"She's busy," I say quickly. "And I doubt she's lonely. She's quite...social."

Our earlier discussion about relationships and intimacy keeps replaying in my mind. I can still see the playful glint in her eyes as she teased me about my "dry spell."

It's been hours since that conversation, yet I can't seem to shake it from my thoughts. Every passing day, Val's presence affects me more. The way she challenges me, even the casual way she brushes stray strands of hair behind her ear when she's thinking—it all lingers in my mind long after our meetings end.

Irritatingly, now she's even dominating my thoughts when she's not around. Here I am, at dinner with my family, and all I can think about is our conversation about sex and relationships. I feel strange, almost like I'm outside myself and at the same time, I've never felt so paradoxically unmoored and anchored. It's as if my consciousness is floating above the table, watching this unfamiliar version of myself navigate dinner, while simultaneously being hyper-aware of my body. I'm a stranger in my own skin, yet never have I felt more physically present.

I try to refocus on the conversation, but as my father launches into another anecdote about his and Candy's adventures, my mind wanders again. What is it about Val that's gotten under my skin? And more importantly, how am I going to get rid of this strange infatuation?

Chapter 26

Val

I settle onto a barstool, savoring the first sip of my ice-cold beer when my phone buzzes. Smiling, I prop it up against the napkin holder and accept the video call.

"Hey, boss lady!" Marcus grins, his face filling my screen. "Look at you, living the life!"

I raise my beer in a mock toast. "Don't let it fool you. I've been fighting with Evelyn Rothschild all day. I've earned this cold one."

Marcus's eyebrows shoot up. "Still butting heads, huh?"

"No, it's not so bad anymore," I admit, tracing a finger through the condensation on my glass. "Evelyn's more lenient now. Her daughter's here and she wants to spend time with her, so she can't afford to waste hours arguing with me."

I consider mentioning Donald Rothschild and his young fiancée, but something stops me. It feels like a violation of Evelyn's trust, so instead, I just shrug and take another sip of my beer.

"Well, that's progress," Marcus says. Behind him is the familiar backdrop of our San Francisco office. The large windows reveal a slice of the city skyline, fog rolling in over the hills in the distance. The walls are adorned with living plant installations, and I can just make out the edge of our reclaimed wood conference table and the whiteboard filled with scribbled ideas and design concepts as he swivels on his chair. "So, is the ice queen finally thawing to our ideas?"

I laugh, shaking my head. "She's actually growing on me. I'll even go as far as to say I like her now."

Marcus rolls his eyes. "Be careful, Val. You know what they say about mixing business with pleasure. She's a beautiful lady. Don't get distracted."

A little flutter of something stirs in my stomach, but I quickly push it aside. Sure, I find Evelyn attractive—I'd have to be blind not to. The memory of her laughing at my lingerie comment still brings a smile to my face, and I've been wondering what she looks like wearing it. I can't help it; I'm a sucker for pretty lingerie.

"It's not like that," I insist, perhaps a bit too quickly.

Marcus holds up his hands in surrender, but there's a knowing twinkle in his eyes. "Whatever you say. Just remember, I've seen that look before."

I roll my eyes, grateful for the distraction as Mateo approaches with a bowl of olives. "Here you go, Val," he says. "On the house."

"Thanks, Mateo." I pop one into my mouth. "You're spoiling me."

"Who's that?" Marcus cranes his neck as if he's trying to see beyond the frame of my phone.

"It's the bartender. He's my Mallorca bestie," I add, shooting Mateo a wink.

Mateo laughs and waves at Marcus as I turn my phone and point my camera at him.

"Hello there, Val's bestie." Marcus waves back. "Take care of her, will you? Don't let her get distracted by women. She's there to work, not to—"

"Marcus!" Turning my phone back, I shoot him a glare as Mateo bursts out in laughter. "Can we just focus on work, please?" He's teased me ever since he caught me making out with one of our female contractors on our Hawaii site. It wasn't anything serious; it was just a bit of fun for both of us, and although I don't make a habit of getting involved with people I work with, Marcus clearly has the wrong idea of me now.

"I'm sorry, I couldn't help myself." He grins. "So, how's the Ibiza trip shaping up?"

"All set," I confirm, grateful for the change of subject. "I'll fly out in two weeks, spend a couple of days checking out the site and sweettalking the local authorities, then head back here." I don't mention that Evelyn will be there too, for her father's wedding. It's not relevant to the business at hand, and again, it feels too personal to share.

"Sounds good." Marcus nods. "I'll email you the deets."

We chat for a few more minutes about the logistics of the Ibiza trip, and as we're wrapping up, I notice two familiar figures approaching the bar.

I end the call just as Evelyn and Mia reach me. Evelyn looks slightly flustered.

"Val," she says. "I'm sorry to invade your territory. I suspected you might be here, but Mia wanted to come here to sample the local cuisine."

"Oh, hush, Mom. Val won't mind." Mia smiles at me. "Why don't you join us for dinner?"

"I think Val might prefer some time to herself," Evelyn says with a nervous glimmer in her eyes. "She's been in meetings with me all day and—"

"Please," Mia insists. "I don't like wasting food and with the three of us, I can order more dishes." Without waiting for an answer, she points to an empty table by the water's edge and turns to Mateo. "Can we sit there?"

"Yes, please sit down." Mateo rushes over and pulls out chairs for Evelyn and Mia.

I contemplate excusing myself, but it feels rude to decline as Mateo pulls out a third chair for me. "Thank you, I'd love to join you." I'm sure Evelyn would rather have dinner with Mia alone, but what can I do?

"Great!" Mia claps her hands together. "I love this little hotel, by the way. It's got so much more charm than that monstrosity of a building you're staying in, Mom."

"I know that's not your thing, honey." She looks out over the water and smiles. "And yes, I agree. This place is rather charming, and the food is very, very good. I've had dinner here with Val before."

"Oh? You didn't tell me that." Mia picks up the menu, her eyes scanning over the options. "Everything looks so good. What should I get?"

"Why don't we let Mateo decide?" I suggest. "Let him surprise you."

"Sure, I love that idea! Mateo?" Mia looks up at him. "We're putting our dinner in your capable hands."

Mateo seems pleased, and after he's checked for allergies and taken our drinks orders, Mia turns back to me. "Val, I have to ask. What have you done to my mother?"

I blink, not quite sure what she's referring to. "I'm sorry?"

Mia nudges Evelyn. "She dresses differently. I've rarely seen her in anything other than a suit, and she's way less uptight."

"Uptight? Excuse me?" Evelyn interjects.

"I don't mean that negatively, Mom." Mia shoots her a sweet smile. "But you're always so focused on work and now you're... I don't know. Different. I don't know how else to put it into words. Is it your influence, Val? I mean, she never spends much time with anyone in particular, and she's been stuck here with you for a while now."

I don't know how to respond to that. My eyes flick to Evelyn, taking in her appearance. Mia's right—Evelyn does look different. Her hair is loose and wavy, and she's wearing a simple sundress that softly frames her curves.

Evelyn seems as taken aback by the comment as I am. Our eyes meet, and I see a flicker of confusion in her gaze that probably mirrors my own.

"I haven't done anything," I say finally, still holding Evelyn's gaze. "Your mom's just...settling into island life, I guess."

Evelyn clears her throat, breaking our eye contact. "It's the climate," she says matter-of-factly. "And I don't think I'm any different than usual. I'm always happy when you're around, Mia." She looks flustered, her cheeks tinting pink. "Now, enough about me. Why don't you tell Val about Vietnam?"

As Mia launches into a story, my attention is divided. Part of me is genuinely interested in Mia's adventures—her passion for food and culture is infectious. But another part of me can't stop thinking about Mia's observations.

Have I really had an effect on Evelyn? I sneak glances at her as Mia talks, noticing little things I hadn't before. The way she gestures more freely when she speaks, the relaxed set of her shoulders. Even the way she laughs seems different—fuller, more uninhibited.

I struggle to tear my eyes away from her and the realization hits me like a punch to the gut. I have a crush on Evelyn Rothschild.

Chapter 27

Evelyn

The boutique in Palma that Candy recommended is awash with soft, feminine fabrics and bohemian designs that make me feel entirely out of my element. Racks of flowing dresses and colorful kaftans surround us, a far cry from the tailored suits I'm accustomed to.

The shop itself is a sensory overload, all dappled sunlight and earthy tones, with dreamcatchers hanging from the ceiling and the faint scent of patchouli in the air. It's as if someone's taken every cliché of a hippie boutique and crammed it into one space. The overly enthusiastic sales assistant, a young woman with more bangles than I've ever seen on one arm, tried to help earlier. Her constant chatter about certain colors matching my aura grated on my nerves until I dismissed her, probably more briskly than necessary.

Mia, of course, loves it. She's already found her brides-maid's dress—a flowing, soft pink number that matches Candy's wedding dress. It hangs in its garment bag near the fitting room, a reminder of why we're here.

"Mom, what about this one?" She holds up a gauzy teal

dress adorned with delicate embroidery. "It's perfect for a beach wedding."

I eye the garment skeptically. "It's see-through, Mia. I might as well show up in my underwear."

"It's meant to be worn with a slip, Mom. Come on, at least try it on."

"I don't think so," I say, running my hand over a rack of dresses. The fabrics feel foreign under my fingertips—too soft, too yielding.

Mia sighs, hanging the dress back on the rack. "Okay, what about something simpler? Less frilly?"

I nod, grateful for her understanding. "That would be better."

We continue our search, Mia occasionally holding up a dress for my inspection. Each time, I find a reason to reject it—too bright, too short, too revealing. I can see frustration building in the set of Mia's shoulders, but she soldiers on.

"You know," she says, rifling through another rack, "it wouldn't kill you to step out of your comfort zone once in a while."

I bristle at her words. "I'm perfectly comfortable in my own clothes, thank you very much." I don't like shopping. My PA always ordered my clothes and when she wasn't available, I left it to a personal shopper. Both were instructed to buy similar items to what I already had.

Mia turns to me and tilts her head. "I know you are. But this isn't a board meeting, it's a wedding. Grandpa's wedding. Don't you want to look like you've gone to a little bit of effort?"

Her words hit home. Am I really so rigid that I can't even dress appropriately for my own father's wedding? Or enjoy shopping with my daughter? The thought is unsettling.

"You're right," I concede. "I'll try to be more open-minded." My eyes land on a simple, long champagne-colored dress. The fabric looks light and airy, and I reach out to touch it, surprised by how smooth it feels.

When I take it off the rack, Mia lets out a sigh of relief. "Yes! That's more like it. It's gorgeous. You have to try it on."

I hesitate, eyeing the thin shoulder straps and the plunging neckline. It's far more revealing than anything I'd normally wear. "I don't know, Mia. It's a bit...daring, don't you think?"

Mia shakes her head. "No, it's perfect! It's casual enough for a beach wedding but still elegant. And the color would look amazing on you now that you've got a tan."

I chew my lower lip, a habit I thought I'd broken years ago. "The neckline is very so low though..."

"That's the point," Mia says with a laugh. "Why not flaunt what you've got?" She grins unrepentantly. "Come on, just try it on. What's the harm?"

Unable to argue with her logic, I reluctantly take the dress and head to the fitting room. As I slip it on, I'm surprised by how comfortable it is. I turn to face the mirror and my breath catches in my throat.

The woman staring back at me is almost a stranger. The color complements my skin tone, making me look sun-kissed and vibrant. The dress hugs my curves before flowing grace-fully to the floor and the slit rides all the way up to my right thigh. But it's the neckline that draws my attention. The plunging V reveals more cleavage than I've shown in years, if ever.

Pulling out my hairclip, I shake my hair loose and study myself, trailing a hand over my body, tracing the seams of the dress. My fingers hesitate at the edge of the neckline, and I can't help but imagine what Val would think if she saw me in this. Would her eyes linger? Would she...

I banish the thought. What am I doing, thinking about Val, and here of all places?

"Mom?" Mia calls from outside. "How does it look? Can I see?" She steps inside without waiting for an answer, and a wide smile spreads across her face. "Oh, Mom," she says softly. "You look beautiful."

I fidget with the straps of the dress, feeling vulnerable. "You don't think it's too much?"

"Not at all. You look like a goddess."

I turn back to the mirror, trying to see myself through Mia's eyes. I must admit, the dress is gorgeous, and I can't deny that it flatters my figure.

"I don't know," I murmur, smoothing my hands over the fabric once again. "It's not really me, is it?"

Mia comes up behind me, meeting my eyes in the mirror. "Maybe it is. You just don't know it yet."

"Has that shop assistant gotten to you?" I ask. "Is this a case of 'you don't choose the dress, the dress chooses you'? Because I don't believe in garment destiny, or any form of destiny for that matter."

"No... Maybe a little. It does look like it was made for you." Mia narrows her eyes at me and nudges me teasingly. "Your aura is speaking to me. It's begging for a break from pantsuits."

I chuckle as I turn to face her. "Ha-ha, smartass. Okay, I'll take it. Now let's get out of here before that shop assistant manages to corrupt you even more." I look down at my feet. "Wait... I need heels, don't I?"

"Nope. It's a barefoot wedding, remember?"

I groan at Mia's reminder. "A barefoot wedding? I thought Candy was joking when she said that." The idea of attending a wedding without shoes feels utterly foreign to me, like showing up at work in pajamas.

Mia laughs. "Nope, she was dead serious." She takes my hand and squeezes it. "You're really not sold on this wedding, are you?"

I sigh, leaning against the dressing room wall. "No, I'm not. She's brainwashed him. It's like he's become a completely different person. Luckily, she won't be able to get her hands on the company, but your grandfather is a very wealthy person and that worries me."

"Is that really what you're worried about?" Mia asks. "Money?"

"Of course, honey. Candy can't possibly be serious about him. This will end in divorce in a few years' time, if not sooner, and your grandfather will be left with half his fortune and a broken heart."

"I'm not so sure about that," Mia says. "Grandpa is a pretty charismatic man. He's not bad looking either now that he's toned up and gained some color."

"And she's twenty-eight," I argue. "But you know your grandfather. Once he's decided on something there's no changing his mind, even though this whole ordeal is ridiculous."

"Is it?" Mia challenges. "Maybe instead of worrying about what Candy might take from Grandpa, you should consider what she's given him. When was the last time you saw him this happy?"

Blowing out my cheeks, I unzip my dress. I'm not going to argue with my daughter over something I can't control. "We'll just have to see how this plays out," I say, avoiding the question. "Now, how about a pedicure? If we're going to be barefoot, we'll have to do something about that chipped nail polish of yours."

Chapter 28

Val

When Evelyn lets me in for our meeting on Monday morning, her hair is pulled back in a loose ponytail, and she's wearing a simple white top tucked into high-waisted linen pants. She's not wearing makeup and looks rested and sun kissed.

"Good morning, Val," she says, stepping aside to let me in. "Right on time, as usual."

I'm still recovering from the realization I had during dinner with her and Mia, and I try to ignore the flutter in my belly as I brush past her. "Morning, Evelyn. I see you sorted out your laundry." It's become a running joke every time I see the dry-cleaning bag hanging on her door. "Good girl."

"Yes, I'm getting good at this. Do I get a medal?" She laughs and gestures for me to take a seat on the terrace, where a pot of coffee and two cups are already waiting on the dining table shaded under a huge parasol.

"Are we working outside today?" I ask, pleasantly surprised. I don't like air-conditioned spaces.

"Yes, if you don't mind," she says, pouring me coffee. "I thought it would be nice."

"I'm all for it." I thank her when she hands me my coffee. "You look like you've been on the beach. How was your weekend?"

"It was...interesting," she says, pouring us each a cup. "Yes, we spent some time on the beach—that was lovely—and yesterday, Mia dragged me to Palma to go dress shopping for the wedding."

My eyebrows shoot up. "You? Dress shopping?"

She rolls her eyes, but there's a hint of amusement in her expression. "I know, I know. It's not exactly my idea of a good time, but Mia insisted."

As I add a splash of milk to my coffee, my gaze lands on a garment bag slung over the back of a chair near the terrace doors. "Is that the dress?" I ask, pointing to it.

Evelyn follows my gaze and nods. "Yes, that's it."

"Can I see it?" The words are out of my mouth before I can stop them, curiosity getting the better of me.

She hesitates for a moment, then shrugs. "I suppose so."

Setting down my coffee, I head over there, unzip the bag and carefully pull out the dress. The champagne-colored fabric shimmers, and I let out a low whistle.

"Wow, Evelyn." I hold the dress up to get a better look. "This is...something else." I turn to her with a mischievous grin. "You're going to make heads turn."

Evelyn lets out a surprised laugh. "Don't be ridiculous," she says, but there's no bite to her words. "It's just a dress."

"Just a dress? This is a weapon of mass distraction." I shoot her a playful wink. "I'd love to see it on." I'm probably crossing a line, but I just can't help myself.

Evelyn still chuckles as she leans back in her chair, crossing her arms. "Nice try, Val. But I think I'll save the grand reveal for the wedding." Her tone is light and teasing, and I have a feeling she's enjoying my subtle flirtations.

Carefully placing the dress back in its bag, I zip it up with exaggerated care. "Can't blame a girl for trying."

Evelyn ignores my comment, but I can see she's blushing.

"Speaking of the wedding," she says, "I wanted to offer you a ride to Ibiza in the company jet. Mia's leaving a few days early to help my father and Candy with preparations, so I'm traveling solo."

"That's...very generous of you," I say slowly. "But I don't take private jets. Or short flights in general. I'm pretty conscious of my carbon footprint."

Evelyn nods. "Of course. I should have thought of that. What's your plan, then?"

"I'm taking the ferry," I say. "Care to join me?" My suggestion was only a joke; I can't see Evelyn Rothschild setting foot on a rusty car carrier, but she doesn't laugh it off. In fact, she seems to seriously consider it as she taps a mani-cured nail against her coffee cup.

"That's not a bad idea," she finally says. "With Roth-schild opening its first eco-friendly resort, I should probably be more mindful of my own habits. We don't want any bad press about the CEO's travel choices conflicting with our changing company image."

I stare at her, genuinely stunned. "Wait, are you seri-ous? You'd actually consider taking the ferry?"

Evelyn tilts her head from side to side and hesitates for a beat. "Why not? It could be...an experience. Although, I'm not too keen on crowds," she adds with her usual dose of sass. "How would you feel about chartering a private yacht instead?"

At that, I throw my head back and laugh. She really is

clueless when it comes to sustainable travel. "Oh, Evelyn... Are we actually negotiating about transportation now?" She grins sheepishly, and I shake my head. "Yachts aren't exactly eco-friendly either. But...if we could make it a sailing yacht, I might be on board. Literally."

Her eyes light up at the suggestion. "A sailing yacht? That could work. I've never been on one before."

"Never?" I ask, leaning forward in my chair.

"Never had the time, I suppose. Or the inclination, until now."

I feel flattered that Evelyn wants to travel with me. She could just take the easy way and use her jet, but it makes sense for her to be more conscious now. Bad press can harm a company in a heartbeat these days, but I have a feeling it's not just the press that's changed her mind.

The rigid boundaries that initially defined our professional relationship have blurred, and we've grown unexpectedly close. There's a subtle flirtation in our exchanges now, a playful banter. I catch myself studying the curve of her smile, the way her eyes crinkle when she laughs. It's not just physical attraction; I genuinely enjoy her company, and I know she enjoys mine too. The way she seeks out my opinion, the lingering glances, the softening of her usually stern demeanor around me—it all points to something more than just a working relationship. We're stepping into uncharted waters, and I'm both curious and a little worried.

"Well then," I say, raising my coffee cup in a mock toast, "here's to new experiences. Shall I book us a sailing yacht for the trip to Ibiza?"

Evelyn clinks her cup against mine, her smile genuine and unguarded. "Why not? Let's do it."

We settle into our usual meeting routine, but I'm distracted. I like the idea of taking a sailing trip with Evelyn, away from work and the rest of the world, a little too much. My mind keeps wandering to images of Evelyn sunbathing on the deck in a bikini. It's a dangerous line of thinking, I know, but I can't help myself.

"Val? Are you listening?" Evelyn's voice snaps me out of my reverie.

I blink, realizing I've been staring. "Sorry, what was that?"

She gives me a curious look, her head tilted slightly to the side. "I was saying you're fucking killing my budget with these solar panels and I'm about to throw a tantrum unless you can assure me it will be worth it." Her words are harsh but she's smiling, perhaps looking forward to the trip as much as I am. "Is everything all right?"

"Everything's fine," I say quickly, forcing myself to focus on the blueprints and cost sheets in front of us. Remembering I brought something, I reach into my bag and hand her the report that Marcus sent over last night. "Here, take a look at this. The solar panels will have paid for them- selves within seventeen months at projected occupancy rates. It's all broken down in there."

Evelyn takes the report and flicks through it, her brow furrowing as she scans the numbers. After a moment, she looks up at me. "Well, you're lucky you had this ready. I was about to give you an earful."

I grin, feeling a small thrill of victory. "Of course. I always come prepared. Wouldn't want to risk getting a spanking from Evelyn Rothschild."

Chapter 29

Evelyn

The sun seeps into my skin as I sit across from Mia at a bar on a nearby beach. It's a quaint little place, all wood and faded blue paint, with strings of seashells dangling from the eaves. It's the kind of place I'd normally avoid, but Mia insisted, and I'm slowly warming to its rustic appeal.

Mia drains the last of her rosé, setting the glass down with a soft thud. "I'd better head to the road," she says. "My taxi will be here soon. This was fun, Mom. I've had a great day."

"Yes, it's been a wonderful day," I agree and finish my own drink before slipping a few bills under the stem of my glass. The crisp, slightly tart wine lingers on my tongue as I stand, my chair scraping against the worn planks. "I'll walk you out," I offer, falling into step beside her as we make our way up the short, sandy path to the street.

When we reach the curb, I turn to Mia, my motherly instincts kicking in. "Be careful, okay? And let me know when you get there."

Mia bursts into laughter. Apparently, she finds my comment hilarious. "Mom, seriously? I've been to over thirty countries, some of them not exactly tourist hotspots. This is a fifty-minute flight to Ibiza, not an expedition to the Amazon."

Her amusement is contagious, and I join in, my laughter bubbling up from deep in my chest. It's a freeing sound, one I'm not used to hearing from myself. "You're right," I concede, wiping a tear from the corner of my eye. "I think I've had a little too much wine in the sun."

Mia pulls me into a tight hug, and I breathe in the scent of her hair—coconut shampoo and sea salt. "I love you, Mom," she murmurs. "Try to relax a bit before the wedding, okay?"

I nod against her shoulder, reluctant to let go. When we finally part, I watch as she climbs into the waiting taxi, waving until the car disappears around a bend in the road. Instead of ordering a taxi for myself, I decide to walk back to the hotel. The wine has left me feeling light and buoyant, and the idea of a stroll along the coast is suddenly appealing.

I set off down the narrow road that winds along the cliffs, my sandals almost sticking to the sunbaked asphalt. To my left, the land falls away, revealing a breathtaking vista of the Mediterranean. The sea stretches out, a canvas of deep blues and greens, shimmering. The air is thick with the scent of salt and lavender growing wild along the roadside, and a light breeze plays with loose strands of my hair, carrying with it the distant cries of seagulls.

As I round a bend, a beautiful bay comes into view, its waters an impossible shade of azure that seems almost otherworldly. It takes me a moment to realize that this is where Val's hotel is located. I've only ever arrived here by taxi, approaching from the other direction, and the view from this vantage point is entirely new.

My eyes are drawn to the small restaurant built on a concrete platform jutting out over the water. Even from this distance, I can make out the figures of people seated at the bar. One of them, a slender silhouette with long dark hair, looks remarkably like Val.

My heart does an unexpected flip in my chest, and knowing that I'm actively looking for her, hoping it's her, worries me. It's a feeling I'm not accustomed to, a mix of anticipation and nervous energy that leaves me a little breathless.

Driven by an impulse I don't fully understand, I make my way down to the hotel. The main road winds down the cliffside, but I spot what looks like a shortcut—a narrow, overgrown trail leading more directly to the beach.

I pause for a moment, considering the wisdom of attempting such a route in my attire. My sundress and sandals are hardly appropriate for hiking, but the wine-induced bravado wins out, and I step onto the trail, my feet sinking slightly into the loose, sandy soil.

The path is steeper than it appeared from above, and I grab onto scrubby bushes for balance. The scent of wild herbs intensifies as I brush past them, releasing their oils into the warm air.

About halfway down, my foot catches on an exposed root, and I stumble, my arms windmilling as I try to regain my balance. Pain lances through my leg as I feel something sharp scrape against my shin. I manage to stay upright, but when I look down, I see a thin line of blood trickling down my leg. It's only a cut; it's not as bad as it looks, but I have nothing to wipe away the blood with.

Muttering a curse under my breath, I continue my

descent, more carefully now. By the time I reach the beach, my sundress is slightly askew, my hair is a mess, and my leg is still bleeding.

I make my way across the sand toward the restaurant platform, acutely aware of the less-than-graceful figure I must cut. As I draw closer, I confirm that it is indeed Val seated at the bar. She's clearly still working, as her laptop is open in front of her, but she's only wearing a bikini, and this makes me chuckle. Only Val could get away with jumping onto a video call dressed like that.

She spots me, her eyes widening in surprise. "Evelyn?" she calls out, sliding off her barstool while she closes her laptop. "What are you doing here? And what happened to your leg? Are you okay?"

I glance down at my shin, where the cut is still oozing blood. "I, uh, took a shortcut," I explain, feeling silly. "It didn't quite work out as planned, but I'm fine. It's only a little cut."

Val's brow furrows with concern. "Mateo," she calls over her shoulder, "do you have a first-aid kit?"

Mateo nods, disappearing into the back of the bar and returning moments later with a small white box. Val takes it from him, then turns back to me. "Come on," she says, taking my elbow. "Let's get you cleaned up."

She leads me to a nearby table, urging me to sit. Sitting opposite me, she pulls my leg onto her lap, opens the first-aid kit and begins to clean the cut with an antiseptic wipe. The sting makes me hiss through my teeth.

"Sorry," she says, her touch becoming gentler. "I'll try to be quick."

Despite the sting, I'm enjoying Val's close proximity. The sun has brought out golden highlights in her dark hair, and a light sheen of perspiration glistens on her tanned skin.

Her fingers are soothing against my leg, their touch sending little sparks of sensation racing up my thigh.

"There," she says at last, smoothing a bandage over the cut. "That should do it."

But instead of pulling away, her hand lingers on my leg, her thumb absently stroking the skin just above the bandage. The casual intimacy of the gesture sends a wave of heat coursing through my body, settling low in my belly. It's a sensation I haven't felt in years, if ever, and it leaves me feeling both exhilarated and terrified.

"Thank you," I manage.

Val looks up, her eyes meeting mine. There's a question in her gaze, an intensity that arouses me. I don't shy away, and wonder if she feels it too, this thing between us. She's still stroking my leg and it's taking away my ability to think straight.

The spell is broken by Mateo's voice calling out from the bar. "Everything okay over there?"

Val stands quickly, brushing sand from her knees. "Yeah, we're good," she calls back. Then, turning to me with a slightly forced smile, she asks, "Can I get you a drink? You look like you could use one after your adventure."

I nod, grateful for the distraction. "A glass of rosé would be lovely, thank you."

As Val heads to the bar, I take a moment to collect myself. What just happened? Or, more accurately, what *almost* happened? The residual warmth of Val's touch lingers on my skin, and now I long for more.

Val returns with our drinks, settling into the chair next to mine. "So," she says, a hint of amusement in her voice. "Want to tell me what inspired your impromptu hiking expedition?"

I feel a blush creeping up my neck. "I was having a

drink with Mia on a beach down the main road before she left for Ibiza," I explain. "I may have indulged a bit more than usual. I even went into the sea for a swim with her. I don't normally do that as it ruins my hair."

Val chuckles. "Day drinking and taking ill-advised shortcuts? I'm shocked. I thought you never had more than two drinks?"

"Oh, stop," I say playfully. "I made an exception because it was Mia. I'm not always so...rigid."

"No?" Val smiles, and there's a challenge in her eyes. "Prove it."

I consider for a moment, then kick off my sandals and pull my dress over my head, leaving me in my black bikini. Dropping my dress on the chair, I'm aware I'm exposed, but even that doesn't stop me because something—probably the wine—has given me a new sense of body confidence and I simply don't care that much.

"Come on," I say. "Let's jump in." Walking to the edge of the platform, my reason fights with my gut as I ignore the steps farther down. It's totally out of character, but a sense of reckless abandon begs me to let go and immerse myself. Maybe it's because I'm sweating after my hike, or maybe it's just that I want to be near Val, but despite the height, I feel an irresistible urge to jump. I turn to Val, my heart racing.

"Ready?"

Val nods, a wide grin spreading across her face. She takes my hand, her fingers intertwining with mine. The warmth of her touch sends a jolt through me, more electrifying than my nervousness about the jump.

"On three," she says. "One...two..."

I don't wait for three. I squeeze her hand and leap, pulling her with me. For a moment, we're suspended in air, the wind rushing past us. I feel weightless, free, more alive than I have in years. Val's hand is still in mine as we plummet toward the azure water below, and in this breathless instant before we hit the surface, I realize I'm laughing.

Chapter 30

Val

I burst through the surface, gasping for air and blinking salt water from my eyes. The sound of laughter fills my ears, and I turn to see Evelyn beside me, her head thrown back in pure joy. Her hair is slicked back, water droplets glistening on her skin in the fading sunlight. She's radiant, carefree, and utterly captivating.

Our eyes meet, and the laughter dies on her lips. There's a spark in her gaze, a heat that matches the fire burning in my chest, and for a moment, we're suspended in time, treading water and staring at each other. The urge to close the distance between us is overwhelming.

"Race you to the shore?" I challenge, breaking the tension before I do something reckless.

Evelyn grins, a competitive glint in her eye. "You're on."

We swim toward the shallows, our strokes matching each other's pace. The cool water rushes past me, but all I can feel is the heat of Evelyn's presence beside me. As we near the shore, our feet touch the sandy bottom, and we stand, breathless and exhilarated.

Evelyn pushes her wet hair back from her face, and I

follow the movement with my eyes. Water trails down her neck, over her collarbone, and I fight the urge to trace its path with my fingers.

"I won," she declares, her chest heaving slightly from the swim.

I laugh, shaking my head. "I let you win."

"Sure you did," she teases, taking a step closer.

We're standing face-to-face now, close enough that I can see the droplets clinging to her eyelashes. Evelyn's eyes flick down to my lips, then back up to meet my gaze. My heart races.

Slowly, hesitantly, Evelyn reaches out. Her fingertips graze my cheek, feather-light and tentative. I lean into her touch, unable to help myself. Her hand is cool from the water, but it leaves a trail of fire on my skin.

"Evelyn," I murmur, my voice husky. "I don't want you to do anything you'll regret just because you've had a few drinks."

She shakes her head, her fingers still resting on my cheek. "On the contrary," she says softly, "I feel like I've just sobered up." There's a clarity in her eyes that backs up her words. This isn't the impulsive action of someone drunk on wine and sunshine. This is Evelyn, fully present and aware, making a choice.

I search her face for any sign of hesitation, but find none. Instead, I see a woman open, vulnerable, and achingly beautiful.

Evelyn's hand slides to the back of my neck, her fingers tangling in my wet hair. She pulls me closer, pausing when our lips are just a breath apart.

"Val," she whispers.

I press my lips to hers. The kiss is soft at first, tentative, as if we're both afraid the other might pull away. I've kissed many women before, but nothing could have prepared me for this. The softness of Evelyn's mouth, the faint taste of salt and wine, the way she arches into me, the sigh that escapes her—it all combines to create a sensation so intense it leaves me dizzy.

My heart pounds, so hard and fast I'm sure Evelyn must feel it. Every nerve ending in my body seems to come alive, and I'm hyperaware of every point of contact between us as I push my body against hers.

When Evelyn moans louder and deepens the kiss, parting her lips slightly, I feel as if I'm falling and flying at the same time. This woman, who I've admired and argued with, challenged and been challenged by, is kissing me with a passion I never expected, and I'm struck by how right it feels. There's none of the awkwardness of a first kiss—instead, it's as if we've done this a thousand times before and I'm overwhelmed by a rush of emotions. Desire, yes, but also a tenderness that catches me off guard. I want to protect her, cherish her, show her just how amazing she is.

My arms wrap tighter around her, pulling her flush against me, and Evelyn's other hand lowers to my behind, squeezing me hard as if she's afraid I might disappear. And then, she wraps her legs around me and the weight of her, solid and real against me, ignites a fire that threatens to consume me. It feels like we stopped being two separate beings and have become a single entity swaying in the tide.

It's the kiss of a lifetime, the kind of kiss I know will stay with me forever, and as we finally part, both breathing heavily, I'm left in a state of awe.

Evelyn's cheeks are flushed, her lips slightly swollen. She looks dazed, but there's a smile playing at the corners of her mouth.

"Wow," she breathes. "Even better than I imagined."

I laugh, giddy with the realization of what just happened. "You've been imagining this?" Her legs are still wrapped around me and I pull her up higher, needing to feel her as close as I possibly can. "I must admit, I've had a few fantasies of my own..."

"Hmm..." Evelyn tilts her head to study me, but as soon as her eyes lower to my mouth, we're kissing again, and I know there's no chance we'll continue our conversation anytime soon.

She grinds into me, her breath hitching as I brush my thumb over her hardened nipple. It's like she's never been touched like this before, like she's been waiting for this moment with a need that's been bottled up for far too long. I deepen the kiss, tasting her more fully, losing myself in the sweetness of her mouth.

Evelyn's hands aren't idle either. They roam over my back, pulling me closer, as if she can't stand the thought of any distance between us. There's a desperation in her touch, her body responding to every caress with a raw intensity that matches my own.

I slide my hand down her back, over the curve of her behind, squeezing as she lets out a soft moan. God, she feels incredible—every inch of her skin under my hands, her body a perfect fit against mine. I break the kiss, trailing my lips down her neck, and smile at the way she shivers as I press my lips to the sensitive spot just below her ear.

"Val," she breathes, her voice trembling.

I pull back slightly, my hand still resting on her hip, my breath ragged.

"Do you want to go to your room?" she asks.

Do I want to? The thought of being alone with her is almost too much. But there's a part of me that holds back, a small voice of reason fighting against the tide of my desire.

"Evelyn," I murmur, brushing a damp strand of hair away from her face. "Are you sure?" She meets my gaze, and I see so much desire, but there's also a hint of hesitation there and that's something I can't ignore. "We still have to work together," I remind her, even though it feels like I'm tearing myself apart to say it. "This could complicate everything."

Her lips part as if to argue, but then she closes them again. "You're right," she says, peeling herself away from me. "We need to be careful. I don't know what I was think-ing, I got carried away and oh my God..." She buries her face in her hands. "I'm sorry."

"No, don't be," I say, already missing her nearness. "I'm not."

"You're not?" Evelyn lets out a deep sigh, and I take both her hands and kiss them. I want to kiss all of her, and it takes every ounce of self-control I have not to pull her back into my arms. My body is screaming for more—to taste her, to explore her, to show her exactly what she's been missing all these years. But for the first time in my life, I'm holding back. This isn't just another vacation fling or casual encounter. This is Evelyn, who has never even kissed a woman before today, who might wake up tomorrow regret-ting this moment of vulnerability. And we're stuck working together, our professional relationship already complicated enough without adding sex to the mix. The rational part of my brain knows we should stop now, before we cross a line we can't uncross.

"Tomorrow," I say. "We'll meet at the yacht. We'll talk about it on our way to Ibiza, figure it out."

"Okay, tomorrow." She nods, though desire still burns in her gaze. She drifts back, her eyes locked on mine, the echo of our kiss still burning on my lips.

Chapter 31

Evelyn

I arrive at the pier, rolling my small suitcase behind me and carrying my dress bag over my arm. It's only seven a.m., and the Palma marina is still calm at this early hour. Yachts bob in their moorings, their polished hulls reflecting the cloudless sky above. We didn't have to leave this early; it's not that far to Ibiza, but Val thought it would be fun to make a day out of it, as we have the yacht anyway.

My eyes scan the line of vessels until they land on our chartered yacht, *Eleonora*, the name elegantly painted on the stern in navy blue letters. It's a stunning sailing yacht, its gleaming white hull and towering mast cutting an impressive figure against the backdrop of the Mediterranean.

As I approach, a crew member in white shorts and a polo shirt steps forward to greet me. "Good morning, Ms. Rothschild. Welcome aboard *Eleonora*," he says with a polite smile. "May I take your luggage?"

I nod, handing over my suitcase and dress bag. My stomach is in knots, and I haven't slept a wink all night.

Every time I closed my eyes, I saw Val's face, felt the phantom touch of her lips on mine. That kiss... God, that kiss. It's been replaying in my mind on an endless loop, each recollection sending a fresh wave of heat through my body. I've spent hours alternating between worrying about the implications and fantasizing about what might have happened if we hadn't stopped.

Taking a deep breath, I remove my sandals and make my way up the gangplank. The teak deck is warm beneath my feet as I step aboard, the faint scent of varnish and salt air filling my nostrils. I pause for a moment, taking in the yacht.

With four sun loungers, the foredeck is a lovely space for sunbathing, and at the bow is a cozy seating nook with curved benches. Polished stainless steel cup holders and small tables are seamlessly integrated into the design.

I pass the mast with its maze of halyards and sheets. The main salon, visible through large windows, looks inviting, but I resist the urge to explore the interior. Instead, I continue, and there, lounging on a white sofa on the aft deck, is Val.

She's dressed more smartly than usual, in navy palazzo pants and a white shirt. The fabric is just sheer enough that I can make out the triangle bikini top underneath. She looks effortlessly chic, the epitome of casual elegance, sipping a cappuccino in the morning sun.

Val's eyes meet mine, and suddenly, it's as if all the oxygen has been sucked out of the air. The intensity of her gaze is as potent as it was yesterday.

"Hey, there," she says, her soft voice carrying across the deck. She stands, picking up a second cup from the table beside her. "I took the liberty of ordering you a black coffee and arranged for breakfast to be served soon. I hope that's okay."

I nod, not trusting my voice just yet. I'm not used to others taking charge; in my day-to-day life, nothing happens unless I give the final nod of approval, but it's refreshing not having to think about anything. As I make my way over to her, I'm acutely aware of every step, every breath.

"Thank you," I manage as I take the cup from her, our fingers brushing lightly. Even that small contact sends sparks shooting up my arm. I don't understand the effect she has on me. "You look...nice," I add lamely, inwardly cringing at my inability to form a more eloquent compliment.

Val smiles, a hint of amusement dancing in her eyes. "Thank you. So do you."

I glance down at my own outfit—a white linen shirt dress. It's nothing special, but Val's appreciative gaze makes me feel like I'm wearing couture.

"Did you sleep well?" she asks, gesturing for me to take a seat beside her on the sofa.

I let out a small, nervous laugh. "Not really," I admit, settling onto the cushions. "I had a lot on my mind." It feels silly to fall into small talk after what happened yesterday.

"Me too," she says, turning to face me. "About yesterday..."

My heart rate picks up. This is it. The moment I've been dreading. "Yes?" I prompt when she doesn't continue.

Val takes a deep breath. "I don't regret it," she says firmly. "Not for a second. But I meant what I said about complications. Not just work, that's temporary. I mean you've never been with a woman and—"

"I'm not fragile," I interrupt her. "I can handle a storm. You should know that by now."

"I know." Val scoots closer, and a heavy silence falls

between us. Her gaze flicks from my eyes to my lips. I want to reach out, to touch her, to feel the softness of her skin under my fingertips again. But I hold back, my hands clenched tightly around my coffee cup.

"So where do we go from here?" I ask, hating how vulnerable I sound.

"I'm not sure," Val admits. "But I do know that I care about you, Evelyn. And you have no idea how much I want you... I really do." She swallows hard and licks her lips. "But I needed you to sleep on it."

Before I can answer, the captain approaches. "Ms. Rothschild, Ms. Mendoza," he greets us with a nod. "We're ready to cast off if you are. Ibiza with a detour as discussed?"

"That sounds great," Val says, shooting him a smile. "Wherever you'd like to take us."

The crew starts bustling around us, preparing the yacht for departure. Ropes are untied, sails unfurled. The engine rumbles to life, a low vibration beneath our feet. Slowly, we begin to pull away from the pier and I'm still sitting here, trying to find words.

"Technically, I haven't slept on it," I finally say with a chuckle. "But I have been up all night replaying that kiss. I'm not even tired, I'm buzzing, and all I can think is that I want more."

Val's eyes darken and she leans in. We're so close now, I can feel the warmth of her breath on my skin. For a moment, we stay like that, suspended. Then, with a soft groan of surrender, she cups my neck and pulls me in. Her lips meet mine, soft and insistent, and just like that, I'm lost again.

This kiss is slow and deep, filled with a passion that makes my knees weak. Val's hands come up to cup my face, her thumbs stroking my cheeks as she explores my mouth with a thoroughness that makes me squirm.

I melt into her, my arms wrapping around her waist, pulling her closer, and the feel of her body pressed against mine sends waves of heat coursing through me.

I have no idea how long we sit there, making out and exploring each other. I guess part of my brain registers the yacht backing up and turning before setting sail, but it's only when we pull apart that I realize we're already far from the mainland.

Blinking, I'm momentarily disoriented as I take in our surroundings. The marina has disappeared, and the coastline of Mallorca is nothing more than a distant silhouette. It's as if we've sailed into another world, one where time and space have lost all meaning.

Val notices my bewildered expression and chuckles softly. "I hadn't noticed we'd left the harbor either," she whispers, tucking a stray strand of hair behind my ear. "You're beautiful when you're flustered."

I lean into her touch, closing my eyes for a moment. When I open them again, Val is still watching me, her gaze intense and unwavering. I'm not used to this; to someone touching me so gently and telling me I'm beautiful. To someone being so open and honest with me. People are usually wary around me, shifty even. It's not something I'm proud of, and it's not the way I want to be perceived. But not Val. She sees me for who I am.

She takes my hand in hers and brings it to her lips, pressing a soft kiss to my knuckles. It's a courteous gesture, almost old-fashioned, but there's nothing chaste about the way her lips linger on my skin.

We're interrupted by the sound of footsteps approaching.

"Breakfast is served, ladies," one of the crew members announces while beginning to set up the meal on the table in front of us. The spread is impressive—fresh fruit, pastries, eggs prepared in various ways, and freshly squeezed orange juice. I'm hungry but I'm not sure I'll be able to eat. The clink of cutlery against fine china seems distant, drowned out by the thundering of my pulse.

The shoreline retreats, and in its wake, I'm left lost and weightless, anchored only by the gravity of Val's presence.

Chapter 32

Val

Eleonora's anchor splashes into the water off the coast of a tiny, uninhabited island, the jagged cliffs of which rise from the sea like the teeth of some ancient beast, their weathered faces scarred by millennia of wind and waves. The rugged shoreline, with its maze of sea caves and volcanic formations, gives the island a primordial feel—as if we've sailed back to a time when dinosaurs might have roamed these very cliffs. The captain recommended this spot for snorkeling, promising an abundance of marine life around the nearby reef.

I stand at the railing, taking in the view. The water takes on a bright shade of turquoise here, so clear I can see straight to the sandy bottom dotted with dark patches of seagrass. Schools of tiny silver fish dart just beneath the surface, their scales glinting in the sunlight.

"It's beautiful," Evelyn says, coming to stand beside me. Her shoulder brushes against mine, and I turn to look at her, struck anew by her beauty. The wind has tousled her hair, giving her a softer look, and there's a light in her eyes.

"Have you ever been snorkeling before?" I ask.

She shakes her head. "No, never. I've never jumped into the deep either." The way she says it makes me think she's not just talking about snorkeling.

"It's easy," I assure her. "I'll be right there with you."

One of the crew members approaches with our gear—masks, snorkels, and fins.

"Right...I should probably get out of these clothes," Evelyn says. She takes off her shirt dress and the sight of her takes my breath away.

She's wearing a white and navy triangle bikini that accentuates every curve of her body. The contrast against her glowing skin is striking, and as my eyes graze over her, my fingers itch to trace the lines of her collarbones and her full breasts, to run down the smooth plane of her stomach.

Evelyn catches me staring, and a visible shiver runs through her. Her lips part slightly before they pull into a small, flirtatious smile. "Your turn," she says, tugging at the hem of my shirt.

I feel a rush of heat at her boldness, my heart rate quickening as I comply with her request. Slowly, I pull my shirt over my head, then take off my pants, acutely aware of Evelyn's gaze on me. Her eyes travel over my body, lingering on the toned muscles of my abdomen, the curve of my breasts. Her gaze is appreciative, almost hungry, and I fight the urge to close the distance between us, to feel her skin against mine. Instead, I stand there, letting her look and reveling in the intensity of her stare.

"Are you ready?" I ask. This question too suddenly seems loaded.

She hesitates for a beat before she nods, then picks up the mask and places it over her head.

I help her adjust it, and we sit on the edge of the swim platform to put on our fins.

Offering her my hand, we slide into the water together, the coolness a shock against our sun-warmed skin. Evelyn gasps, her grip on my hand tightening. As we lower ourselves beneath the surface and swim toward the reef, the color beneath us deepens, changing from turquoise to a rich azure, and the sandy bottom gives way to a landscape of coral and rock formations teeming with life.

The reef is a patchwork of hard and soft corals in shades of brown, yellow, and purple. Fan-like gorgonians sway in the current, their branches home to tiny, jewel-like fish.

A school of saddled sea bream swims by, their silver bodies marked with distinctive black saddles. They move as one, creating mesmerizing patterns in the water. Nearby, a pair of painted combers dart in and out of a crevice in the reef.

A large dusky grouper hovers near a rock formation and watches us warily as we pass. In a patch of seagrass, I spot movement and point it out to Evelyn. A small green turtle is grazing, its head bobbing as it tears at the grass. We watch, transfixed, as it goes about its meal, seemingly unbothered by our presence.

Evelyn squeezes my hand, and when I look at her, I can see the joy radiating from her eyes even through the mask.

I love snorkeling. There's something incredibly soothing about gliding through the water, enveloped in a world of tranquility. The usual noise of life above the surface fades away, replaced by the rhythmic sound of my own breathing.

Everything moves with a dreamlike slowness, as if the water itself is bending time. The weightlessness of my body creates an illusion of flying, rather than swimming, through this alien landscape. It's a sensory cocoon, where sight becomes heightened and touch is muted, save for the constant pressure of water against skin as the boundaries between myself and the environment blur.

I'm so glad to do this with Evelyn; experiences are always better shared, but I wanted her to see the beauty of the reefs for herself, to appreciate what's below the surface. Perhaps then she'll feel more connected to nature and understand my life's mission.

We continue our exploration, marveling at the diversity of life around us. An octopus changes color before our eyes, shifting from reddish-brown to match the coral it's resting on. Tiny cleaner wrasses set up shop on a large grouper, darting in and out of its gills and mouth.

As we round a large coral formation, I spot something that makes me pause. There, hovering just above the reef, is a seahorse. Its long snout and curled tail are unmistakable, its body a pale yellow that almost glows in the filtered sunlight.

I tap Evelyn's arm, pointing excitedly, and her grip on my hand tightens. We float there, quietly, watching this delicate creature sway in the current until it finally drifts away, disappearing into the maze of the reef. We surface together, pulling off our masks.

Evelyn is wide-eyed with wonder when she resurfaces. "This is incredible!" she exclaims. "I can't believe it!"

I laugh, caught up in her enthusiasm. "I know! And seahorses are so rare to spot. We got so lucky."

A droplet of water clings to Evelyn's eyelash, and I reach out to brush it away, my thumb grazing her cheek.

Evelyn's eyes flutter closed for a moment, and she leans into my hand. "Val," she whispers. "What are we doing?"

"I don't know," I admit, adjusting my mask around my neck to buy time. The waves rock us, and I watch a seabird dive into the water nearby, wishing I had its certainty of purpose. "We should head back to the yacht."

Evelyn nods, but neither of us moves. We stay there, suspended in the water.

What are we doing? That's the question I've been asking myself too. This thing between us has snuck up on me. I didn't see it coming, and now that it's here, I don't know what to do with it. I've never wanted anyone the way I want Evelyn, and it terrifies me.

After our first kiss, I firmly told myself to back off, to maintain a professional distance. It all happened so fast, so unexpectedly that I hadn't given myself time to think it through properly.

Last night, I lay awake for hours, my mind racing with thoughts of Evelyn and the complications that would inevitably arise if we allowed ourselves to pursue this attraction. But this morning, when Evelyn walked onto the yacht, all my carefully laid plans and rational arguments crumbled and now I find myself adrift.

I swallow hard, torn between the desire to pull her close and the nagging voice in my head reminding me of all the reasons this is a bad idea. But as I look into Evelyn's eyes, seeing the want there, I find it harder and harder to remember those reasons.

Chapter 33

Evelyn

This is madness, I think as I climb onto the bowsprit of the yacht, carefully making my way to the netting suspended over the water. Val is already there, waiting for me to join her. She reaches out a hand to help me, and I settle between her legs, leaning back against her chest.

The sailing yacht cuts through the waves, sending up sprays of salty mist that cool my skin. The vast expanse of the Mediterranean stretches out before us, an endless canvas of blue meeting the horizon.

The sea is rough out here and it's a little scary, but I know we're perfectly safe. We've been snorkeling and sunbathing all day, and kissing whenever we get a moment alone. There's a constant hesitation between us, as if we both know this is a bad idea, yet the undercurrent of desire wins every single time.

Val's arms encircle me, her chin resting on my shoulder. It's intimate, comfortable, and utterly foreign all at once.

Suddenly, the reality of my situation hits me. I'm here, cradled in the arms of a woman I've been kissing all day. A woman who, just five weeks ago, I saw as nothing more than a business associate—and an irritating one at that. Now, her touch makes me melt, her laughter makes my heart beat faster, and her kisses... God, her kisses make me feel things I've never felt before.

This is the most romantic thing I've ever experienced, and that thought alone is enough to make my head spin. I'm participating in a scene straight out of a romance novel. The setting sun painting the sky in hues of pink and orange, the swaying of the boat, the intimacy of our position—it's all so surreal that part of me wonders if I'm dreaming.

"Are you okay?" Val murmurs. "You've gone very quiet."

I nod, not trusting my voice just yet. How can I explain the whirlwind of thoughts and emotions inside me?

Why now? I wonder. I've never been attracted to women before. In fact, I've never been particularly attracted to anyone. Relationships, romance, intimacy—they've always seemed like unnecessary complications, distractions from work, motherhood, and my ambitions. And yet here I am, sinking into Val's embrace, and I don't want it to end.

And why Val? She's twenty-odd years younger and the complete opposite to me. She challenges me, frustrates me, pushes me out of my comfort zone at every turn. She's the last person I should be falling for. *And* she's a woman.

Falling for. The phrase echoes in my mind, sending a jolt of panic through me. Is that what this is? Am I falling for Val?

"Val," I whisper. "What are we doing?"

It's not the first time I've asked that question today and Val doesn't seem to have a clue either.

She tightens her arms around me, a gesture that's both

reassuring and unsettling. "I don't know," she says. "But it feels good, right?"

And that's the crux of it. As illogical and unexpected as this is, it does feel good, great even. And that scares me more than anything.

Am I losing it? The thought creeps in, unbidden. *Is this some sort of midlife crisis? Am I turning into my father, losing my sanity over a whirlwind romance with someone far too young for me? Was I lonely? Did I just need someone to hold me after decades alone?* The warmth of Val's embrace, the comfort of her presence fills an emptiness inside me I didn't know existed and perhaps I've simply been starved for affection. So many questions...

The yacht challenges a large wave, and we're momentarily airborne before crashing back down. The jolt brings me back to the present and I turn slightly to meet Val's gaze. "My family can't know about this."

She stares at me for a long moment, her expression unreadable. Then she nods. "Of course." Her lips graze mine and a jolt of arousal shoots between my thighs. The physical reaction she evokes in me is beyond my comprehension. "I don't expect anything from you," she whispers against my mouth. "This is on your terms, so don't worry, okay? If you decide this was only a phase, that's okay. I understand. I imagine it's not easy for you. But if you want more, I'm open to that."

I wonder how she can be so calm and composed about this. Her words are reassuring, but they also stir up a mix of emotions I can't untangle. Part of me is grateful for her understanding, for giving me space to figure this out. But another part feels a twinge of disappointment. Does she really think this could just be a phase for me? Could she be right about that? The intensity of what I'm feeling seems too profound, too all-consuming to be dismissed so easily.

"Thank you," I finally say. "I know this isn't a big thing to you—being with a woman—but it is to me. I'm not sure how to deal with it."

Val smiles. "How about you don't deal with anything at all? Just enjoy it while it lasts." She shrugs. "I may be comfortable with women, but attraction like this is very rare. It's not something you can rationalize, so don't try to over-think it."

"Easier said than done." I return her smile and hesitate for a beat. "I can't stop thinking about what it would be like to..." Biting my lip, I take a deep breath. I can't even let my mind go there without burning up inside.

"To what?" Val arches a brow. There's a teasing glimmer in her eyes.

"You know what I mean," I shoot back. "Don't make me say it."

Val chuckles. "You can't say the word sex? Are you really that much of a prude, Ms. Rothschild?" She wedges a hand into my bikini top and strokes my breast. When her thumb skims my nipple, I gasp, my back arching. There's no doubt that I want this; my whole body screams out for her.

"I guess I'm a little prudish," I say through heavy breaths, tilting my head to the side when she starts kissing and sucking my neck.

Val's lips are relentless, teasing and tasting, and my breath hitches in my throat as I give in to the sensations. Her hands are warm, firm against my skin as they trail down my ribcage and my belly, frustratingly far from where I need them most. I want to beg her, to guide her, but the crew is close enough to see us, and Val, sensing my restraint, pulls back. Her eyes meet mine, and she smirks, knowing exactly what she's doing to me.

"I'm sorry, I'll behave. We're not alone," she murmurs, her voice a low, seductive whisper against my ear. "But soon, when we have some privacy..." Her hand trails down my arm in a way that promises more before she laces her fingers with mine. "I'm going to make you feel things you've never felt before."

Her words make my heart race so fast, I'm struggling to breathe. It's all I can think of now. Val, naked and all over me.

Feeling an overwhelming need for something solid and familiar, I stare at the horizon as if it might calm me down. But it doesn't. It just sits there, steady, indifferent to the storm brewing inside me.

The coastline of Ibiza comes into view, and I sigh deeply, the tension in my chest loosening just a fraction. The island's cliffs rise from the water, their rugged edges softened by the setting sun. Whitewashed buildings are scattered like pearls along the shoreline, and the vegetation that surrounds them is lush, covering the island in a blanket of green.

I should feel some measure of peace, seeing this beauty laid out before me, but all it does is heighten my reluctance. I don't want to step onto that island—not just because my father's wedding is waiting for me, but because I don't want this day to end. This strange, unsettling, but beautiful day.

"Where are you staying?" I ask. My voice sounds tentative, almost shy. I'm self-conscious around Val, and I hate myself for it.

"My hotel is near the plot of land I'm viewing. It's about half an hour from the wedding venue."

I nod, absorbing that information like it's a lifeline.

Somehow, I like the idea of her being near, even if we won't see each other. We haven't spoken much about her possible new venture. It feels like a no-go considering we're competitors. "Would you like to sail back to Mallorca together?" I ask. "If you need more time, I can stay at the venue for an extra night."

"Yeah, I'd like that. Let's keep in touch. I'm not sure how long this will take until I'm there." Val squeezes my hand. "And try not to worry about your father," she adds. "Just try and enjoy the wedding. This is beyond your control. He's going to get married no matter what, and if he's happy for now, isn't that enough?"

I want to argue, to tell her she doesn't understand, that he used to be a man of reason and that he lost his brain to a woman half his age. But that would make me a hypocrite. Who am I to judge my father when I'm displaying the exact same irrational behavior?

"I suppose so," I say. "You're right. I'll try to let it go."

Chapter 34

Val

The full moon bathes the landscape in an ethereal glow as I make my way across the rugged terrain. The real estate agent isn't expecting me until tomorrow morning—but I couldn't wait. After the intensity of the day with Evelyn, I need some time to clear my head and refocus on why I'm really here.

The plot of land is a hidden gem nestled between rolling hills and pristine coastline. Even in the moonlight, I can see its potential. The natural terraces formed by years of erosion, the sheltered coves below—it's as if Nature herself designed this spot for our resort. The contour of the land offers exciting possibilities, from solar-powered villas nestled into the hillside to a wind-sheltered infinity pool overlooking the sea.

I close my eyes and breathe in deeply, letting the scent of wild herbs and sea air fill my lungs. The quiet is profound, broken only by the distant crash of waves and the occasional rustle of wind. This, I think, is what our guests will experience—this sense of connection with nature, of peace and solitude.

Opening my eyes, I turn my back to the shore and scan the hills. In the distance, I can just make out the twinkling lights of the nearest town, far enough away to ensure privacy but close enough for convenience.

I pull out my phone, unable to contain my excitement. Marcus picks up on the third ring.

"Val? Is everything okay?"

"Everything's great," I say. "I'm at the plot."

There's a pause. "At the plot? Now? It's late there, Val."

"I know, I know. But I couldn't wait. Marcus, it's perfect. The location, the terrain, everything. And the views —God, the views are incredible."

"That good, huh?" I can hear the smile in his voice now. "Tell me more."

As I describe the layout of the land, the natural features we can incorporate into our design, and my initial ideas for the resort layout, I can feel Marcus's excitement growing to match my own. This is why we work so well together—we share the same vision, the same passion for creating sustainable, beautiful spaces.

"It sounds amazing," he says when I finally pause for breath. "I can't wait to see it myself. But maybe next time, wait for daylight before you go trespassing, yeah?"

I laugh, feeling a little sheepish. "Yeah, yeah. I'll call you tomorrow after I've met the agent here."

"Great. Can't wait." He clears his throat. "Well, I'm about to call it a day and head home. How was your journey? Did you end up taking the ferry?"

"Actually, I sailed here," I say. "With Evelyn. She has some..." I pause. "She had some private business to take care of on Ibiza."

"Evelyn?" Marcus's tone sharpens with interest. "Are

you sure it's private business? Be careful. She might be after the same plot. We don't want her to beat us twice."

"No, I'm not worried about that. Please, trust me, Marcus. The land doesn't even lend itself for large developments. She genuinely had to be here too, and it seemed nice to travel together."

"Nice?" There's a moment of silence, and then Marcus lets out a long sigh. "Oh, Val." He groans. "You slept with her, didn't you?"

"No!" I protest, perhaps a bit too quickly. "No, we didn't sleep together. We just... I like her." I glance around, half expecting to see Marcus behind a tree or something. How come he's always on to me?

"I don't believe you." His voice rises in pitch. "You're fooling around with our client. Don't lie to me, Val."

I run a hand through my hair, frustration bubbling up. "Whatever I do outside work is my business."

Marcus is quiet for a long moment, and I brace myself for a lecture. It's coming, I can feel it. "Val," he says, his voice softer than I expected, almost cautious. "You're playing with fire."

I sigh, sitting down on a rock. "It's private."

"That's not entirely true and you know it," he shoots back. "You're getting involved with a woman who—correct me if I'm wrong—has never shown interest in other women before. And she's our client. Her business is incredibly valuable, especially if you ever want to set up a consultancy subbrand within the company."

I close my eyes, trying to clear away the tangled web of emotions and complications swirling in my head. "I promise I won't let it get messy."

"Sure." There's a long pause on the other end of the line, and I can practically see Marcus rubbing a hand over his face, trying to figure out how to deal with his stubborn, headstrong boss who's clearly gone off the deep end.

I appreciate Marcus, I really do. He's the one who pulls me back, the one who tells me I'm getting carried away and reminds me to think things through before diving into a project. I hired him because he's older with a wealth of experience in the industry, but there are some situations I'd rather figure out for myself, and Evelyn is one of them.

"Look, Val," he continues. "I know you. When you set your mind on something, you go all in, and that's what's so great about you. Just...be careful, okay? Because this isn't just about you anymore. It's about the company, our employees, our investors. We can't afford a scandal or complications. She's not some random contractor, she's Evelyn Rothschild."

"I know that. I'll be careful," I say, mainly to get him off my back. "I'll call you tomorrow, okay? Go home and enjoy your night."

After I hang up, I hike back to the main road where my taxi driver is snoring behind the wheel. I paid him to wait for two hours, and he seems almost disappointed that I'm back already and disturbing his sleep.

I roll down the window, letting the warm night air rush over me as we drive off. My mind drifts to Evelyn, as it has been doing with increasing frequency. I wonder what she's doing right now. Is she fast asleep, exhausted from the day's journey? Or is she lying awake, her thoughts as restless as mine?

The events of today feel surreal—like a dream I'm afraid to wake from. I've had my share of romantic encounters, sure. Quick liaisons in paradise locations, heated moments stolen between business meetings. But this is different.

I think about how Evelyn trembled under my touch,

how her breath caught when I kissed her neck. The way she fought to maintain control even as she was clearly losing it. Everything about her fascinates me—her strength, her vulnerability, the walls she's built around herself that crumble only when we're alone.

The women I've been with before knew exactly what they wanted. They were confident in their sexuality, comfortable with casual encounters. But Evelyn...she's discovering herself, taking tentative steps into unknown territory. The trust she's placing in me feels so significant I should be running in the opposite direction. Instead, I find myself wanting to be worthy of that trust.

I picture her in a luxurious hotel room, sitting on the edge of a plush king-size bed, perhaps wearing silk pajamas —no, that doesn't seem like Evelyn. A satin nightgown, maybe? Or does she prefer to sleep naked?

The thought of Evelyn in bed, possibly naked, sends a jolt of heat through my body, and I shift in the back seat. The memory of her soft skin, her intoxicating scent, and the way she melted into my arms on the yacht keeps flooding back.

I'm struck by a sudden urge to call her. To hear her voice, to make sure she's okay. I imagine she's feeling overwhelmed and confused, and she's got no one to talk to. Not about this.

As the taxi pulls up to my hotel, I make a decision. I pull out my phone and type a quick message to her: *Thinking of you. Hope you're okay. Call me if you need to talk.* I hit send before I can change my mind. Whatever happens next, at least she knows she's not alone.

Chapter 35

Evelyn

The sea breeze ruffles my hair as I sit in the front row, about to watch my father marry a woman young enough to be his granddaughter. The wooden chair digs into my back, but I barely notice, transfixed by the surreal scene before me.

Fifty or so guests are arranged in a half-circle facing the floral wedding arch, a gaudy creation dripping with white orchids and trailing vines. Behind it, the Mediterranean stretches to the horizon, a beautiful backdrop that seems to mock the gravity of this moment with its carefree beauty.

Mia sits beside me in her pale-pink dress. Her long dreads are adorned with a crown of tiny white flowers, and she's beaming, clearly caught up in the romance of it all.

I shift slightly, feeling the soft fabric of my own dress move against my skin. When I bought it, I felt uncertain about wearing something so daring. But today, memories of Val's appreciative gaze and gentle touches flood my mind, making me feel desired and sensual in a whole new way, and I sit up straighter, embracing the unfamiliar confidence she's given me.

The celebrant, a middle-aged woman with long gray hair and a flowing kaftan, steps up to the arch. Her bare feet sink into the sand as she raises her arms, calling for silence.

"Friends, family, beloved ones," she intones, her voice carrying a hint of an Australian accent. "We are gathered here today to witness the union of Donald Rothschild and Candy Seacrest in the sacred bond of marriage."

I resist the urge to roll my eyes at the word "sacred." There's nothing sacred about this farce.

My father steps into view, and I have to stifle a gasp. He's wearing loose linen pants rolled up at the ankles and a white cotton shirt with the sleeves pushed up to his elbows. A lei of white flowers hangs around his neck.

The guests collectively turn as Candy makes her entrance. She glides down the makeshift aisle, in a bohemian dream of a dress—all flowing silk and delicate lace with off-the-shoulder sleeves and a train that trails behind her. Her blonde hair is styled in loose, beachy waves, adorned with a crown of flowers that matches my father's lei.

As much as I hate to admit it, she looks beautiful. Radiant, even. The cynical part of me wants to dismiss it as the glow of a gold digger who's hit the jackpot, but there's an unmistakable joy in her eyes that gives me pause.

My father's face lights up as he sees her, and for a moment, I'm transported back to my childhood. I remember him looking at my mother that way, with a mix of awe and adoration that I'd forgotten he was capable of.

Candy reaches the arch, taking my father's hands in hers, and they smile at each other, seemingly oblivious to the crowd watching them.

The celebrant begins again. "Donald and Candy have

chosen to write their own vows, to express the unique love they share. Donald, would you like to go first?"

My father nods, clearing his throat. When he speaks, his voice is thick with emotion. "Candy, my ray of sunshine. Before I met you, I thought my best days were behind me. I was set in my ways, focused only on work and what I thought was success. But you showed me that there's so much more to life. You taught me to slow down, to appreciate the little things—like the feeling of sand between my toes and the beauty of a sunset. You've brought laughter and joy back into my world."

Beside me, Mia lets out a quiet, "Aww."

"I promise to always cherish your free spirit," my father says. "To support your dreams and adventures, even when they take us off the beaten path. I promise to be your partner in all things, to face life's challenges and celebrate its joys together. I love you, Candy, and I can't wait to start this new chapter of our lives."

There's a collective sigh from the audience before the celebrant turns to Candy. "And now, Candy, your vows to Donald."

Candy's voice is clear and steady as she begins. "Donald, my devilishly handsome silver fox." There's a ripple of laughter from the guests. "When we first met, I never imagined I'd fall in love with you. But life has a funny way of surprising us, doesn't it?"

I can't argue with that. My mind drifts to Val, to her lips on mine.

"You've shown me that age really is just a number," Candy continues. "That wisdom and youth can coexist beautifully. You ground me when I need it, but you also encourage me to fly. Your kindness, your humor, your willingness to try new things—these are just a few of the reasons I fall more in love with you every day."

I watch my father's face, seeing the naked adoration there. It's disconcerting, like watching a stranger wear my father's skin.

"I promise to always push you out of your comfort zone," Candy says with a grin. "To remind you to play and explore and never take life too seriously. I promise to be your biggest cheerleader, your trusted confidant, and your partner in crime. I love you, Donald, wrinkles and all."

There's more laughter, and even I find myself smiling reluctantly. Their vows are sickeningly sweet, but there's a genuineness to them that I wasn't expecting.

Mia steps forward, presenting a small velvet box. My father takes out a delicate gold band, inlaid with tiny diamonds. His hands tremble as he slides it onto Candy's finger.

"With this ring, I thee wed," he says, his voice husky with emotion.

Candy then takes a thicker gold band from the box and slides it on my father's finger. "With this ring, I thee wed," she echoes.

Their hands remain clasped as the celebrant continues, "By the power vested in me by the Universal Life Church and the island of Ibiza, I now pronounce you husband and wife. Donald, you may kiss your bride!"

My father doesn't need to be told twice. He pulls Candy close, dipping her dramatically as he kisses her. The guests erupt in cheers and applause. Mia claps enthusiastically, and after a moment's hesitation, I stand too, offering a more restrained applause.

As my father and his new wife make their way back down the aisle, showered with flower petals thrown by guests, I grapple with conflicting emotions. Part of me still wants to dismiss this as a midlife crisis, a foolish decision that will end in heartbreak and financial ruin. But another part—a part that's grown louder in the past twenty-four hours—wonders if I've been too quick to judge.

When Mia and I head to the bar to congratulate the newlyweds, my phone vibrates in my purse. It's Val. My heart skips and I stop dead in my tracks, causing a small traffic jam of guests behind me. Someone bumps into my back with a muffled, "Sorry," but I barely register it, my attention completely captured by those three letters on my screen.

It was great, very promising. Try to have fun today. I bet you look stunning in that dress... x. The message is in answer to my previous one, asking her how the plot was looking. We messaged back and forth a few times yesterday, and every time I hear from her, I'm aware of the stupid smile that spreads across my face.

Glad it was worth the trip. Wedding's not so bad and I'm rocking the dress. I end with a wink emoji, then quickly put my phone back in my purse when I see Mia glancing at me.

"Who was that?" she asks, signaling a waiter holding a tray of champagne flutes.

"No one. It's not important." I take two flutes and hand one to her. "Let's go give your grandfather a hug." Giddy after Val's message, my terrible sense of humor kicks in and I add, "And let's not forget your new grandmother."

"Oh my God, Mom! Don't say that." Mia laughs and shakes her head. "But seriously, who was that?" she asks again as she follows me. "You've been on your phone a lot today and you're smiling."

"Are you saying I never smile?"

"No..." She frowns and looks me over. "Wait. Are you

sure you haven't met someone? I swear, there's something different about you..."

I feel my cheeks heat up and take a long drink of my champagne. *Is it really that obvious?* "Of course not. It was just Val. She's funny, that's all."

"Oh." Mia seems content with that explanation, but she's still giving me a weird look. "Well, I'm glad you made a new friend. How is she?"

"She's great." I leave it at that, relieved the crowd in front of my father and Candy has cleared so we can end the conversation. "Congratulations to you both. That was a beautiful ceremony," I say, sounding somewhat genuine, even as I turn to Candy. "Welcome to the family. You truly look radiant."

Chapter 36

Val

I slip through the hotel lobby, my heart pounding. The marble floors echo under my sandals as I make my way to the elevators, hyperaware of every person I pass. I should have dressed more appropriately; my denim shorts and T-shirt make me stand out in this high-end place.

Evelyn has called ahead for the staff to let me up in the elevator, and the ride to the top floor feels interminable. I check my phone again, re-reading Evelyn's message for the hundredth time. *Room 1201. I know it's late, but maybe we could talk?*

Talk. Right. I suspect she's starting to panic now that she's had time to process everything, and I don't blame her.

I step out into a hushed hallway and 1201 is right at the end. For a moment, I hesitate. Is this a bad idea? The two of us alone? Am I really about to knock on Evelyn Rothschild's hotel room door in the middle of the night?

Before I can overthink it, I raise my hand and knock softly. Three quick taps.

There's a pause, then the sound of movement inside. The door opens and Evelyn is there, backlit by the warm

229

glow of the room behind her. My breath catches. She's wearing that champagne-colored dress she bought for the wedding, and she looks stunning. Her hair is slightly mussed, and there's a flush high on her cheekbones.

"Val," she says softly. "You came."

"Of course I came. Are you okay?"

Evelyn nods, stepping back to let me in. "I had one too many glasses of champagne earlier," she admits. "But that was two hours ago. I'm clear-headed now."

I shoot her a grin, not quite sure she's as sober as she claims, and enter the room, taking in the opulent suite. It's all creamy whites and soft golds, with a massive bed dominating one wall and floor-to-ceiling windows overlooking the sea. Sliding doors open up to a spacious balcony, letting in the warm night air and the distant sound of music. "Is the wedding still going?"

Evelyn nods. "There are still a few guests left but I snuck out." She closes the door behind me with a soft thud. We stand there, mere feet apart.

My eyes wander over her form. The dress is even more stunning on her body, the fabric shimmering in the dim light. It dips low between her breasts, revealing a tantalizing amount of cleavage. Her chest rises and falls rapidly, betraying her nerves.

"So...you wanted to talk?"

"I..." Evelyn starts, then stops. She takes a shaky breath. "I'm not very good at this."

I step closer, close enough to catch the scent of her perfume—something light and floral. "At what?" I ask gently, even though I think I know the answer.

Evelyn gestures vaguely between us, her usually eloquent speech failing her. "This. Asking for what I want."

I take her hand. "And what is it that you want, Evelyn?

Tell me." My heart is racing, and my stomach is doing flips. I want her so badly I can barely stop myself from kissing her.

She stares at me, her eyes flicking down to my lips and back up. Another silence. Heavy breaths. The space between us crackles, every inch shrinking as sexual tension pulls us closer.

Then she surges forward, pressing her lips to mine. The kiss is almost desperate in its intensity, and I respond immediately, my hands coming up to cup her face. Evelyn moans, the sound sending a jolt of heat through me.

Her lips are soft but insistent, and when I slide my tongue against hers, it feels like lighting a fuse. The heat between us is instantaneous, building as her hands grip my waist, pulling me flush against her. I bite her lower lip gently, teasing, and she gasps into my mouth, the sound fueling the fire spreading through my veins. My fingers tangle in her hair, tugging just enough to tilt her head, giving me control as I kiss her harder, deeper.

When we finally part, we're both breathing heavily. "Does that answer your question?" she asks, a hint of her usual sass returning.

"Crystal clear," I murmur, leaning in to kiss her again, slower this time. I take my time exploring her mouth, savoring the lingering taste of champagne on her tongue.

Evelyn's hands find their way to my waist again, slipping under my T-shirt. Her touch is intoxicating, and she gasps when I lower my hands to her behind and squeeze it gently.

"Val," Evelyn breathes when we part again. "I...I've never done this before. With a woman, I mean."

"I know." Brushing a strand of hair behind her ear, I

give her a small smile. "We can take this as slow as you want. Or we can just talk..."

"I don't want to talk. I want you," she says, her fingers grazing my bare skin. I feel the heat of her palms, tentative yet eager, and it's like every nerve in me is awake, hyper-aware of her touch. My pulse races, and for a second, I just stand there, eyes closed, letting the sensation wash over me.

I've imagined it a hundred different ways, but nothing could have prepared me for how it feels to finally be alone with her. There's a vulnerability in the way she touches me, like she's both nervous and desperate to explore, and it makes me want to go slow, to savor every second.

I touch her in return, sliding my hands up her sides, over the smooth fabric of that champagne-colored dress, and Evelyn lets out a small, breathy sound that undoes me. Her skin is hot under the thin fabric, and when my hands find the zipper at her back, she gasps softly against my neck.

"Undress me," she whispers, her voice thick with need.

The sound of the zipper sliding down cuts through out heavy breaths, and as I slowly push the fabric off her shoulders, the dress slips down her body, pooling at her feet in a silken heap.

Evelyn stands there in nothing but a pair of white lace panties, and I'm speechless. She's exquisite. Her body is a work of art—the soft curves of her hips, the gentle rise of her breasts, the way her skin catches the dim light from the lamp on her nightstand.

I want to tell her she's beautiful, but the words feel inadequate, so instead, I let my touch speak for me. I brush my fingers down her arms, across the smooth expanse of her stomach, reveling in the way she shivers under my touch.

"I want... I want you to undress," she whispers, tugging at the hem of my T-shirt.

I nod, swallowing hard as I take a small step back, peel off my T-shirt and let it drop to the floor. My denim shorts follow quickly, and her eyes trail over me, taking me in.

When she finally meets my eyes again, her lips part slightly. I can feel her want, it's almost tangible, but I wait patiently, allowing her to see me like this, to see a woman near naked for the first time.

When I lean in to kiss her again, she responds immediately, her mouth opening to mine, her hands grasping at my hips, pulling me closer until there's nothing between us but heat and the promise of what's to come. The kiss is intense, our lips moving desperately, and I feel her body arching against mine, needing contact, needing everything.

Guiding her to the bed, I push her gently onto the soft covers, and she falls back, her hair splayed out around her. The sight of her there, vulnerable and waiting, takes my breath away. I crawl up to meet her mouth and lower myself on top of her. My body pressing against hers feels heavenly and so right.

"Val...yes..." she whispers, her voice breaking as I kiss my way down her neck, across her collarbone, and lower. Her hands are in my hair, urging me on, and the way she responds to every touch, every kiss, is overwhelming. She trembles beneath me, like she's never been touched before, like every sensation is new and raw and impossibly intense.

I let my hands glide over her chest, and Evelyn gasps when I brush my thumb over one of her nipples, watching it harden at my touch. The sound of her sharp inhale pushes me further, so I lower my mouth to her breast, teasing her with slow, deliberate kisses until I finally take her nipple into my mouth. Her body jerks in response, a quiet moan spilling from her lips as I swirl my tongue around it. She's shaking now, her fingers gripping my hair tightly. I can feel her hips shift, seeking more even as I linger here, savoring the way she reacts to every flick of my tongue.

When my hand slides lower, over the curve of her hip and down to the waistband of her panties, Evelyn lets out a shaky breath, her back arching off the bed. I hesitate, waiting for some sign that this is what she wants, and then, when she nods, I slide the delicate fabric down her legs and toss it aside.

I stare at her, taking in the way her body moves with each breath, the way her skin flushes under my gaze. She's stunning.

When I touch her again, trailing a finger over her thigh and up between her legs, her response is immediate—her hips lifting to meet my touch, a soft moan escaping her lips. I move up to kiss her again while my hand moves slowly, exploring her, and the way she reacts—the way her body tenses and releases, the way she gasps—is almost enough to undo me.

Evelyn's breathing becomes ragged, her hands clutching at my back as I move against her. Her responses are so raw, and it only drives me to take her higher.

I slide my fingers over her clit, circling with a slow, deliberate rhythm. A throaty moan escapes her. The way she moves under me is intoxicating, and I can tell by her breathing that tension is building in her.

I keep up the slow, steady motions as her hands grip the sheets, fingers curling around the fabric like she's trying to anchor herself to something solid. But there's no grounding here, no holding back. She's unraveling, and I'm with her, completely lost in the moment, in her.

I kiss her again, swallowing the soft sounds she's making, my lips brushing against hers as my fingers continue their careful, teasing circles. Her mouth opens to mine, and the kiss is frantic, messy, full of need. It's like she's trying to convey everything she's feeling, everything she wants, through the press of her lips, the way she pulls me closer, like she can't get enough.

When I slowly slip two fingers inside her, she gasps against my mouth, her entire body tensing for a moment before she relaxes, hips pushing forward to meet my hand. She's so warm and wet and tight around my fingers that it makes me squirm. I start to move slowly, in and out, my thumb still circling her clit, and she moans, her voice shaky.

The feeling of being inside her, of having her so open and vulnerable beneath me, slays me. I've never wanted anyone like this, never felt this kind of intensity before. Every gasp, every moan, every movement of her hips sends a wave of heat through me, and I'm drowning in her.

"Val," she says, her voice trembling, her arms wrapping around me. "Oh God, I..."

I kiss her again, silencing her, feeling her body tighten around my fingers as I move a little faster, thrusting deeper. Her legs wrap around me too, her hips rocking in time with my movements, and I can feel how close she is, how badly she needs this.

Evelyn tilts her head back as her breathing becomes erratic, her moans growing louder, more desperate. She feels incredible, and every little tremor of her body drives me closer to the edge of my own control.

When she finally breaks, when her body tenses, I watch her come undone. She cries out, her body trembling as she clutches at me, and I keep moving inside her, my fingers thrusting slowly as her orgasm crashes over her. She pulses, clings to me like I'm her only anchor, and I drink her in, my lips pressed against her neck, my fingers still deep inside her, still moving slowly, drawing out every last wave of her pleasure. Evelyn says my name again, softer this time, and her legs tighten around me as if she never wants to let go.

When her breathing starts to slow, I pull back just enough to look at her, to take in the flushed, blissed-out expression on her face. Her eyes are heavy-lidded, her lips parted, and she looks utterly wrecked, in the best possible way.

I kiss her forehead, her cheek, the corner of her lips, and she looks up at me with a beautiful softness in her eyes. A tear slips down her cheek before she brushes it away, almost embarrassed.

"I didn't know I could feel like this," she whispers, her voice breaking. She smiles, a real, genuine smile. "Good tears," she adds, and something inside me melts as I cup her face and press a kiss to her temple.

I can't find the words to respond, so I just hold her and hope she understands everything I'm feeling in the warmth of my embrace.

Chapter 37

Evelyn

I lie there, my body humming, still catching my breath from what just happened. I'm overwhelmed, and my mind is racing—part pleasure, part disbelief. I didn't know it was possible to feel so... I don't even know how to describe it.

Val is beside me now, her fingertips brushing against my arm as I lay with my head nestled on the pillow, facing her. I can't even think straight. All I can feel is the lingering ache, this new kind of warmth that spreads through my chest and pulses through my veins. I want to move, but completely undone, I can't.

"You're quiet," Val murmurs, her voice husky. "Are you okay?"

I blink up at her, dazed. "More than okay," I whisper. "I —" I trail off. "I want to touch you," I finally manage.

Val's lips curve into that small, knowing smile of hers, the one that always makes my heart flutter. "You can do anything you want," she says softly, taking my hand and guiding it to her chest.

I'm nervous, my fingers trembling as I let my hand roam

over her bare skin. I've never touched a woman, never thought I ever would. But the softness, the way she feels blows my mind. Her warmth seeps into my fingertips, and I let out a deep sigh.

My hand glides over the swell of her breast, and her breath hitches just slightly, enough to make my pulse quicken. I glance up at her, worried I'm not doing it right, but her eyes are dark with need, her lips parted as if she's waiting for more.

"Does that feel good?"

"Yes. That feels amazing," Val whispers, her head tipping back slightly. She looks so beautiful, so effortless. I trail my fingers around her nipple, watching as it hardens beneath my touch. She sighs, her body arching just a little, silently asking for more.

I can't believe how good she feels. How perfect. My thumb brushes over her nipple again, and this time, I take it between my fingers, rolling it gently, loving the way her body responds to me. The sound she makes—a soft, low moan—urges me on and I lean forward, my lips hovering above her skin. I want to kiss her, to taste her.

Val looks up at me, her eyes half-lidded, pupils blown wide. "Please," she says, and I lower my mouth to her breast, taking her nipple between my lips.

The instant I do, Val gasps, her hand tangling in my hair. Her body rolls and I'm overtaken by want. She tastes like salt and warmth and something distinctly her. I suck gently, teasing her with my tongue, and she moans again, her body restless beneath mine.

The sound of her pleasure is everything, and I want more. I want all of her.

My hand moves lower, my fingers grazing the smooth

skin of her stomach before they slip into her panties. I pause for just a moment, my heart pounding. "Are you sure?"

Val's hand tightens in my hair, her lips parting as she breathes, "Yes." She lifts her hips so I can pull down her panties and I'm staring at her, in awe of her naked beauty.

I can feel her heat, feel how ready she is. And when I slide my fingers lower, finding her, she lets out a soft cry, pressing her hips into my touch. She's so wet, and warm, and I can hardly believe I'm doing this, touching her like this. Touching a woman and making her feel this way.

"Just like that," she whispers. "Don't stop."

I don't. I keep going, exploring her as my fingers move over her sex. Val's breath quickens, her body writhing beneath me, and I'm mesmerized by the way she moves, the way her body responds. Her skin is flushed, her chest rising and falling fast, and she's never looked more beautiful.

I watch as she bites her lip, her eyes fluttering closed, and I know she's close. My fingers move with purpose now, determined to take her over the edge. But just as I feel her body tense beneath me, Val's hand closes around my wrist, stopping me.

I freeze, pulling back slightly, my heart lurching in my chest. Did I do something wrong? "I'm sorry," I say, searching her face for any hint of what I might have done, but all I see is warmth in her eyes.

"No... You didn't do anything wrong," Val says softly. She leans up, kissing me gently, as if to reassure me. "Trust me, you're perfect, but..." She smiles, brushing a stray lock of hair from my face. "I want us to come together."

She rolls us over, her body pressing me into the mattress as she moves on top of me. My breath catches at the sensation of her weight, her skin, her heat—everything about her feels like fire against me. She shifts, spreading my thighs apart, and my heart pounds, anticipation flooding my veins.

Val's lips brush mine as she whispers, "I want to feel you. All of you."

I can't breathe. I can't think. All I can do is nod, my lips trembling against hers.

Slowly, Val presses herself into me, and the moment her heat meets mine, I cry out. I'm hypersensitive and it feels sensational, this friction.

She starts to move, her hips rocking, and I gasp. The pressure, the delicious slide of her against me, it's enough to send shockwaves through my entire body.

My fingers dig into her back, desperate to hold on as she sets a slow rhythm. The friction is maddening, the pleasure building with every grind of her hips. I'm lost in her, in the way she feels, the way she makes me feel.

Val's breathing is ragged, her chest heaving against mine as she moves faster, her hips pressing harder into me. The slick heat between us grows, the sensation building to something almost unbearable, and I cling to her, my nails raking down her back as my body responds to every movement she makes.

My body trembles beneath her, and I can't get enough of her, of the way she moves, the way she touches me. I press up into her and Val meets my movements with equal intensity.

"Come with me," she whispers, and I can hear the need in her voice, the desperation. She leans down, capturing my lips in a deep, heated kiss. Her moans mix with mine as our hips move in sync. She grinds harder, faster, and I'm teetering on the brink of something immense.

And then, like a wave crashing over me, the pleasure hits. I cry out, my entire body convulsing as the orgasm rips through me, and I can feel Val falling apart right along with me. Her body shudders, her hips grinding into mine one last time before she collapses against me, her breath hot and ragged in my ear.

We fall together, both of us shaking, our bodies spent and intertwined. I'm still gasping for air as aftershocks pulse through me. I can't even describe how it feels to be this close to someone, to share something so intimate.

Val's eyes meet mine. "You're incredible," she whispers, brushing her fingers over my cheek.

I smile up at her, my heart still racing from the high of it all, and she collapses beside me, pulling me into her arms. I curl against her, my head resting on her chest. I can hear the steady thump of her heartbeat, feel the warmth of her body wrapped around mine.

Val's arms tighten around me, our bodies still tangled. Her fingers trail lazily along my back, creating soft, feather-light sensations. The music outside has stopped and there's a stillness in the room, a quiet intimacy that feels sacred.

I close my eyes, letting Val's scent fill my senses. I've never felt so safe, so content.

Chapter 38

Val

A soft knock on the door pulls me from sleep. For a moment, I'm disoriented, unsure where I am. The room is unfamiliar but there's a warm body pressed against me. Then I remember: Evelyn's suite. Her presence beside me is a steady, soothing reminder that this isn't some dream.

I smile to myself, the memories of last night flooding back in a warm rush. Evelyn's touch, the way she looked at me—like I was the only thing in the world that mattered. I glance over at her now, curled up in the sheets, looking so sweet and peaceful.

There's another knock, and I sit up carefully, trying not to disturb her. Room service, I assume. It can't be anything else, right? The light pouring into the room hints that it's late in the morning. We didn't fall asleep until the early hours and forgot to set our alarms.

Evelyn stirs next to me, mumbling something in her sleep, and I slip out of bed, grabbing a robe from the chair. I'll send them away quietly, maybe ask for coffee later when Evelyn wakes up.

But when I open the door, it's not room service. It's Mia.

Mia, standing there, eyes wide with confusion and surprise. Her gaze sweeps over me, taking in the robe, the fact that I'm very clearly not supposed to be here.

I freeze. Words fail me. I should say something, anything. But all I can do is stand there, holding the door open, heart pounding. I open my mouth, but nothing coherent comes out.

"Val?" Mia shifts in an attempt to see into the room. "What are you doing here?"

I blink. I've never been great at quick thinking, but this? This is beyond anything I've prepared for. Evelyn's daughter is standing here, staring at me, and I can't even find the words to explain why I'm in her mother's hotel room.

Before I can attempt an answer, I hear Evelyn stirring behind me.

"Val?" Her voice is groggy, and I turn just as she's crossing the room, her hair messy from sleep, eyes still bleary as she rubs at them. "Is that coffee?" she asks, wrapping a towel around her.

I glance back at Mia, then at Evelyn, my throat suddenly dry. Evelyn moves to the door. There's nothing I can do, so I step aside, allowing her a full view of her daughter.

Evelyn's reaction is immediate. She goes pale, her shoulders tensing. Then she stammers, "M-Mia... I..."

Mia's eyes flick between the two of us, her confusion deepening, but she says nothing.

Evelyn is clearly panicking. Her hand clutches at the towel, white-knuckled. "This... It's not what you think."

I cringe. It's exactly what she thinks, and we both know it. But Evelyn, flustered, barrels on, her words spilling out too quickly, as if she can talk her way out of this. "We were just...working. On the project, you know?" She gestures vaguely between us, her expression pleading. "It's not... I mean, it's nothing."

Mia's brow furrows, clearly unconvinced. She glances at me, as if I might offer a more coherent explanation. I wish I could. I wish I had the ability to diffuse this, to say something that would make it all make sense. But I can't.

Evelyn's face flushes as she tries again. "Mia, sweetheart, this is just... Val and I, we were working late, and... It's not—"

"Working late?" Mia holds up a hand, stopping Evelyn mid-sentence. "Please. Have you already forgotten we were at the wedding last night?" Her voice is calm, but there's an edge to it, a tone that cuts through Evelyn's frantic rambling.

I watch as Mia exhales slowly, her eyes narrowing as she looks at Evelyn. "I came to check on you because you didn't show up for breakfast." She holds up a box of Advil. "I thought you might need something to sooth your hangover with, but I see it wasn't alcohol that kept you in bed."

Evelyn bites her lip, her gaze dropping to the floor. For a moment, it looks like she's going to keep denying it, but then she deflates as she leans against the doorframe. "Mia... I'm... I'm sorry. I didn't mean for you to find out like this. I mean, there was nothing to find out anyway. Well, until now, I guess."

"So...it is what I think. Really, Mom? You?"

Neither of us answers. We don't need to. The silence is enough.

"Oh my God." Mia covers her mouth with her hand. "You are literally such a hypocrite. The way you've talked about Grandpa lately..."

"I didn't think... I mean, I..." Evelyn sighs and shakes her head. "Can we talk about this later, Mia? And don't tell anyone. Please?"

"Sure. Whatever." Mia shrugs. "The yacht is about to depart, but you'll never be ready in time. I guess I'll see you when I get back."

"The yacht?" Evelyn asks.

"Yes, the trip, remember? We were all supposed to sail along the coast today. With Grandpa and Candy and ten other guests."

"Oh, of course." Evelyn blows out her cheeks. "Perhaps it's better if I skip that today. I'm feeling a little awkward."

"You should," Mia says. And with that, she turns on her heel and walks away, leaving us standing there in the doorway, watching her retreat down the hallway.

Evelyn closes the door, and we stand there in silence. I can feel the weight of what just happened settling over us like a heavy blanket, and I don't know what to say. I don't know how to fix this.

She slumps against the wall, her hands coming up to cover her face. "Oh God," she whispers. "What have I done?"

I take a deep breath and shake my head, my heart squeezing uncomfortably. "You haven't done anything wrong," I say. "Mia's just shocked. She'll get over it."

Evelyn's eyes harden, her expression unreadable. "Mia is right, and you know it."

My heart sinks. I can feel the tension building, swirling around us. "Right about what?"

"I'm a hypocrite," Evelyn says, frustration simmering behind her eyes. "I don't take my father's relationship seriously, but now I'm doing the same thing. Sleeping with a much younger woman. It's ridiculous."

I flinch at her words, the sting of them more potent than I'd expected. "Do you really think what's happened between us is ridiculous?"

Evelyn's gaze falters for a moment, and I see something flicker in her eyes—regret, perhaps, or panic. But she's good at keeping her composure. "I didn't mean that," she says, softer now, almost apologetic. "It's just...it's not possible for this to be more. We can't..." She trails off, looking away, her fingers nervously fidgeting with the sheets.

"Why?" I ask. "Why can't it be more if that's what we both want?"

Evelyn looks at me again, and this time, I see the panic fully taking over. "Because people won't take me seriously," she says. "The way I don't take my father seriously."

I blow out my cheeks and run a hand through my hair. There's a sharp ache in my chest, a raw feeling, and it's clawing at me, making it hard to think straight.

Evelyn's shoulders slump. "You don't get it. I can't afford to lose my reputation over a fling."

"A fling?" I inch closer and take her hand. I understand she's in shock after her daughter just found out we slept together, but I won't let her dismiss our connection. "Correct me if I'm wrong, but this doesn't feel like a fling to me."

She stares at me and hesitates. "Don't tell me you're genuinely into me, Val. You're this gorgeous young thing, bright and talented with the world at your feet. And I'm..." She pauses. "I'm a middle-aged straight woman with a daughter older than you."

I open my mouth to protest, but Evelyn stops me.

"Please. I can't do this. It's not right." A hint of regret passes over her features. "I think you should leave. I'm so sorry, but I need some space."

I'm not sure what she means by "not right." It's not like

we're breaking the law. We're both grown women in a free world. Sensing there's nothing I can do or say to make her change her mind, though, at least not right now, I nod and start gathering my clothes. "I'll see you back in Mallorca?"

"Yes. It's probably best if I travel back alone. I might stay a few extra days." Evelyn meets my gaze and swallows hard. Her eyes are glassy; she looks like she's about to burst into tears, but she composes herself. "I'm sorry," she says again. "But I can't do this."

Chapter 39

Evelyn

"No." Val stands firm, crossing her arms. "I'm not leaving until we talk about this properly." Something in her stance tells me she won't back down easily. "You're scared, I get that. But pushing me away isn't the answer."

I sink onto the edge of the bed, suddenly exhausted. I wince against the sun streaming in. Everything feels too bright, too raw. The sheets are still rumpled from our night together, and the scent of her lingers on my skin. It's too much—this visceral reminder of what I'm trying to walk away from.

The faint sounds of life drift up from the beach below— voices, the distant cry of seagulls. Normal sounds. Ordinary life continuing as if my world hasn't just been turned upside down. As if my daughter didn't just find me in bed with a woman barely older than she is.

"What is there to talk about?" I gesture helplessly. "You saw Mia's face. My own daughter caught me in bed with someone her age. Do you have any idea how that feels?"

The memory of Mia's expression hits me again—that

mix of shock and confusion that I never wanted to see on my daughter's face. We've always been close, always understood each other. Or at least, I thought we did.

Val moves closer but doesn't touch me. "Mia's an adult. She'll understand if you give her a chance."

"Will she? My daughter just found out her mother's having some sort of midlife crisis. And it's not just Mia." I get up again and start pacing, my bare feet silent on the plush carpet. I feel so restless and the ball of anxiety in the pit of my stomach continues to grow. "What happens when word gets out? When my family, friends and coworkers find out?"

I pause by the window, wrapping my arms around myself. "I've spent decades building my reputation. Do you know how hard it is for a woman to be taken seriously in this industry? One hint of scandal and they'll use it against me. They'll say I'm unstable, unreliable. That I'm going through some sort of identity crisis."

"Is that what you think this is?" Val's voice catches slightly. "A crisis?"

The hurt in her tone makes me turn. She's standing there, lit by the sun, and for a moment, I can't breathe. How can I explain what she does to me? How she makes me feel things I've never felt before? How terrifying that is?

"No," I admit softly. "But maybe it should be. It would be easier that way."

Val closes the distance between us and takes my hand in hers. "Tell me what you're really afraid of."

Her touch anchors me, even as everything else is spinning out of control. "Everything," I whisper. "I'm afraid of everything."

"Be specific."

I take a shaky breath. "You're twenty-eight, Val. You

have your whole life ahead of you. You probably want children someday—"

"Is that what this is about?" She squeezes my hands. "Kids?"

"Among many other things." I pull my hands away, needing space. "You might not be thinking about it now, but in a few years? You're at that age where people start wanting families. And I'm..." I swallow hard. "I'm past that."

"You don't know what I want," Val says quietly. Something in her tone makes me turn to look at her. There's a shadow in her eyes I haven't seen before.

"Tell me then."

She's quiet for a moment, and I can see her wrestling with something. Her fingers drum against her thigh. "I don't want kids," she finally says. "I never have."

"You say that now, but—"

"No." She cuts me off, and there's a rawness to her voice that stops me short. "This isn't about my age or about changing my mind later. I made this decision a long time ago." She takes a deep breath, moving to sit on the edge of the bed. "When you lose your parents young, it...changes how you see things. You said so yourself. For me, the idea of having children, of possibly leaving them alone like that..." She shakes her head, and I see tears in her eyes. "I can't risk that. I won't."

The vulnerability in her voice makes my chest ache. I move to sit beside her, close but not touching. "That's fear talking," I say softly. "You can't let fear stop you from living."

"Isn't that exactly what you're doing right now?"

Her words hit home with uncomfortable accuracy. "It's different."

251

"Is it?" She moves to stand beside me. "You're letting fear of what might happen stop you from being happy. How is that different?"

"Because I have more to lose!" The words burst out of me. "My relationship with Mia, my reputation..."

"Fuck reputation. What about happiness? Love?"

I shake my head. "You make it sound so simple."

"It's not simple, but it doesn't have to be as complicated as you're making it." She shrugs. "Yes, there will be challenges. Yes, some people might talk. But are you really willing to give up something real because you're afraid of what others might think?"

"It's not just that," I say. "You're a different generation. We're different."

Val's eyes stay locked on mine, unflinching, and I can feel the weight of her determination. It's like she's daring me to push her away again, to keep pretending that this can't work. I swallow hard, trying to steady myself, but the fear inside me keeps twisting, knotting tighter.

"We're different," I say again, my voice quieter this time, almost pleading. "You're younger, Val. You haven't lived through what I have."

"You keep saying that like it's some insurmountable gap. Like the years between us make it impossible for me to understand you. But you don't get to decide what I can or can't handle, Evelyn. That's not your call to make." She sighs. "You don't know the half of what I've lived through. Losing your mom was hard, I get that, but you still had your dad, money, security. Losing both parents...it forces you to grow up fast. Faster than you should have to."

Her words hit me like a punch to the chest, and I'm frozen, unable to interrupt as she continues.

"I didn't have time to drift through life or figure myself

252

out. I didn't have the luxury of making mistakes and starting over. I've built a hugely successful business from the ground up. Not many people my age can say that."

She takes a breath, her voice softening, though the intensity of her gaze doesn't falter. "So, no, I'm not some young girl trying to find herself, and I'm not inexperienced or fragile. I know exactly who I am and what I want."

I'm silent, caught off guard by the raw honesty in her words. "I'm sorry," I whisper, the words weak and inadequate.

Val shrugs, but there's no bitterness in the gesture. "I don't dwell on the past, but it has shaped me into the woman I am today. And I believe we're compatible."

I look at her, really look at her, and it's like seeing her for the first time. The strength in her, the resilience, the courage it must have taken to not only survive but thrive. And yet there's still a part of me that clings to the fear, to the what-ifs.

"I hear you," I say. "And you're right. We probably are compatible. But when you're forty-five, I'll be in my sixties. And when you're in your late fifties, well...that's when..." My voice catches, but I force myself to keep going. "That's when the age gap becomes a burden on you. When I can't do certain things anymore, or when other health problems start to occur. You'll be full of life, and I...I'll be holding you back."

Val doesn't flinch. "And you think you can predict the future?" she asks. "Evelyn, nothing is set in stone. I could die tomorrow. Or next year. Or maybe I'll be the one with health problems at sixty. You can't base your choices on what might happen decades from now."

Her words hang in the air, heavy with truth. She's right —I've been letting fear of the unknown paralyze me. The uncertainties, the worst-case scenarios, they're all I can see. But Val's not afraid of them. She's standing here, willing to face them head-on, and she's asking me to do the same.

"You're not holding me back, Evelyn," she says softly. "You're giving me something to look forward to. Someone to share my life with, no matter how long or short it might be. That's what matters. Not the number of years between us, but the time we have together. Isn't that worth it?"

Tears prick at my eyes, but I blink them away, my chest tight with emotion. I want to believe her. I want to believe that this can work, that love can outweigh the fears and uncertainties. But right now, this is all too fresh, too raw. I think of Mia again and shake my head.

"I'm scared," I admit. "I'm so scared, and I need time. My mind...it's muddled. I need to be alone to think."

Val's face softens, though there's a flicker of hurt in her eyes. She nods, taking a step back. "I understand," she says. "Take the time you need. I'll see you back in Mallorca."

Chapter 40

Val

The waves lap at my feet as I walk along the Ibiza plot we're about to acquire. It's a stunning piece of land—the kind of place that would normally make my heart race with possibilities.

The shoreline is smooth, sun-warmed rocks glistening under the Mediterranean sun, and the waves lap against them with a soft, rhythmic sound. The water shimmers in shades of azure and turquoise, so clear it's almost impossible to distinguish where the sea ends and the sky begins.

In the daylight, the land unveils its secrets. The slopes are alive with color—wild herbs like rosemary and thyme scatter the air with their fragrant perfume, and pine trees twist and stretch toward the sky, their gnarled trunks painted in warm tones by the sun's golden rays. Little tufts of hardy grass peek through sandy soil, thriving in the embrace of nature's untouched beauty.

From the higher points, the views are even more breathtaking. The horizon stretches endlessly, dotted with distant islets, the sea reflecting the sun like a mirror. Looking inland, the terrain offers limitless possibilities—a place where sustainable structures could harmonize with the landscape, creating a true sanctuary.

I should be excited, at least a little bit. I guess that's why I came here, to lift my mood. This plot has everything I look for, but still, I feel sad, so incredibly sad.

Finding a flat stone warmed by the sun, I sink down and let my feet dangle over the edge. The rhythmic sound of waves against rock usually soothes me, but today, it triggers something else—a memory I constantly fight to keep locked away.

The grief always comes back to bite me and maybe I shouldn't have brought it up today, but there was no other way to explain to Evelyn that I'm wise beyond my years. That I had no choice but to grow up and deal with life from a young age.

I was fifteen the day my life shattered, sprawled on my bed at my aunt and uncle's house, reading a book. I remember everything about that moment with crystal clarity—the weight of the book in my hands, the sound of cars passing on the street outside, the way sunlight filtered through the curtains, painting stripes across my bedspread. Especially the stripes, they're etched in my mind for some reason.

The knock on my door was soft, hesitant, and when I looked up, my aunt was standing in the doorway, and something about her expression made my stomach drop. Her face was pale, her hands clasped tightly in front of her. I knew before she spoke. I knew from the way she couldn't quite meet my eyes, from the slight tremor in her voice when she said my name.

"Val, honey..."

A seagull's cry pulls me back to the present, and I realize I'm shaking. I wrap my arms around myself, trying to hold in the emotion threatening to spill over. I've gotten so good at pushing it down, at channeling everything into work and forward momentum. But sometimes, like now, it all comes rushing back.

I remember how the world seemed to tilt on its axis as my aunt delivered the news. A storm. A capsized boat. No survivors found. Words that didn't make sense, that couldn't be real. My parents were just documenting ocean pollution. They were supposed to come back in three days. I had their whole itinerary mapped out on my wall calendar.

The sob catches me by surprise—raw and unfamiliar in my throat. I haven't cried since that day. Not at the memorial service, not during the months that followed, not in all the years since. I've been too busy moving forward to look back.

But here, on this sun-warmed rock, everything I've held in for so many years finally breaks free. Tears stream down my face as I remember my mother's laugh, my father's gentle encouragement of my dreams. The way they lived their convictions, fighting to protect the oceans they loved. The future we'll never share.

I envisage my mother in her favorite yellow dress, my father in his jeans and lumberjacks. That's how I'll always remember them, eternalized in my mind's eye.

The breeze picks up, carrying the sound of distant boat engines. Somewhere out there, a family is having an ordinary day on the water. Parents are watching their children, making memories.

I take a shuddering breath, wiping my eyes with the back of my hand. My parents would have loved this spot—would have seen the same potential I see, the same chance to create something meaningful while preserving nature's beauty.

"I miss you," I whisper to the wind. "I miss you so much."

For the first time in many, many years, I let myself feel the full weight of that loss. But mixed with the grief is something else—a deep gratitude for the legacy they left me, for the passion they instilled. Everything I've fought for carries a piece of them forward.

"Mommy!" some kid calls, and I look over my shoulder.

Behind me, a little girl with wild curls is running toward her mother, arms outstretched, face lit up with pure joy. She can't be more than five or six, wearing a purple swimsuit dotted with tiny stars. Her mother scoops her up, spinning her around in a dance before they follow the path down to the nearest beach. The girl's small hands cup her mother's face with such innocent trust, such complete certainty that this love will always be there.

Mommy. Just that one simple word I will never say out loud again gets to me, and grief pours out of me in waves that feel as though they will never end. It's unfiltered, all-consuming, and my body shakes with each sob. Years of restraint unravel, as though every tear I didn't shed back then has been waiting for this exact time and place to spill over. It's not just sadness—it's anger, too. Anger at the storm, at the sea, at the universe for stealing them away.

I curl in on myself, my knees drawn to my chest, and my arms wrap tighter around them. My breath hitches as I rock back and forth, trying to steady the torrent of emotion but failing miserably. Images flash behind my closed eyes, unbidden but vivid. My mother's hand brushing my cheek, my father's voice telling me I could do anything if I put my mind to it. Their faces, so alive, feel so close I could almost reach out and touch them, but they fade as quickly as they come, leaving a void that feels impossible to fill.

The weight of the lost years presses down on me—the birthdays they missed, the milestones they never got to see, the laughter we'll never share again. I think of all the times I've needed them, the countless moments I've wished for their guidance, their hugs, their words of wisdom. The ache is unbearable, a physical pain that cuts through my chest like a knife. It's a void I've carried silently for so long, but now it feels as if it might consume me entirely.

Memories emerge like glimmers of light breaking through a stormy sky. The way my parents danced in the kitchen to old records, completely lost in each other. The endless summer evenings spent on the beach, where their passion for the ocean became mine.

I'd never put another human being through this crushing, overwhelming sense of loss. The thought of leaving a child behind, of causing this kind of pain...it's unthinkable.

Evelyn doesn't understand. She thinks our age difference is what could tear us apart, as if years between us matter more than the connection we share. She worries about what people might think, about her reputation, about growing old. It makes me want to shake her, to make her see that none of that matters. She of all people should know better—she lost her mother young too. Every day is precious, every moment counts, and she's willing to throw it all away because of what? Social standards? Fear of judgment?

My tears slow as anger rises, hot and fierce in my chest. I welcome it—anything is better than pain. While she's worried about her image, I'm sitting here breaking apart because I know—I know with devastating clarity—how quickly it can all be taken away. How one storm, one moment, one twist of fate can shatter everything you thought was certain.

I wipe my eyes roughly with the back of my hand. My parents taught me to live boldly, to fight for what matters. They died doing what they believed in, trying to make the world better. And here I am, letting the woman I'm crazy about push me away because she's scared of what others might think.

The waves continue their endless rhythm, and I realize something—I'm not just grieving my parents anymore. I'm grieving for all the moments Evelyn and I could have, all the joy we could share, if she'd just be brave enough to take this chance. If she could see that time isn't guaranteed, that waiting for the perfect moment, the perfect circumstances, is a luxury we don't have.

Standing up, I brush the sand from my clothes. The tears have left me feeling hollow but somehow stronger, like a storm that clears the air. I know what I want—not just for this piece of land, but for my life. I want to build something beautiful here, yes, but more than that, I want to build a life with someone who understands that love isn't about playing it safe. Because if losing my parents taught me anything, it's that life is too short to let fear dictate your choices.

Chapter 41

Evelyn

I smooth down my dress as I step outside. The sound of laughter and clinking glasses drifts from the hotel's restaurant terrace, and my stomach churns with anxiety. I've faced countless high-stakes business meetings, but nothing has made me feel as nervous as I do right now.

I spot them immediately. My father, Candy, Mia, and a handful of remaining wedding guests are seated around a large table, their faces flushed with the warmth of good wine. Mia is sitting next to my father, laughing at something he's saying, and for a moment, I freeze. Has she told them?

I force myself to move forward, plastering on what I hope is a convincing smile. "Good evening, everyone," I say.

My father looks up, his face breaking into a wide grin. "There she is! We were beginning to think you'd abandoned us, princess."

I lean down to kiss his cheek, then Candy's, before taking my seat next to Mia. My daughter gives me a brief smile, but I'm not sure if it's genuine. I clear my throat. "I'm sorry I couldn't make it to the boat trip. How was everyone's day?"

The table erupts into excited chatter, and I feel a wave of relief wash over me. Maybe Mia hasn't said anything after all.

"Oh, Evelyn, you missed out on the most incredible experience!" Candy gushes. "We saw dolphins! They were swimming right alongside the boat!"

My father nods enthusiastically. "It was spectacular. They were so playful, jumping and diving."

"We even got to swim with them for a bit," Mia chimes in, and I turn to look at her, surprised by her casual tone. "It was beautiful, Mom. You should have been there."

I swallow hard, guilt and relief warring inside me. "That sounds wonderful," I manage. "I'm sorry I missed it."

"Why couldn't you make it, dear?" my father asks. "Are you feeling all right?"

I open my mouth, ready to claim illness, but I catch Mia's eye and the words die in my throat. I can't lie, not now. "I...had some personal matters to attend to," I say. "Just...things I needed to sort out."

My father's frown deepens. "Care to share? You know you can talk to us if something's bothering you."

"I'm fine, Dad," I assure him. "I've taken care of it. Let's just enjoy dinner."

The conversation shifts to other topics, and I'm only half-listening. Was I wrong sending Val away? Was it rude or will she understand? I missed her the moment she walked out the door and I still feel her absence in my gut, but what choice did I have? Yes, we have fiery chemistry, and physically, I can't get enough of her, but sitting here now, surrounded by my family, I find it impossible to imagine her by my side, holding my hand under the table or sharing private smiles. It's simply not an option, and besides, she can't possibly be that serious about me.

The waiter arrives to take our orders, and I'm grateful for the distraction. As I peruse the menu, I can feel Mia's eyes on me. When I glance up, she quickly looks away, but not before I catch a flicker of...something. Concern? Disappointment? Or is it curiosity?

"So, Evelyn," Candy says. "Have you given any thought to where you might want to go for your next vacation? Donald and I were thinking of planning a family trip once we're back from our honeymoon. It's been so nice spending time with the two of you, we thought we should do it again. Perhaps Vietnam? We could go and visit Mia while she's there."

I blink, caught off guard by the question. "Oh, I...that's a nice idea," I say politely, mentally scrolling through my list of standard excuses. "Work is busy at the moment, though."

"But you can leave Majorca soon, right?" Candy presses on. "After the planning stage, your project managers will be there."

"True, but the planning is taking a little longer than expected as I have to go through a ton of revisions with our consultant."

"Of course. Val." my father says. "I like Val."

Candy nods. "She seemed so passionate about her work. It must be exciting to collaborate with someone like her."

I take a sip of wine, buying myself a moment. Just the mention of Val's name gives me butterflies, even now with my anxiety through the roof. "Yes, it's...it's been an interesting experience," I say. "Val brings a unique perspective to the project."

"I bet she does," Mia mutters under her breath, and I feel my cheeks flush.

"Well, I think it's wonderful that you're open to new ideas. Change is good. No business survives without adapting to its time. I'm all for it." My father raises his glass. "To new beginnings!"

"And to the newlyweds," I add, shifting the topic away from Val. "That was a beautiful wedding yesterday."

"Totally. So romantic," Mia agrees. "And I like you, Candy. I think you're great for Grandpa. He's really changed for the better." She winks at her grandfather when he raises a brow at her. "Come on, admit it. You were a little too serious for your own good before you met her."

My father laughs. "I suppose you're right." He sits back and drapes an arm around Candy. "Life is for living. Candy taught me that."

"Exactly! You should take a page from Grandpa's book," Mia says, turning to me. "I think that family vacation is a great idea. Let's do it after you finish up in Mallorca. You need to live a little. And perhaps you'd like to bring someone special too?"

I stare at Mia, my mind racing. What is she doing? Is she trying to get a reaction from me? I can't read her, and it's unsettling.

"I...well..." I stammer, feeling heat rise to my cheeks. "You know I don't date, Mia. I'm far too busy for that sort of thing."

My father chuckles. "Everyone knows Evelyn doesn't date. I don't think I've ever seen you in love, princess."

I ignore the comment and refill my wine glass. If only he knew.

"Speaking of which," my father continues, "Mia, you don't seem to date much either. Did you get that from your mother?"

Mia shrugs. "Oh, I date," she says matter-of-factly. "I just wouldn't bring anyone home unless I'm serious about them. I've dated both men and women, actually." I nearly choke on my wine, but Mia sits back casually as if she hasn't just dropped a bomb.

"You've dated women?" This is news to me, and I wonder if she's making it up. "Why have you never told me this before?"

"I didn't think you'd be open-minded enough to understand," she says, meeting my gaze.

"Of course she would." My father reaches out to pat Mia's hand. "Your mother would understand, wouldn't you, princess?"

"Yeah... You can tell me anything, you know that," I say. Mia's admission about her dating life has thrown me off balance. How did I not know this about my own daughter? I've always prided myself on being close to her, but now I'm realizing there's so much I don't know.

"Thank you. And the same counts for you, Mom. You can talk to me." Mia is clearly making a point and I have no idea how to handle the situation. "Sometimes I feel like I don't know you at all."

I stare at Mia, my heart pounding. Everyone at the table has fallen silent, their eyes darting between us. I can feel their gazes on me, questioning, curious.

Mia calmly pours herself more wine. Her nonchalance is infuriating, and I struggle to keep my composure. What is she playing at? Does she want me to confess everything right here, right now? In front of everyone?

What can I possibly say? The silence stretches on, becoming more uncomfortable with each passing second.

Just as I'm about to stammer out some weak response, my father's voice cuts through the tension. "Mia, honey, how can you say that? We all know your mother. She's nothing but consistent. Dependable and reliable, pragmatic, sensible, and set in her ways. You always know exactly what to expect from her."

Mia mumbles a half-hearted reply in apology and I let out a soft sigh of relief. Leave it to Dad to unknowingly come to my rescue. His words, meant to be complimentary, feel mildly insulting, though. Consistent. Reliable. Sensible. Is that really all I am? I force a smile, hoping Mia will let it rest.

As the conversation slowly picks up again, Mia's words echo in my mind: *"Sometimes I feel like I don't know you at all."* The truth is, it seems I don't know myself either.

Chapter 42

Val

It's been years since I cried. Years of holding it together, staying strong, moving forward. The last time was when my parents died, and that was different. That was justified. But this? Standing on the deck of a crowded ferry, my tears blurring the horizon—this is ridiculous. I'm ridiculous.

The wind whips my hair around my face, carrying the scent of salt and diesel. All around me, tourists jostle for the best spots along the railing, their phones raised to capture a shot of the sunset. A group of young backpackers sprawl nearby on their oversized packs, passing around a bag of chips and laughing at something on their phones.

I could have chartered a sailing yacht back to Mallorca. I can afford it, and God knows it would have been more comfortable than this packed ferry. But I've never been one for unnecessary luxury. Even after my resorts started turning serious profit, I kept traveling like this—by public transport, always choosing the option with the lowest environmental impact.

Right now, though, I wish I had some privacy. Another

tear rolls down my cheek, and I swipe it away angrily. What is wrong with me? I don't do this. I don't get attached easily and I don't let people get under my skin. Especially not straight women.

I've had my share of romantic encounters—passionate nights in exotic locations, brief connections that burned bright and fast. There was Maria in Hawaii, who surfed like a goddess and left me with nothing but tan lines and memories. And Sarah, the contractor who helped build my first resort—that could have been something real, if either of us had wanted it to be.

But I learned early on to keep things light, uncomplicated. No promises, no expectations. It was easier that way, cleaner. After my parents died, I built walls around my heart so thick and high that no one could scale them. I threw myself into work, and relationships were just pleasant distractions, brief interludes between projects.

It worked until now. Until I met Evelyn. She didn't try to scale those walls—she simply walked through them as if they didn't exist. With her sharp mind and sharper tongue, her vulnerability hidden beneath layers of control, the way she challenged me, frustrated me, fascinated me...

The memory of her in that champagne-colored dress, the way she looked at me, the vulnerability in her eyes when she pulled me close—it all comes rushing back, making my chest ache. How did she manage to slip past all my defenses so quickly?

I remember how her hands shook as she gathered my clothes, how she couldn't quite meet my eyes. The silence as I dressed was deafening. No gentle touches, no soft morning kisses—just the harsh reality of day breaking through our bubble. I wanted to say something, anything, to make it better, but what could I say? Her panic was palpable, filling the room like a physical presence.

A child's shriek pierces the air, and I turn to see a little girl pointing at a pod of dolphins playing in the ferry's wake. Her mother lifts her up for a better view, both of them laughing. The sight triggers another memory—watching dolphins with Evelyn during our sailing trip. Was that really just days ago?

"Excuse me." An elderly couple squeezes past me to get to the railing, the woman steadying herself on her husband's arm. They stand close together, sharing the view, and I have to look away. It's too much right now, too raw.

I find a quieter spot near the stern, away from most of the crowd. The wake stretches out behind us like a road leading back to Ibiza, back to her. But there's no going back, is there? Evelyn made that perfectly clear.

"I can't do this," she'd said, her voice tight with panic. "It's not right." As if what we shared could be reduced to right or wrong, as if the connection between us was something that could be rationalized away or dismissed as a mistake.

I pull out my phone, half hoping to see a message from her, knowing there won't be one. Instead, there's an email from Marcus about the Ibiza property. Right. Work. Reality. I should focus on that instead of dwelling on...whatever this is.

The plot on Ibiza works well for us—the location, the potential, everything we've been looking for. I should be buzzing with ideas and plans, but all I can think about is how I'll somehow have to face Evelyn again, have to maintain a professional facade while pretending last night never happened. The consultancy contract isn't finished, and I've never been one to leave things half-done.

A wave crashes against the ferry's hull, sending up a spray of saltwater. Some of it catches me in the face, mingling with the tears I can't seem to stop. Thirteen years. Thirteen years since I last felt this vulnerable, this exposed. Back then, I at least understood why. Losing your parents is the kind of pain that demands tears. But this? This shouldn't hurt so much. I barely know her, really. A few weeks of working together, one night of intimacy, that's all it was.

Except it wasn't. It was more than that, and we both know it. It was early morning conversations over coffee, heated arguments that turned into deeper understanding. It was watching her walls come down, piece by piece. It was feeling her tremble in my arms, hearing her whisper my name.

My phone buzzes—Marcus calling. I consider letting it go to voicemail, but he'll just keep trying.

"Hey," I answer, clearing my throat.

"Val! I've been trying to get hold of you."

"Sorry, terrible reception," I lie.

"No worries. Tell me about the plot. Is it as good as it looked in the photos?"

I turn away from the wind so he can hear me better. "Even better. The terraced landscape is ideal for what we want to do. We could build right into the natural contours, minimal disruption to the land. And the views are incredible—every villa would have an unobstructed view of the sea."

"That's what I wanted to hear. Should I start putting out feelers for contractors?"

"Not yet. I'm on the ferry back to Mallorca now. Let me get my thoughts together and we'll discuss next steps tomorrow." I force myself to sound enthusiastic. "But yeah, the location is ideal—close enough to amenities but completely private. And there's this hidden cove that would be great for a beach club."

"Weren't you supposed to sail back with Evelyn Rothschild? Did something come up?"

My heart clenches, but I keep my voice steady. "Change of plans. Listen, Marcus, the connection's pretty bad out here. I'll call you tomorrow, okay?"

"Sure thing. Talk tomorrow."

I end the call and slip my phone back into my pocket, grateful he didn't push further. The last thing I need right now is Marcus's concern. Or worse, his "I told you so."

A voice comes over the ferry's speakers, announcing our approaching arrival in Palma. Around me, people start gathering their belongings, children are called back to their parents, and conversations grow louder with the excitement of arrival. I stay where I am, watching Mallorca grow larger on the horizon.

The last tear dries on my cheek, and I take a deep breath of salt air. Enough. No more crying. What's done is done, and I have work to do. I'll give Evelyn the space she needs, keep things strictly professional from now on. That's all it ever should have been anyway.

I fish my sunglasses out of my bag and slip them on, hiding my red eyes. Time to put on my game face. There are contracts to fulfill, meetings to attend, a resort to build. Life goes on. It always does.

Chapter 43

Evelyn

I sit curled up in a corner of my balcony, hidden from view by a large potted palm. From this vantage point, I can see the marina below without being seen. Under different circumstances, I might appreciate the beauty of the sunset, but right now, everything feels wrong. Off-kilter. Like I'm watching the world through a cracked lens.

The yacht has just docked, and I watch as my family and the remaining wedding guests disembark. Mia heads off with a group of younger guests, probably to one of the beachfront bars. A few others linger on the pier, chatting before gradually dispersing in different directions. Their voices carry up to me on the evening breeze, fragments of conversations about dinner plans and departures.

Only my father and Candy remain. They stand at the end of the pier, his arm is wrapped around her waist as they gaze out at the water. There's something intimate about the way they lean into each other, something that makes my chest tighten with an emotion I can't quite name. Envy? Regret? Or maybe it's just recognition of something I pushed away this morning.

Candy's head rests on my father's shoulder, her blonde hair catching the last rays of sunlight. She's wearing a simple white sundress that floats around her in the evening breeze, and her feet are bare. Gone is the Instagram-ready poise she usually maintains, the curated image of the influencer.

My father whispers something in her ear, and she laughs—not the high-pitched, performative giggle, but something quieter, more genuine. He pulls her closer, pressing a kiss to her temple, and the tenderness of the gesture brings a lump to my throat. His hand moves to the small of her back, a gesture I saw him make a thousand times with my mother.

I've been so quick to dismiss their relationship as a midlife crisis on his part and a calculated move on hers. But watching them now, when they think no one's looking, I'm struck by how natural they seem together. There's no audience here, no one to impress. Just two people, standing close, sharing a moment that feels almost too intimate to witness.

My father's laughing and even the way he stands has changed, less rigid and formal than I remember. His usual straight posture has softened, curved slightly to accommodate Candy's presence at his side.

When was the last time I heard him laugh like that, so free and unguarded? It reminds me of my childhood, of summer days spent on various beaches around the world, before business became everything, before we lost Mom.

They begin to walk along the pier, taking their time, still wrapped up in each other. Candy stumbles on a loose board, and my father steadies her. She looks up at him with warmth and affection, and I have to look away for a moment. I feel as if I'm intruding on their intimacy.

My mind drifts to Val, and I push the thought away, but

it persists, like a splinter I can't quite reach. The memory of her hands on my skin, her lips against mine, the way she made me feel both safe and thrillingly alive—it all comes rushing back.

Could I have been wrong about my father and Candy? About everything? I've been so certain that this marriage is a mistake, that Candy must have ulterior motives. But watching them now, I'm forced to consider another possibility—that maybe this is actually love. Real, messy, inconvenient love that doesn't care about age differences or social expectations.

Below, Candy stops to take off the light cardigan she's wearing. My father helps her, and she says something that makes him smile again, that same smile that transforms his whole face. They look...content. At peace with each other and the world. It's a stark contrast to the chaos churning inside me.

I think about Val again, about the way she made me feel —seen, understood. Everything. Is this how my father feels with Candy? This sense of discovering a new part of yourself through someone else's eyes? The thought brings fresh tears to my eyes, but I blink them back. I've done enough crying today.

The evening breeze carries the sound of their voices up to me, not clear enough to make out words, but I can hear the tone—soft, intimate, filled with shared jokes and private meanings. They've created their own little world together, and I've been so busy judging it from the outside that I never bothered to really look at what was happening within it.

My father reaches out to brush a strand of hair from Candy's face, tucking it behind her ear. I remember Val doing the same thing to me, her fingers lingering against my cheek, and my heart aches with the memory. How quickly we fell into those small, intimate gestures. How natural it felt.

They're heading toward the hotel now. My father is barefoot and carries his shoes in his free hand, swinging them carelessly as they walk.

I watch as they pause at the end of the pier. Candy turns to face my father, rising on her tiptoes to kiss him. There's nothing showy about it, nothing designed to attract attention. It's simply a moment of connection. The kind of moment I pushed away this morning when I sent Val from my room.

The setting sun casts long shadows across the pier, and in this light, the age difference between them seems less stark, less important. They're just two people who found each other, who bring out something special in each other. Why has it taken me so long to see it? And why does recognizing it now feel like such a profound loss?

Was I really protecting my reputation, or was I just scared? My father isn't having a midlife crisis. He's just brave enough to grab happiness when he finds it, regardless of what anyone else might think. Maybe he's wiser than I've given him credit for.

I watch until they disappear from view. The sun has almost set now, the sky darkening to deep purple, but I remain where I am, hidden behind the palm tree on my balcony. The air has grown cooler, but I barely notice. I'm too caught up in the realization that I might have made a terrible mistake this morning.

My phone sits on the table beside me, silent and dark. I pick it up, unlock it, stare at Val's name in my contact list. My finger hovers over it for a long moment before I set the phone down again. What would I even say?

The first sob catches me by surprise, raw and unfamiliar in my throat. Something inside me ruptures, and suddenly I'm crying like I haven't since I was fourteen, since the day they told me Mom wasn't coming home from the hospital. My whole body shakes with it, grief and regret and longing all tangled together.

I press my face into my hands, letting the tears fall. All the years of control, of being the responsible one, the sensible one, crumble away. I think about Val's smile, about the way she looked at me this morning, hope and hurt warring in her eyes. I think about my father, finding joy again after decades of going through the motions. I think about all the walls I've built, all the chances I've refused to take.

The sound of music drifts up from somewhere along the beach, a melody I don't recognize. Down in the marina, lights twinkle on the boats, and the world goes about its business while I fall apart in my hidden corner. I remember Val's hands in my hair, the way she held me like I was precious, like I mattered beyond my name.

My nose runs, my eyes burn, and I probably look like hell, but for once I don't care. I let myself feel everything I've been holding back—the terror of wanting something I don't understand, the ache of pushing it away, the crushing weight of always, always doing what's expected instead of what I want. The tears feel endless, but with each one that falls, something inside me shifts, like a door slowly opening to let in light.

Chapter 44

Val

The small boat cuts through the waves as I make my way toward Cormoran Island. The sun beats down, hot and unforgiving, but I barely notice. My mind is a thousand miles away, replaying that night on Ibiza over and over again.

Evelyn's face when Mia opened the door. The panic in her eyes. The way she told me to leave.

I shake my head, as if I can physically dislodge the memories. It's been two days, and I still haven't heard from her. Not a word. No call, no text, nothing. The silence speaks volumes and it hurts.

I'm trying to clear my head, to get some space from everything that's happened. Maybe the peaceful isolation of Cormoran will help me get my thoughts in order. I know it's a long shot. How can I possibly sort through this mess when I can't stop thinking about her? About us? Our connection was intense, special. Or at least, I thought it was. Now, I'm not so sure. Maybe Evelyn wishes she'd never met me at all.

As I approach the island, I make a split-second decision. Instead of heading to my usual spot, I steer the boat around the rocky shore to the other side. I need a change of scenery, something different to shake me out of this funk. Besides, I haven't explored the north side of the island yet, as it's difficult to navigate unless you're a goat.

The boat rocks as I navigate through choppy waters. This side of the island takes the full force of the Mediterranean, and the currents are stronger here, pushing against the bow. I keep a safe distance from the cliffs, watching for submerged rocks that could tear through the hull. White water churns where waves crash against the shore, sending spray high into the air.

The landscape changes dramatically as I round the northeastern point. Gone are the gentler slopes I'm familiar with, replaced by sheer walls of limestone that rise straight from the sea. Wind and water have carved deep fissures in the rock face, creating strange formations. Seabirds nest in the crevices, their calls echoing off the stone.

A school of fish breaks the surface, their silver bodies catching the sunlight as they leap in unison, fleeing from some unseen predator below. I cut the engine to avoid disturbing the hunt playing out before me, letting the current carry me.

The cliffs here tell a different story than the southern side of the island. These rocks have been battered by countless storms, sculpted by centuries of wind and waves. Hardy plants cling to impossible perches, their roots finding purchase in the smallest cracks. Even here, life finds a way to thrive.

Cormoran Island looks different from this angle. The cliffs are steeper, more imposing with small trees growing out at a horizontal angle. A small, secluded cove is tucked away between two rocky outcroppings. It's hard to reach from the land, but I might be able to get there from here.

Sliding into the water, the current tugs at me as I swim toward the rocks. It's jagged and slippery, covered in a thin film of algae, and it takes me a few tries to push myself up onto the land.

Catching my breath, I survey my surroundings. The cove is small, maybe twenty feet across, enclosed on three sides by high cliffs. It's quiet here, the sound of the waves muffled by the rock formations. A seagull flying low overhead startles me, causing me to turn, and that's when I notice it—a dark opening in the cliff face, partially hidden behind a jutting rock. My curiosity piqued, I make my way toward it, careful not to slip on the wet stones.

As I get closer, I can feel a cool breeze emanating from the opening. I'm about to reach for my phone to use as a flashlight when I realize it's in the boat along with my other belongings. Climbing inside anyway, it seems I don't need a light after all. Sunlight filters through the narrow entrance, creating a soft, diffused glow that illuminates the cave interior. The light dances on the rough walls, casting intricate shadows that shift and change. After a few feet, it opens up into a cavern, and what I see takes my breath away.

The walls are covered in crystals that catch and reflect the light. They're celestite, their pale-blue color unmistakable. I've seen small clusters before, but never anything like this. The formation must have taken hundreds of thousands of years to develop, undisturbed by human hands.

I find a relatively flat area and sit down to take it all in. It's mesmerizing, like being surrounded by stars. The celestite is phosphorescent, giving off a soft, blue-white light that pulses in the shadows.

Small pools of water are scattered throughout the cave, so still they look like mirrors. The reflection of the celestite creates an illusion of infinite depth on the surface, and I imagine falling right through into another world.

This cave has been undiscovered for so long, its beauty hidden away. And here I am, stumbling upon it by chance. The implications hit me then. It changes everything for Evelyn's project.

The presence of a significant celestite cave system will trigger immediate geological surveys and environmental impact studies that would likely lead to the site being classified as a protected geological heritage site.

The irony isn't lost on me. I came here to escape thoughts of Evelyn, only to discover something that will directly impact her plans. The resort project she's poured so much into, the one that's brought us together and torn us apart—it might never happen now.

Once I report the cave's existence to the local authorities—and I must, it's the law—everything will change. The environmental protection agencies will get involved. Geologists will want to study the formation. Marine biologists will need to assess the impact of development on the cave's ecosystem. The bureaucratic wheels will start turning, and Evelyn's plans will grind to a halt indefinitely.

A drop of water falls from the ceiling, landing in one of the pools with a soft plunk that echoes through the chamber. The ripples distort the reflected crystals, making them dance and shimmer.

I don't know how long I sit there, lost in the glow of the crystals and my own tangled thoughts. Time seems to lose all meaning in this place. Eventually, I become aware of the growing ache in my back from sitting on the hard stone, and I stand up, stretching.

I make my way deeper into the cave system, following a narrow passage that slopes downward. The temperature drops noticeably, and the air grows thicker with moisture. The passage twists and turns, occasionally opening into smaller chambers, each with its own crystal formations. In some places, the celestite has formed patterns, like frozen waterfalls cascading down the walls. Water drips steadily somewhere ahead of me, the sound amplified by the cave's acoustics.

My foot slips on the wet rock, and I catch myself against the wall. The sharp edge of a crystal cuts into my palm. Blood wells up, and I curse under my breath. The sting brings me back to reality—I'm alone in an unexplored cave system without proper equipment or anyone knowing where I am. Not smart.

Reluctantly, I turn back toward the entrance. As much as I want to explore further, it's not safe. Blood drips onto the stone floor, and I wonder if I'm the first person to leave a mark in this place.

The sun is blinding after the cave's dimness, and I shield my eyes, waiting for them to adjust. The cut on my palm is still bleeding, a jagged line across my skin. The salt stings my cut as I swim back to the boat, mentally planning my next steps. I need to tell the authorities and I need to tell Evelyn. Perhaps I should tell Evelyn first; that only seems fair. I realize—this discovery doesn't just end her project. It ends my time with her. Life has other plans, I guess.

Chapter 45

Evelyn

The past three days have been torture. After sending Val away, I couldn't bear the thought of returning to Mallorca, of facing her, so I made excuses to stay on Ibiza longer. "I need a break," I told everyone, then talked about plans to explore the island. In reality, I've been hiding in my suite, drowning in guilt and confusion.

What's worse is how Mia's been acting. She's been perfectly polite, joining me for meals, making appropriate small talk, but there's a distance that wasn't there before. The careful courtesy hurts more than anger would. At least anger would be real, something I could push against. This polite facade feels like a wall between us, and it's killing me.

Mia leaves for Vietnam tomorrow, and I can't let her go with this unresolved tension between us. I spent the early hours of the morning pacing my room, rehearsing what to say, but every practiced speech feels hollow.

Finally, I force myself to act. I stand outside Mia's door, shifting my weight from one foot to the other, trying to gather my courage.

I knock, and when Mia opens the door, she's already dressed, her dreads pulled back in a loose ponytail. She looks at me with an expression I can't quite read.

"Can we talk?" I ask, hating how uncertain my voice sounds.

Mia leans against the doorframe, crossing her arms. "That depends. Are you going to be honest with me?"

I swallow hard. "Yes. I'll tell you everything."

She studies me for a moment longer, then steps back, gesturing for me to enter. Her room is smaller than mine but still very nice, with a private balcony overlooking the sea. I notice her suitcase is packed, waiting by the door.

"Do you want coffee?" she asks, motioning to the room service cart where a fresh pot sits steaming.

I nod. "Please."

Mia pours two cups, adding milk to hers while leaving mine black, and we settle on the balcony. Below us, the beach is still quiet, just a few early morning swimmers braving the waves.

"So," Mia says, taking a sip of her coffee. "Val."

I close my eyes briefly. "Yes. Val."

"How long has this been going on?"

"It hasn't been... I mean, it only just..." I trail off, frustrated with my inability to find the right words. "That night was the first time."

"But you've had feelings for her longer than that," Mia says. It's not a question.

I stare into my coffee cup, watching the steam rise in delicate spirals. "I didn't recognize them at first. Or maybe I didn't want to. Everything with Val has been...unexpected."

"Because she's a woman?"

"Yes." I look up at Mia. "I've never... I mean, I didn't think I was..." The words stick in my throat.

"Gay?" Mia supplies, and I flinch at the directness of it.

"I don't know what I am," I admit. "I've never felt this way about anyone before, man or woman. It's terrifying."

Mia's expression softens. "Why didn't you tell me you were struggling with this?"

"How could I?" I let out a bitter laugh. "I couldn't even admit it to myself. And then when you found us... God, Mia, I wasn't anywhere near ready for anyone to find out and I panicked. I just... I was scared. I still am."

"Of what?"

"Everything." The word comes out in a rush. "Of what people will think. Of losing respect. Of making a fool of myself. Of getting hurt." I pause. "Of losing you."

Mia shakes her head. "Mom, why would you think that?"

"Because I'm supposed to be the strong one. The one who has everything figured out. And instead, I'm..." I gesture helplessly. "I'm a mess. I'm having some sort of midlife crisis, falling for a woman who's younger than you, questioning everything I thought I knew about myself."

"First of all," Mia says, reaching across the table to take my hand, "you're not having a midlife crisis. You're finally letting yourself feel something real. And second, you could never lose me. Ever."

Tears prick at my eyes, and I blink them back. "I felt sick at first when I saw pictures of my father and Candy together. I assumed you'd feel the same way about me and Val."

Mia tilts her head from side to side. "I'll admit, it's a little weird," she says. "With Grandpa, it was kind of funny and cute, you know? But now that it's you, my own mom... I get why you freaked out about Grandpa. I needed a few days to get used to the idea of you and Val myself." She pauses. "But you're not doing anything wrong."

"No..."

"So, what are you going to do about her?"

I look away. "Nothing." My own words cut through me like a knife.

"Why?"

"Because it's impossible. I can't... We can't..."

"Can't what?" Mia challenges. "Can't be happy? Can't let yourself feel something real for once in your life?"

"It's not that simple."

"Actually, it is that simple. You're just making it complicated because you're scared." Mia leans forward. "Mom, I saw the way you were around Val that night at dinner. It makes so much sense now, I just didn't see it."

Heat rises to my cheeks. "Am I really that different around her?"

"From what I've seen, yes." She smiles. "You lit up whenever she spoke. You laughed—really laughed, not that fake social laugh you usually do. You looked...happy."

"I was," I admit. "I am, when I'm with her. But Mia, she's so much younger than me. She deserves someone who can match her energy, someone who isn't weighed down by responsibilities and expectations."

"Don't you think that should be her choice?" Mia asks. "You're not giving her enough credit. Or yourself, for that matter."

I take a shaky breath. "I sent her away. After you found us, I panicked and told her to leave. I think I came across as...I don't know. Cold, dismissive, I suppose. I haven't spoken to her since."

"Oh, Mom." Mia shakes her head. "You need to talk to her. You can't just leave things like this."

"I know. But what would I even say?"

"How about the truth?" Mia suggests. "That you're scared but you care about her. That you need time to figure things out, but you don't want to lose her."

I sigh and stare at my daughter, wondering when she became so mature, so wise about matters of the heart. "Can I ask you something? Why didn't you tell me you were bisexual?

Mia shrugs. "I wasn't hiding it. It just never seemed like the right time, and I wasn't even sure if you could relate. You've been single all my life, so honestly, you wouldn't be the first person I'd go to for relationship advice."

"I'm sorry," I whisper. "I'm sorry I made you feel that way."

"It's okay, Mom. I should have been more open with you." Mia stands up and moves around the table, pulling me into a hug. "You've spent your whole life being what everyone else needed you to be—the in-charge CEO, the responsible single mother, the dutiful daughter. Maybe it's time to just be yourself."

I lean into her embrace, letting the tears fall freely. "I love you so much," I whisper into her hair.

"I love you too," she says. "Even when you're being stubborn and ridiculous."

I laugh through my tears, holding her tighter. "I don't know what to do," I admit.

"Yes, you do," she says, pulling back to look at me.

And she's right, of course. I know exactly what I need to do. The question is, will I be brave enough?

Chapter 46

Val

A seagull walks toward me, tilting its head. I throw a piece of bread and it hops forward, snatching the morsel with quick precision before scurrying away. The motion draws my attention to the waves, their rhythm steady as they kiss the shoreline.

The sun is setting and each passing minute marks the end of something that could have been. My time in Mallorca is coming to an end, and while part of me aches at the thought of leaving, maybe it's for the best.

Tomorrow, I'll report the celestite cave to the local authorities. It will likely halt all development plans for months, maybe even years. There's no point in either of us staying here, waiting for bureaucrats to decide the fate of Cormoran Island. Better to make a clean break, to let the memories fade.

A familiar presence settles over me before I catch the subtle scent of her perfume. My heart skips, then steadies. *It's her.* Even without turning, I know it's her. I've become attuned to Evelyn's presence in a way I can't explain.

"I've been looking for you," she says. "Is it okay if I join you?"

"Of course." I gesture to the sand beside me, still not meeting her gaze. I'm afraid of what I might see in her eyes —or worse, what she might see in mine.

She settles next to me, maintaining a careful distance, and we sit in silence for a while, watching the sun sink lower into the sea. Finally, I turn to her. "How are you?"

Evelyn opens her mouth, then closes it again. Her fingers fidget with the hem of her dress. She looks beautiful in the golden light, but tired, like she hasn't been sleeping well.

"We need to talk," I say, deciding to rip off the Band-Aid.

"Yes..." She pauses. "We do."

I clear my throat. "I found something on Cormoran Island that will impact your project."

Evelyn's brow furrows in confusion. "What do you mean?"

"There's a cave system on the north side of the island," I say. "It's filled with celestite formations—some of the most impressive I've ever seen. We have to report it to the authorities, which means all development plans will come to a halt pending environmental impact studies."

"Wait..." Evelyn studies me. "Is that what you wanted to talk about? The project?"

I turn to face her fully, frustrated that she doesn't seem to grasp the significance. "Do you understand what I'm saying? This could be the end of your resort. It likely will be."

"Oh." Evelyn's reaction isn't what I expected. There's no flash of anger, no tightening of her jaw, none of the signs I've come to recognize when she's holding back frustration.

Instead, she just looks at me with those dark eyes and God, I wish I knew what was going through her mind.

"I actually wanted to apologize," she says quietly, as if she still hasn't processed my message. "I shouldn't have sent you away like that on Ibiza. I panicked when Mia found us, and I handled it badly. I'm truly sorry."

"It's okay," I say, though the memory still stings. "I understand."

"No, you don't." Evelyn shifts closer, her knee brushing against mine. "I want this, Val. I want you."

I freeze, thrown by her words. I thought this was it. I thought we'd go our separate ways from here. Just minutes ago, I was ready to accept that whatever we had was over before it really began. But now she's here, saying exactly what I've been longing to hear, and it feels surreal. I search her face for any hint of doubt or hesitation but find none.

"Evelyn—"

"Wait, let me finish." She holds up a hand. "I was scared. I still am. But I'm more scared of letting you go without telling you how I feel. Without at least trying to explain."

"And how do you feel?" I ask, barely breathing.

Evelyn reaches for my hand. "Like I'm waking up for the first time in years." She laughs softly. "God, that sounds ridiculous, doesn't it?"

I squeeze her hand, smiling despite the tears threatening to spill. "It's not ridiculous at all."

"I told Mia everything. We talked for hours this morning before she left for Vietnam," she continues. "I want you, Val. I want to see where this goes, even if it terrifies me. Even if I have no idea what I'm doing. I don't expect you to feel the same, but..." She sighs. "Well, I want you to know, that's all."

The last rays of sunlight catch in her hair, turning it to spun gold. She looks vulnerable and strong all at once, and I've never wanted to kiss her more than I do in this moment.

"I think you know how I feel," I whisper. "But what about all the reasons you gave for why this couldn't work?"

"I don't care anymore." Evelyn shakes her head. "Well, that's not entirely true—I do care. But I care about you more. And maybe it's time I stopped letting fear and reputation dictate my choices."

I reach up to brush her cheek and let my hand linger there. "Are you sure? Because if we do this—if we really do this—I want all of you, Evelyn." I pause, swallowing hard. "In a way, this is new for me too."

"How so?" she asks, leaning into my touch.

"Because I can't do casual. Not with you. I always preferred the idea of casual, it suited my lifestyle." I let out a chuckle. "I don't know what you've done to me, but I miss you when you're not with me, and I don't think I can handle being halfway with you."

Evelyn's eyes well up as they catch mine and I soften my tone, squeezing her hand. "That being said, I know this is big for you, and I don't want to rush you into anything you're not ready for. We can take it slow, as slow as you need. Just...let me be there for you. Let me be with you."

"That's all I want," she says, her voice cracking.

"I don't expect you to tell anyone until you're ready," I continue. "Just don't push me away."

Evelyn nods and she smiles, a real smile. "So what do we do now?"

"Now?" I tug her closer, until our foreheads are nearly touching. "We take it one day at a time."

"San Francisco to New York isn't exactly ideal," she whispers. "That's a lot of miles." After a moment, a hint of mischief crosses her face. "I suppose I could ask my boss about working remote."

I laugh. It's these little moments of playfulness from her that catch me off guard, that make me want to discover every hidden side of her. "Yeah, I'll do the same. See if me, myself, and I can come to an arrangement. We'll figure it out as we go along." I lift her hand and kiss it. "I'm willing to travel anywhere to see you."

"So am I," Evelyn says.

"And we'll have some free time now," I say with a wince.

"Yeah, about the cave..." She raises her brows. "Are you fucking kidding me?"

The tension breaks and we both burst out laughing, falling back into the sand together. The ground is still warm from the day's heat, and I can feel the vibration of her laughter against me.

"At least we won't have to argue anymore." I roll onto my side and pull her into my arms.

She hums against my lips. "True. I don't like arguing with you." Her fingers find the collar of my shirt, playing with the fabric. "Let's agree to never collaborate again."

"Sounds good to me." I shoot her a smirk. "I might have a new project to focus on while you work your way out of this pickle."

"The Ibiza plot?" she asks.

"Yeah, it's very nice. We're going for it."

"Good for you." Evelyn cups my face and kisses me. "I guess we both got something out of our stay here. You got a new plot, and I got you."

"And I got you. Double-win for me." I run a hand through her hair and breathe in her scent; proof that she's really here. That this is really happening. Stars are starting to appear in the darkening sky, and the sea has taken on that deep, mysterious blue that comes with twilight. "Let me show you the cave tomorrow," I say. "You should see it before we report it. We may not get a chance otherwise, and it's beautiful."

"It better be." Evelyn rolls her eyes good-naturedly and chuckles. "After everything, it better be fucking spectacular." Her expression softens. "All joking aside, I'd love to go see it with you. One last visit to our island."

Chapter 47

Evelyn

"My hotel," Val suggested, and I followed her. I'm so happy to have her back, I'd sleep anywhere with her. I'd sleep on the beach or in a hammock.

But it's not basic, like I imagined. Her hotel is up three flights of stone steps from the beach. We pass the bar and say hello to Mateo, who's closing down for the night, then pass another bar farther up by the entrance.

It's bohemian, I suppose. Bohemian with simplicity as its strength. Smooth, weathered stone walls meet warm wooden accents, and tropical plants cascade from planters along the staircases, giving it an organic, almost treehouse-like feel.

The steps are uneven but worn smooth over the years, each landing lit by lanterns made of woven rattan. At the top, a modest wooden sign announces the hotel's name in hand-painted letters, with a few blooming hibiscus bushes lining the entryway.

There's a small sitting area, with low, handmade wooden tables surrounded by cushions. A bookshelf stocked with well-loved paperbacks stands next to the reception desk, inviting guests to linger.

Val's door is painted a soft teal, chipped around the edges, giving it character rather than shabbiness. The walls are painted a soft cream, and a single colorful tapestry hangs above the bed, depicting a sunburst in earthy tones. A ceiling fan spins lazily overhead, its hum blending with the ever-present sound of the ocean through the shuttered windows.

The bed is low, with crisp white sheets and a throw blanket made of handwoven fabric in shades of deep blue and green, and a small wooden desk sits against the far wall, its surface adorned with a simple clay vase holding fresh flowers. A hammock is strung in the corner by the sliding doors, positioned to catch the breeze.

It's calm and pretty. This was her sanctuary, and I never came here, too stuck in my own ways to venture outside my hotel room.

"Do you want some water?" Val asks, and I almost laugh at the mundane question in this charged moment.

"No." I step closer, drawn by the scent of her skin, salt and sunscreen and something fruity. It's so perfect I wish I could bottle it. "I want you."

Her eyes darken at my directness. She reaches for me, but I catch her hands, holding them still. "Let me," I whisper.

My fingers find the buttons of her shirt, working them free one by one. I take my time, savoring the reveal of tanned skin, the subtle shift in her breathing as my knuckles brush against her stomach. When the fabric falls away, I pause, studying the constellation of freckles across her shoulders, the defined muscles of her arms.

I unbutton her shorts and push them down over her

hips along with her panties, then walk around her to take her in again. Val's body is a map I want to memorize—the small scar on her hip, the dimples at the base of her spine, the soft curve of her breasts. Brushing her hair to the side, I'm struck by how different this feels from our night on Ibiza. That was urgent, desperate. This is deliberate. Conscious.

Val shivers as my lips brush the nape of her neck, and I run my hands down her sides, resting them on her hips. I press closer, molding my body against her back while my mouth traces a path across her shoulder. She moans softly, and I swallow down the lump in my throat. This power to affect her moves me and I want to savor it.

She turns in my arms, and the look in her eyes steals my breath—desire, yes, but also tenderness, a whole new depth of emotion. Her fingers find the zipper of my dress, but she pauses, watching my face. When I nod, she slowly draws it down, the whisper of the zipper loud in the quiet room. The dress slips from my shoulders, pooling at my feet, and Val's gaze travels over my body with such open appreciation that I feel myself flush. But there's no urge to cover myself, no self-consciousness under her admiring eyes. Instead, I feel beautiful, desired, cherished. I unclip my bra and add it to the garments on the floor along with my panties.

Val steps closer, and this time when our bodies meet, skin against skin, the sensation is overwhelming. Her hands trace patterns on my back, feather-light touches. The ceiling fan stirs the air around us, raising goosebumps on my exposed skin, but I barely notice. All my attention is focused on the points where our bodies connect, on the gentle pressure of her fingers as they trail down my spine.

"You're so soft," she whispers against my neck, and something about the wonder in her voice makes my heart clench. Her hands move lower, cupping my behind, pulling me closer as her mouth finds that sensitive spot just below my ear. I gasp, my fingers tightening on her shoulders.

She guides me backward until my legs hit the edge of the bed. Moonlight spills through the shutters, painting stripes across our skin as we sink down onto the crisp sheets together. Her body covers mine, and the weight of her is all I'll ever need.

Bracing herself on her elbows, she looks down at me with such intensity that I almost have to look away. But I don't. Instead, I reach up to trace the line of her jaw, marveling at how this feels both familiar and entirely new. Here, in this simple room with its spinning fan and ocean sounds, time seems to slow. Each touch lingers, each kiss deepens, as if we're learning each other all over again.

Val shifts, and her thigh slips between mine, drawing a gasp from my throat. I'm wet and I know she can feel it. Her lips find my neck, my collarbone, trailing lower with delicious slowness. When her mouth closes around my nipple, my back arches off the bed, seeking more contact. Her hand slides up my side, her thumb brushing the underside of my breast, and pleasure spirals through me, sharp and sweet.

Val's hands are everywhere—mapping, claiming, worshiping—and I feel like I'm coming undone under her touch. Her fingers splay across my hip, grounding me, while her lips chart a slow, reverent path lower, leaving a trail of heat in their wake. When her lips press just above the apex of my thighs, I moan, anticipation pooling low in my belly.

She glances up at me, her eyes catching mine in the dim light. There's a question in them and I lift my hips in answer, my fingers threading through her hair to guide her closer. The first brush of her mouth is gentle and achingly tender, but it feels like I'm being struck by lightning. The effect she has on me is beyond anything I've felt, like she knows my body better than I do.

The air seems to still around us as her mouth and tongue move against me, and it feels so good I don't know what to do with myself. It's not just the touch but the reverence in it, like she's unearthing a secret and savoring every piece of it. Each kiss, each flick of her tongue, sends ripples of heat spiraling outward, seeping into my skin, my bones. I bite my lip, the sensation a sharp thread pulled taut, trembling on the edge of unraveling. My hands are restless, finding purchase in her hair—anything to anchor me as I'm about to fall.

I can't help but watch her, the way her dark hair spills over my thighs, the moonlight catching on the curve of her cheekbone. Her hands grip my hips just firm enough to keep me grounded as I twist beneath her. My body answers to her touch instinctively, hips lifting, chasing her, the pleasure she draws from me almost too much to bear and yet never enough. My heart thunders in my chest, and when she moans softly against me, the vibration shatters me. My head falls back against the pillow, and the world fractures, nothing but white-hot sensation.

I cry out, my voice breaking, my body clenching, trembling, caught in the exquisite pull of release that seems to go on forever. And through it all, she doesn't stop—her touch softens, her movements slowing, guiding me back down from the crest with infinite care, like she's cradling something fragile. Her touch is slow and unrelenting, as if she has all the time in the world to unravel me, piece by trembling piece, just a little more, drawing out every last shiver and moan.

When I finally still, my chest rising and falling with ragged breaths, she looks up at me, her lips flushed, her eyes soft and full of something I can't quite name but feel in every inch of my being. It's overwhelming, this connection, this tenderness, and as she rises to kiss me, her taste still on my lips, I feel entirely hers. This is what it feels like to belong.

Chapter 48

Val

I guide the boat around the northern edge of Cormoran Island. Evelyn sits across from me, her hair whipping in the wind, and when our eyes meet, warmth floods through me. My body tingles with memories of last night—the tenderness in her touch, the way she learned every inch of me with such devotion, the soft sounds she made. Even now, sitting on the hard bench of the boat, I can feel echoes of her presence on my skin.

"This side looks completely different," Evelyn says, breaking my reverie. "The landscape here is wilder, more dramatic."

I cut the engine, letting us drift closer. "Yeah. It's hard to move around but it's doable. We'll have to swim up there, though," I tell her. "We can leave everything in the boat."

Evelyn nods, already slipping off her sandals. A movement ahead catches her attention, and she points to a group of dark birds perched on an outcropping. "What are those?"

"Cormorants," I say, smiling. "That's actually where the island got its name—Cormoran in Spanish."

"Oh!" Evelyn shoots me a goofy look. "I never even looked up the meaning of the name. I feel a bit silly now."

"Don't," I say with a chuckle. "We never see them on the south side because there's too much boat traffic, and honestly, I didn't spot them last time I came here. They like their privacy."

"They're beautiful," she says, watching as one of the birds spreads its wings. The birds are sleek and dark, their feathers gleaming with an almost blue-black iridescence.

A wave rocks the boat, and Evelyn steadies herself with a hand on my knee. The casual touch sends a shiver through me, and when she catches my eye, I know she feels it too. Everything between us feels heightened, charged with new meaning.

"Ready to swim?" I ask, trying to focus on why we're here. The cave awaits, its crystals hidden in darkness, but right now, all I can think about is the way the sunlight catches in Evelyn's hair, how her eyes sparkle with anticipation of what I'm about to show her.

"Ready," she says, then leans across the space between us. Her lips find mine, soft and sure, and I marvel at how natural this feels now. When she pulls back, her eyes are bright with something that makes my heart skip, and I almost forget to take my shorts off until she points at them.

We dive in, and the swim is easier than during my first visit—the tide has risen enough that we can slip onto the rocky surface without fighting the current. Evelyn follows me through the narrow entrance of the cave, and I hear her sharp intake of breath as the chamber opens up before us.

"Oh my God," she whispers, her voice echoing off the walls. "Val, this is..." She trails off, turning slowly to take in the crystalline formations that surround us. The celestite catches what little light filters through the entrance, creating an ethereal blue glow that dances across the walls.

I watch her face as she absorbs it all—the towering crystal formations, the still pools that mirror the cave's ceiling, the delicate structures. Her expression of pure wonder makes my chest tighten. This is why I wanted to show her first, to share this moment of discovery.

"I've never seen anything like it," she says softly, reaching out to touch one of the crystal walls.

"Neither had I," I admit, moving closer to her. "And I've explored a few caves. This one's special."

Evelyn turns to me, her eyes reflecting the soft blue light. "You're absolutely right. This needs to be reported." There's no bitterness in her voice, just acceptance and understanding. "Thank you for showing me first. It's..." Her voice trails off, and she sits on one of the rocks.

I sink down next to her, our backs against the cave wall. Our breathing echoes, a steady rhythm as I put an arm around her and pull her in. "I've always loved places like this—quiet, unyielding, untouched by time," I say. "It's not just the natural beauty of it all. This place has an energy. There's something almost sacred about the stillness."

"Yes, it does feel sacred." She looks around in wonderment once more, then turns to me. "How big is it?"

"I have no idea and it's not safe to explore." I take her hand and squeeze it. "I wouldn't want anything to happen to you."

"And I want you to be safe too." Evelyn smiles. "Isn't it amazing? Just for now, this is our secret. No one in the world knows about this cave but us."

The weight of her words settles over me. "Our secret," I repeat in a whisper. "It's the kind of thing people search for their whole lives and never find—a place untouched by anyone else. I wanted to share it with you while I still could."

"Thank you." Evelyn reaches for my hand, threading her fingers through mine. "Maybe we were meant to be here." She hesitates. "It feels like everything before now was just a prelude to this. To you."

I brush my thumb over the back of her hand. I understand what she means; I couldn't have phrased it better myself.

"I'll carry it with me forever," I say, placing a soft kiss to her temple. "It's a part of us now."

The faint blue glow of the crystals plays across Evelyn's face. Her damp hair clings to her skin in tendrils, her cheeks flushed from the swim. She looks gorgeous. "What?" she asks when she catches me staring, her voice lilting with amusement.

"You're beautiful," I whisper, but the words don't do it justice. "You're so, so beautiful."

Evelyn opens her mouth to say something, but then she shakes her head, deciding against it. "Charmer," she jokes. She gets up, pulls me up too, and kisses me.

"You don't know how to take a compliment," I mumble against her lips.

"I'm not used to compliments," she retorts and glances around again. "I wish we could take a picture here. I doubt we'll ever come back, at least not anytime soon."

I squeeze her hand. "I'll get my phone from the boat. I have a waterproof cover."

"Wait..." She follows me. "I'm coming with you."

As we move toward the entrance, the celestite's blue glow gives way to bright daylight. The cormorants we saw earlier wheel overhead, their wings dark against the bright sky. Evelyn pauses to watch, and I study the way wonder transforms her face. One of the birds dives suddenly, breaking the surface of the water below with barely a splash, and emerges moments later with a silvery fish in its beak.

I freeze as my eyes are drawn to the water, an unnerving feeling creeping up on me. Something is missing. Scanning the water again, my stomach lurches. The boat is gone. Evelyn notices the shift in my expression, her hand tightening around mine.

"Val...where's the boat?" she asks, her voice laced with concern.

I blink, wincing against the light. Oh, God. My mind was so consumed with Evelyn that it completely slipped my mind to secure the boat. Now, it's drifted away, nowhere in sight. We're stranded on this narrow outcropping of rock with no way back to the main shore.

"I...I'm so sorry," I say. "I forgot to drop the anchor."

Chapter 49

Evelyn

"There has to be a way up." Val's eyes trace the cliff face, searching for handholds.

The rock wall towers above us, a sheer expanse of weathered limestone mottled with patches of vegetation. My heart pounds just looking at it. I've never been good with heights, but right now, we don't have much choice.

"Here," Val points to a narrow fissure that cuts diagonally across the rock face. "See how it creates a kind of natural path? We can use that."

I nod, trying to keep my voice steady. "Okay. You go first?"

She reaches for the first handhold, testing it before pulling herself up. I watch how she places her feet, trying to memorize the pattern. The sun beats down on us, and I can already feel sweat trickling down my back. We're still in our swimsuits and don't even have shoes.

"The rock's pretty solid," Val calls down. "Just take it slow and follow my path exactly."

I take a deep breath and reach for the first hold. The limestone is warm under my fingers, rough enough to provide decent grip. *Don't look down*, I tell myself. *Just focus on what's directly in front of you. One move at a time.*

Val has climbed about fifteen feet up when she pauses. "You're doing great," she says, and I can hear the careful neutrality in her voice. She's trying not to spook me. Under normal circumstances, I'd probably be frozen in terror by now, unable to move up or down. But there's something about this situation—maybe the adrenaline, maybe the absolute necessity of it—that's keeping the worst of my fear at bay.

"This next part's a bit tricky," Val warns. "There's a good foothold just to your right, about knee height. Yeah, that one."

I find it, testing my weight before committing. The height is starting to get to me, making my head swim. I press myself closer to the rock face, focusing on my breathing. In through the nose, out through the mouth. Just like that yoga class I take once in a blue moon.

"Almost to the first ledge," Val says. "Just a few more feet."

The ledge she's talking about is more of a slight widening in the fissure, barely wide enough for us to stand on. But it's a break from climbing, and that's all I care about. I haul myself up beside her, pressing my back against the cool rock wall. We're maybe thirty feet up now, and the boat's former anchoring spot looks impossibly far below.

"You okay?" Val asks.

I manage a smile. "Ask me again when we're on solid ground."

The next section looks even steeper, but I can see where

the fissure widens near the top. If we can just make it there, we might find an easier path. Val starts climbing again, moving with a confidence I envy. I follow more slowly, painfully aware of every shift in the rock beneath my hands and feet.

"There's a weird move here," Val calls down. "You'll need to reach up and right—there's a really good hold just past where you can see."

I stretch my arm out, fingers searching blindly until they find the hold she's talking about. It is good—a deep pocket in the rock that takes my whole hand—but using it requires me to lean out from the wall, and my stomach lurches at the exposure.

"I've got you," Val says, and I realize she's braced herself above me, one hand extended down. "Just push through it. You're almost there."

I take another deep breath and make the move. For a heart-stopping moment, I feel completely off-balance. Then my feet find new holds and I'm stable again. The relief is so intense it makes me dizzy.

The final section is easier, the angle of the rock finally starting to ease back. When Val pulls herself over the top edge, I almost cry with joy. A moment later, she's helping me up and we're both lying on solid ground, chests heaving, staring up at the cloudless sky.

That's when I hear the bleating. I turn my head and there they are—three goats standing a few yards away, watching us.

A laugh bubbles up from somewhere deep in my chest. It's so absurd. Here we are, having just completed this terrifying climb, and our welcoming committee is a bunch of goats.

Val props herself up on one elbow, staring at me with concern. "Evelyn, are you okay?"

"Look at their faces," I gasp between laughs. "They're just standing there, chewing."

A smile tugs at the corner of Val's mouth. "I was worried you were having a nervous breakdown."

"Oh, I'm definitely going to panic later," I assure her, wiping tears of laughter from my eyes. "But right now, this whole situation is just too ridiculous."

One of the goats takes a step closer, sniffing the air, then bleats.

Val arches a brow as she regards me. "Not scared of the goats anymore?"

"After that climb?" I shake my head, still laughing. "Trust me, the goats are the least of my concerns."

Val chuckles. "I'm really sorry. This is all my fault and I'll fix it. I'll get us off this island, I promise."

"It's okay. I didn't think about the anchor either." I steal a kiss, still buzzing with adrenaline. "If anything, I've just overcome my fear of heights and that almost makes up for everything."

Val smiles as she pushes herself to her feet, then helps me up. "We might see the boat if we start walking along the ridge, and if we don't, it's about a twenty-minute walk to the south side. There might be some boats there."

My legs are shaky as I stand, a combination of adrenaline crash and muscle fatigue. I can see why the goats like it up here—it's like their own private paradise, complete with an impressive view of the surrounding ocean.

We start walking, our path taking us through patches of tough grass and around weather-worn boulders. The goats follow at a distance; there are many more of them now.

We reach the spring about halfway across the island and

get on our knees to splash it across our faces and drink enough to get us through the next few hours. It's refreshing and I'm slowly starting to feel like myself again.

There's no sign of the boat so far, and I suspect it may have floated around the other side of the island. When we reach the southern tip, we head to a spot where the rock forms a natural lookout point. It's high enough to be visible from the water but sheltered enough that we won't be completely exposed to the sun.

"No boats apart from that one," I say, pointing to one that is too far out for people to notice us.

Val winces. "Yeah...I think that might be my boat. See that red stripe across the side?" She settles onto a relatively flat rock. "At least it's drifting toward the bay. Someone will notice we're missing eventually, but we might get lucky and spot a boat before that."

"Either way, I don't mind being stuck with you for a while," I say.

Val pulls me closer, and I rest my head on her shoulder. The breeze carries the salty smell of the ocean, and somewhere behind us, the goats bleat. It feels surreal. No phones, no distractions. My muscles ache from the climb, my skin is sticky with salt and sweat, and I should be terrified about being stranded. Instead, I feel peaceful, as if we've stepped outside of normal time into something quieter, something that belongs only to us.

I lean into her, letting her solid presence ground me.

"What are you thinking about?" Val asks, noticing my silence.

I watch a seabird wheel past our perch, riding the thermal currents with effortless grace. "Just that I'm glad to be here with you."

She laughs, pressing a kiss to my temple. "Even though

we're stranded?" Her smile softens, and she leans in to kiss me properly this time. When we break apart, she rests her forehead against mine. "For the record," she murmurs, "I don't mind being stuck with you either."

Chapter 50

Val

It's dark and that worries me. Typical. Today of all days, when we're stranded, not a single boat has passed close enough to spot us, and no one will venture out on the water at night.

I mentally calculate distances again, working angles in my head. I'm a good swimmer—I've done multiple open water competitions, even placed in a few. But the shore is at least three miles away and the currents are strong.

"I can hear you thinking," Evelyn says, and I realize I've been staring at the water for several minutes.

"Just trying to figure out options."

She shifts closer on our rocky perch, her skin cool now in the evening air. "Please tell me you're not still considering swimming for it."

"Not anymore." I wrap an arm around her shoulders. "It's too far."

"Good." She leans into me. "Because I'd have to jump in after you, and then we'd both drown, and the goats would be very disappointed in us."

I can't help but laugh. This is the thing that keeps

surprising me—how she's handling all of this. The Evelyn I first met would have been cursing and screaming before doing everything in her power to control the situation. But ever since she came back from Ibiza, it's like something's shifted. She's accepted her fate today, and she's willing to let things unfold as they will.

"I was going to take you out for dinner tonight," I say. "I even made a reservation before we left this morning. Now instead of a white tablecloth, candlelight, and amazing food, we're stuck here with empty stomachs."

"Please don't mention food." Evelyn pats her stomach. "It'll only make me hungrier."

"Sorry," I say, but I can't help myself. "What's the first thing you want to eat when we get back?"

"Seriously, don't." She groans. "But since you asked…I wouldn't mind a huge breakfast platter with crispy bacon and buttery scrambled eggs."

"And pancakes," I add, making it worse. "With real maple syrup."

"Stop it." Evelyn pokes my ribs. "Though now that you mention it, yes. Pancakes. And a massive cappuccino." She sighs. "What if we get stuck here for days? Weeks?"

"We have water and shelter from the sun," I say, then shake my head. "But that's not going to happen."

"What if it does, though? What would we eat?"

I turn to her and shoot her a smirk. "Goats?"

She laughs. "That's assuming we survive the goats."

The laughter fades into silence. The temperature is dropping now, and Evelyn shivers beside me. I'm a little chilly myself and I wish I had more than just a bikini to cover up the essentials.

"We should probably find somewhere more comfortable to sleep," I say, standing and offering her my hand. "There's softer ground near the spring, with grass." She takes my hand and rises gracefully, despite having spent hours perched on hard rock. "Have you ever slept under the stars before?" I ask as we start walking.

"Of course not." Evelyn's voice is rich with amusement. "I've never slept in anything less than five stars." She pauses for effect. "Well, until last night."

"Excuse me?" I feign offense. "My hotel room is perfectly fine."

"Mm, the bathroom amenities were lacking. And that mint on the pillow? Nowhere to be found."

"Hey, I offered you something much sweeter than a mint," I say, and even in the darkness, I can sense her smile.

We pick our way across the rocky ground, hands linked. The spring's trickle guides us forward until we reach the patch of vegetation surrounding it. In the starlight, the water gleams like liquid silver. We kneel to drink, and the water is cool and sweet against my tongue.

There's more grass here, sheltered from the harsh island winds that have weathered everything else to stubborn survival. Through the darkness, I can make out the shapes of small wildflowers, the kind that thrive in impossible places. The sound of the waves is less violent than the cliff face where we climbed, and it feels peaceful.

"At least we've secured a water source," Evelyn says, sitting back. "That's Survival 101, right?"

"Look who's suddenly an expert." I settle beside her. "What's next on the survival checklist?"

"Let's see...we have water, we have shelter—sort of." She counts on her fingers. "No food, unless we get desperate enough to try eating grass. No way to make fire. I left my matches in my other bikini."

"Shame. I was planning to send smoke signals." I shift

position, trying to get comfortable on the ground. "Marcus will have noticed something's wrong by now. I was supposed to catch up with him today and he'll have checked with the hotel since I didn't answer his calls."

"The hotel staff might not be as quick to worry about me," Evelyn says with a slight wince. "God, I should have been nicer to them. I'm always telling them to leave me alone."

"Don't worry. There's always the boat. It might wash up somewhere with our phones and belongings," I add. "Unless someone decides to help themselves to a free boat, there'll be a search-and-rescue operation once they find it."

We lie back in the grass and the sky above us is infinite. Out here, away from any artificial light, the stars are brightly scattered across the darkness. The Milky Way stretches overhead in a glittering band, and I hear Evelyn's soft intake of breath.

"Okay," she whispers, "maybe this beats five stars."

"More like a billion stars." I turn my head to look at her and my chest tightens with emotion. The goats have wandered off to wherever they spend their nights, leaving us alone in our own private world.

"I used to know all the constellations," she says. "My father taught me when I was little. That's Cassiopeia." She points to a distinctive W-shape above us. "And there's the Big Dipper...and if you follow those stars, they point to the North Star." Suddenly, she gasps and points upward. A shooting star traces a brilliant path across the sky, its tail lingering for a moment before fading away.

"Did you make a wish?" I ask.

"Yeah. I wished for pizza." She laughs, then grows quiet. After a moment, she turns on her side to face me. "But in all honesty...if I wished for anything for myself—not for Mia—it would be to feel the way I feel right now, forever."

Her words hang in the night air, weighted with meaning.

"I actually feel happy," she continues. "Not the kind of happiness that comes from achieving something or checking boxes off a list. Just...happy. Content." She shifts closer, one hand finding mine in the darkness. "I always thought I could make my life perfect through careful planning and hard work. And now here I am, stranded on an island in nothing but a bikini, drinking from a spring, and I've never felt more at peace because I'm with you."

I turn too and pull her closer, wrapping my arms around her. I want to say so much, but I don't know where to start. Maybe holding her says enough, for now. I hope she feels how much I care about her.

"Mm. That's nice." Evelyn nestles deeper into our shared warmth. She takes a deep breath and buries her face against my neck. "What did you wish for?" she whispers.

Evelyn's hair tickles my chin, and I breathe in the scent of salt and sunshine that clings to her skin.

"I didn't make a wish," I say softly, pressing a kiss to her temple. "I've got everything I want right here."

Chapter 51

Evelyn

The first thing I notice as I drift into consciousness is the unfamiliar sensation of something tickling my skin. Something feels off—the surface beneath me is far too hard, and there's a breeze. My back is stiff from sleeping on the ground, but I'm surprisingly warm, cocooned in Val's embrace. Then the events of yesterday flood back—the cave with its ethereal blue crystals, the missing boat, our terrifying climb up the cliff face, the night spent under the stars. It wasn't a dream.

Something makes me open my eyes—that peculiar sensation of being watched that sets off primitive alarms in the human brain. I'm met with a sight so surreal that for a moment, I wonder if I'm dreaming after all. A dozen or so goats are arranged in a loose semicircle around us, their pupils fixed on our sleeping forms with an unsettling intensity. They stand perfectly still, like some sort of bizarre honor guard. Their faces hold that same inscrutable expression I remember from our first encounter on the island, but they feel less threatening now.

"Val," I whisper, nudging her. Her skin is warm against mine, and I hate to wake her, but I don't know what to do and Val is better with goat management. "Val, wake up."

She stirs, mumbling something unintelligible against my neck. Her arms tighten around me for a moment, and I feel her body tense. Her breath tickles my skin as she slowly comes to consciousness.

"What's going on?" she murmurs, then her eyes flutter open. It takes her a few seconds to process the scene before us—the goats standing sentinel, the spring gurgling behind us, the morning sun. A laugh bubbles up from her chest, rich and warm. "Oh, right. Of course."

"We have an audience," I say, nodding toward our observers. My voice comes out shakier than I'd like. Even though these goats have proved harmless, there's something unnerving about waking up surrounded by them. "Is it safe to move?"

Val's laugh deepens. "They're just curious. Probably wondering why we're sleeping in their bedroom." She sits up slowly, stretching her arms above her head, completely unfazed by them. "Good morning, everyone," she calls out to the goats, who continue their unblinking surveillance.

I follow her lead, wincing as my muscles protest. Every part of me aches—sleeping on the ground is definitely not something I want to make a habit of, though waking up in Val's arms almost makes it worth it. The morning air is cool, and I remember that I'm wearing nothing but a bikini. At least no one from the board can see me sprawled on the ground, covered in grass stains, surrounded by goats.

"I don't suppose any of you brought coffee?" I ask the goats. "I'd kill for a coffee."

"I don't think they're the sharing type," Val says, then

points behind the adult goats. "Look at the little ones, though."

Several kid goats are engaged in play, bouncing and headbutting each other with infectious enthusiasm. One particularly energetic youngster attempts a sort of midair twist that ends in an ungraceful tumble, but it springs right back up, undeterred. Another one prances in circles, seemingly just for the joy of movement. Their play is mesmerizing—pure, uncomplicated happiness without any concern for dignity.

"They're totally adorable," I admit, watching as two of them engage in a jumping competition. Their tiny hooves kick up bits of grass as they bounce, and their ears flop with each landing. "Like puppies with hooves."

"Amazing what a night under the stars can do for your perspective, isn't it?" Val stands and offers me her hand. "Come on, let's make use of the spring while we're here. I have no idea what time it is, but it's best to get to the lookout point sooner rather than later."

Our peculiar audience parts to let us through like a formal reception line and stare while we drink and splash water over our faces. I catch my reflection in the small pool and have to laugh. My hair is a wild mess of tangles, there are grass stains on my knees, bruises on my legs, and my bikini is slightly askew.

"What's so funny?" Val asks, wiping water from her chin.

"Just thinking about how far I am from my usual morning routine," I say, gesturing to my disheveled state. "No coffee, no shower, no pressed suit. No email checking, no conference calls, no schedule."

"No morning room service and no mint on your pillow,"

Val teases. She reaches out to brush a blade of grass from my hair, her touch lingering. Her eyes are soft as they meet mine. "You're beautiful like this. All natural. Just you."

My heart does that funny little flip it reserves just for her. I'm about to respond when Val extends her hand. "Shall we?"

Val leads the way with the sure-footedness she seems to have acquired from the goats, and our furry companions follow. The sun is already warm on my skin, and I'm grateful we have access to fresh water.

My feet are tender and sore from walking barefoot on the rocky ground—another sensation I'm not used to. Every step reminds me how far I am from my usual world of luxury carpets and designer heels, but somehow, I don't mind. There's something almost primal about feeling the earth directly beneath my feet, even if it does hurt.

We're almost at the tip of the island when Val suddenly lets out a scream. But before panic can fully take hold, I notice she's waving her arms wildly, jumping up and down with excitement.

"Mateo!" she shouts, and as I hurry to catch up with her, I see it—a small fishing boat approaching the island, and at its helm, the familiar figure of the bartender. Relief floods through me so intensely it makes my knees weak.

Without discussion, we both scramble down to the water's edge and dive in. The sea is cool but not cold, and the swim to the boat is nothing compared to what we faced yesterday. Soon, we're being helped aboard by a grinning Mateo.

"There you are," he says as I pull myself onto the deck and, in a very un-Evelyn-like move, immediately throw my arms around him in gratitude. He seems startled by my enthusiasm but returns the hug with a chuckle. "The coast guard is out looking for you. I'll let them know you're safe. I thought I'd check here first."

"I'm so glad you did," Val says, wringing water from her hair. Small rivulets run down her shoulders, drawing my gaze to her toned arms. "You have no idea how happy we are to see you. How did you know we were here?"

"Your boat with your purses, phones, and clothes washed up near the marina early this morning," he explains. "When the hotel said you hadn't come back last night, I put two and two together."

"Thank you. Thank you so, so much," I say, still buzzing. "I don't fancy another night of sleeping on the ground, though the company was excellent."

Mateo starts the engine, turning the boat toward the mainland. "Let's get you both back so you can get dressed and—"

"No," Val and I say in unison, then look at each other and burst out laughing.

"Breakfast first," I say firmly, surprising myself with how much I sound like Val in this moment. "I haven't eaten since yesterday morning, and I want coffee and pancakes."

"And eggs," Val adds. "Don't forget the buttery scrambled eggs."

Mateo shakes his head, clearly amused by our priorities. "Breakfast it is." He looks us up and down. "It will have to be somewhere low-key where dress code isn't a priority."

As we pull away from Cormoran, I look back at the island that has become significant in ways I never expected. The goats have gathered at the edge of the cliff, watching our departure. In the morning light, they're almost regal, like guardians of their rocky kingdom. I'll never look at them the same way again.

I lean into Val and rest my head on her shoulder. Sometimes the best moments in life are the ones you never planned for, the ones that come when you finally let go of control and just let yourself be. I'm beginning to understand that now, and it feels like freedom.

Chapter 52

Val

My shoulders ache from the climb, and there's sand in places I'd rather not think about. My skin feels tight from salt and sun, and every movement reminds me of our adventure. But watching Evelyn across the table, I wouldn't change a thing. She shifts in her chair, wincing slightly—clearly as sore as I am—as she attacks her pancakes.

My first sip of coffee is heavenly. Our table is crowded with plates—stacks of fluffy pancakes drowned in maple syrup, scrambled eggs glistening with butter, crispy bacon, fresh fruit, warm croissants, and local specialties I can't even name. Mateo's kitchen staff has outdone themselves, preparing a feast.

I watch as Evelyn takes another bite of pancake, closing her eyes in pure bliss. Her hair is still damp from the sea, curling naturally around her face, and she's wrapped in a soft cotton robe the hotel provided. There's something incredibly endearing about seeing her like this—stripped of her usual polish, barefoot and hungry, completely unself-conscious about the way she's devouring her breakfast.

"I don't think I've ever been this hungry in my life," she says. "Everything tastes amazing."

"That's what happens when you skip lunch and dinner and sleep on the ground." Mateo chuckles, sipping his coffee as he watches us eat with obvious amusement. He's pulled up a chair, enjoying the show.

Evelyn reaches for the last pancake on my plate, then freezes mid-motion when I catch her eye. "Sorry," she says, looking adorably guilty.

"The great Evelyn Rothschild, stealing food from my plate?" I tease. "What would your board of directors say?"

She withdraws her hand with exaggerated dignity. "I would never. I was merely...inspecting the quality of your breakfast."

"With your fingers?"

"Quality control is a very hands-on process." She maintains her serious expression for about two seconds before breaking into laughter. "Okay, fine. I was stealing your pancake."

"Here." I push my plate toward her. "You can have it all. I'll just eat your eggs instead." I reach for her plate, and she quickly pulls it away, clutching it protectively.

"Don't you dare," she warns, but her eyes are sparkling. "I've been dreaming about these eggs since yesterday."

Mateo watches this exchange with unconcealed amusement. "Should I order more of everything?" he asks innocently. "Before it comes to blows?"

"Yes, please," we both say, then dissolve into laughter again.

"And this chair," Evelyn exclaims, shifting in her seat. "Have chairs always been this comfortable?"

I laugh, watching her face light up with genuine

wonder. "You mean you prefer it to a rocky outcrop with a side of goat droppings?"

"You don't understand," she says earnestly, running her hands along the armrests. "It has a back. And cushions. And it's not trying to impale me with limestone." She leans back with exaggerated pleasure. "I've sat in thousand-dollar ergonomic office chairs that weren't this magnificent."

"Wait until you rediscover your bed," I tease. "You might never leave it."

Her eyes go wide as she bites into a piece of bacon. "A bed. With actual pillows." She looks at me with mock seriousness. "Val, I need you to understand something. I will never, ever take pillows for granted again. Or plumbing. Or..." She glances down at her coffee cup with newfound appreciation. "Hot beverages that someone else makes for you."

Mateo, who's been trying not to laugh, finally loses it. "Should I give you two a moment alone with the furniture?"

My phone buzzes on the table—the coast guard kindly brought back my things and has returned Evelyn's purse and phone to her hotel. It's probably Marcus, who's left multiple voicemails and messages. I silence it without checking. I've sent him a message letting him know I'm okay, so whatever crisis awaits can hold for a little longer. Right now, all I want is this moment: the warm morning breeze, the taste of strong coffee, and Evelyn's bare foot brushing against mine under the table.

"So, tell me about this cave," Mateo says, leaning back in his chair. "It's crazy to think no one found it before."

Evelyn pauses, chewing another mouthful. "It's beautiful," she finally says. "Unreal. The crystals, the way they catch the light..." She trails off and smiles at me.

"That must be terrible for you, though," Mateo says to

her, genuine sympathy in his voice. "After all the work you've put into the plans."

Evelyn shrugs, surprising me with her casualness. "Some things aren't meant to be." She reaches for her coffee cup—her third already. "There will be other resorts. Cormoran belongs to the goats, and I bet it will stay that way."

"And the occasional stranded visitor," I add with a smirk.

Mateo looks between us. "You two seem so different. More relaxed," he observes. "Especially you, Evelyn. Maybe getting stranded was good for you."

"A lot of things that have happened lately have been good for me." Under the table, Evelyn's foot hooks around my ankle.

The morning sun grows stronger, casting long shadows across our table. The breakfast crowd is starting to filter in now—other hotel guests casting curious glances at our impromptu feast.

Mateo stands, stretching. "Well, I'm going to take a nap before I start my shift. If you want anything else, ask one of my lovely colleagues, and take your time with breakfast."

"Thank you," Evelyn says. "I won't forget this. Maybe Val and I can take you out for dinner to thank you before we leave?"

"I would love that." Mateo smiles. "But when are you leaving?"

Evelyn and I exchange glances, realizing we haven't discussed this.

"We'll leave after we've taken you out? How about that?" Evelyn suggests.

Mateo grins and shakes his head as he pushes back his chair. "You two are hopeless," he says with affection. "I'm free on Monday nights. I'd love to see you both before you leave." He drains the last of his coffee. "But for now, I need sleep. Some of us were up at dawn searching the coastline for stranded CEOs."

As he turns to leave, he pauses and looks back at us. "I'm glad it worked out. You're good for each other."

I watch him disappear, feeling a wave of gratitude for this man who's become a close friend. When I turn back to Evelyn, she's watching me with soft eyes. "So," I say, reaching for her hand across the table. "About our travel plans..."

"I was thinking of staying another week," Evelyn says. "How would you feel about that? Just to relax and spend time together before real life kicks in again."

"Yeah, that would be—" My phone pings again, and this time, I reluctantly pick it up, knowing Marcus won't give up. Scrolling through his messages, I smile. "Actually," I say, "how about a few more days here, and then a week on Ibiza? I need to meet Marcus there to finalize some details about the plot."

Evelyn's face lights up, and before she can respond, I add, "We could stay at the wedding venue if you want— make some new memories there."

She shoots me a mischievous look. "Deal. But only if I get to pick our next destination after that." When I look at her questioningly, she grins. "How about Vietnam? I hear the street food is amazing, and I know someone who could show us around."

Chapter 53

Evelyn

The mahogany conference table gleams in front of me. I'm sitting in the same room where we first presented our proposals, and I recognize all the committee members' faces. They look nervous as if they expect me to snap at the news I know they're about to deliver.

The Director of Sustainable Tourism leans forward with a regretful expression. "This discovery is remarkable. A cave system of this significance..." He clears his throat. "The Environmental Protection Office is preparing the paperwork to designate it as a protected site. Therefore, we regret to inform you that development is now off limits on Cormoran Island."

"I understand," I say. "I expected as much."

The mayor smiles warmly at us. "We appreciate your integrity in reporting this discovery. Many developers might have...overlooked such complications."

My stomach tightens at his words. My past self would have done exactly that—found a way to work around it, to preserve profit over preservation. The thought makes me slightly queasy now.

Val sits beside me, her foot finding mine under the table. "The cave belongs to the island," she says. "Just like the goats."

Laughter ripples around us. They've all heard about our adventure by now. Two CEOs stranded overnight on Cormoran Island. I imagine the story has grown with each retelling.

As we conclude the meeting and shake hands, I notice how differently they look at us now. There's respect there, yes, but also something warmer. More human.

"I guess that's that," Val says as we step into the sun, adjusting her bag on her shoulder. I stare at her, struck by how beautiful she is.

Our taxi driver is loading our luggage—my designer suitcase looking comically out of place next to Val's well-traveled backpack. I've shipped most of my things back to New York; everything I need for the next few weeks fits in one case.

"Are you sure about taking the ferry?" Val asks as we slide into the back seat. I notice she's watching me carefully, probably remembering my initial reactions to anything less than five-star travel.

"Hmm..." I turn to her with exaggerated seriousness. "Tell me—will there be plumbing?"

"Yes." She laughs, her eyes crinkling at the corners.

"Coffee?"

"Definitely."

"Chairs?"

"With backs and everything."

"Well, then," I say airily, settling back against the seat.

"I don't see what all the fuss is about. I'm practically a seasoned adventurer now."

Val's laughter fills the taxi and I find her hand between us. Through the window, I watch Palma's streets scroll past. Everything looks different to me now—softer, friendlier, like a blur around sharp edges. The same buildings I barely noticed before now tell stories: the way the sun catches on weathered stone, the splash of bougainvillea against white walls, the flutter of laundry strung between balconies. I notice more. I see more.

"They might name it after you," I say, turning back to Val. "The cave. Since you discovered it."

"Really? She pretends to consider this. "I don't know... The Mendoza-Rothschild Cave sounds pretty good too. Our little love child."

I laugh. "That's not how it works. You can't name it after someone who had to be dragged in."

"I didn't exactly drag you in, though, did I?"

The taxi slows to a stop at the ferry terminal before I can respond. I step out onto the sidewalk, taking in the scene before me. The sun turns the water to hammered gold, and a salt-laden breeze tugs at my hair. Somewhere across that sparkling expanse, Ibiza waits. A year ago—even a month ago—I would have seen only the distance to be crossed, the time to be managed. Now I see possibility stretching out before us like the sun's path on the water.

Val appears beside me, our shoulders brushing. "Having second thoughts about the ferry after all?"

"No." I turn to look at her, really look at her. A strand of dark hair dances across her cheek in the breeze. "I was just thinking about the first time I set foot here."

"When you arrived?"

"Mm. I was so sure of everything then. My plans, my

priorities, my whole life..." I shake my head, smiling. "I had no idea."

"Regrets?" Val's voice is light, but I hear the question underneath.

"Only that I almost missed out on you."

She smiles then, one of her radiant smiles that transform her entire face, and my heart sings.

The ferry towers above us, massive and industrial—nothing like the yachts I'm used to. Val leads the way up the metal gangplank and I take her hand and let her guide me through the crowd of passengers settling into their seats in the main cabin.

"Not in here," she says, tugging me toward a door marked "Exterior Deck." "The best views are outside."

The railing at the stern is less crowded, offering an unobstructed view of the harbor. A deep horn sounds, vibrating through the deck beneath our feet, and the engines rumble to life.

"Last chance to change your mind," Val teases. "You could still call a helicopter."

I laugh and move closer to her. "I'm exactly where I want to be."

The ferry pulls away from the dock with a lurch and the wake churns behind us, a ribbon of white foam stretching back toward the shore we're leaving. There's something symbolic about watching a place shrink into the distance, especially one that's changed you so completely. The harbor grows smaller, buildings blending into a watercolor wash of whites and terra-cottas.

"I was terrified of the goats that first day," I say. "But I think I'm going to miss them."

"They'll guard the cave," Val says, and I notice how the

wind plays with her hair, lifting strands that catch the sunlight.

A group of children race past, their excited chatter carried away by the wind. Their parents call after them in rapid Spanish, and I realize I've picked up enough of the language to understand their warnings about running on deck.

"I learned more here than I expected," I tell her. "About myself, mainly."

She turns to face me, her back against the railing. "Like what?"

I consider this carefully. "That control is overrated. That sometimes the best things in life happen when your plans fall apart." I pause, watching a seabird glide alongside us. "That I'm braver than I thought."

Val's hand finds mine on the railing, our fingers intertwining. The gesture feels natural now, when once it would have terrified me. "You were always brave," she says. "You just didn't know it."

The coastline is a thin line now, Cormoran Island barely visible to our left. It's strange to think that such a small piece of rock could alter the course of our lives.

An older couple passes us, the woman wearing a flowing kaftan that ripples in the wind. They speak softly to each other in French, sharing private jokes that make them smile. I watch them disappear around the corner and think about how differently I see people now. Before, I would have noticed their clothes, made assumptions about their wealth or status. Now I see their connection, the easy comfort between them. I hope we'll be them one day.

The ferry cuts steadily through the waves, each rise and fall marking another moment farther from shore. I close my eyes and feel the sun on my face, the salt spray settling on my skin. When I open them again, Val is watching me with a knowing look. She's the first person to see past every wall I ever built. To her, I'm not Evelyn Rothschild, the heiress and CEO, but just Evelyn, standing barefoot in a cave, sleeping under stars, learning to trust the unknown. Mallorca will become a memory, but I carry its lessons with me.

Sometimes the bravest thing is to let go of who you were and embrace who you're becoming.

Epilogue – Val

The humidity hits me like a wall as we step out of our taxi into the fading light. The hotel Mia arranged for us sits at the edge of a small street market, its weathered facade partially hidden behind laundry strung between French balconies. Tangles of electrical wires crisscross overhead, and hand-painted signs in Vietnamese script advertise the restaurant below. The building's pale-yellow paint is peeling in places, revealing patches of the original colonial architecture beneath decades of tropical weather and grime.

The Rothschilds staying in a hotel with no valet service, no doorman, and a sleeping dog as the closest thing to security seems like an absurd notion. But here we are, and somehow, it feels exactly right.

I spot them immediately—Mia, Donald, and Candy seated at a table in the open-air restaurant that spills onto the street. The space is alive with energy—fans whirring, locals chattering at nearby tables, the clatter of plates and cutlery mingling with distant traffic sounds and the occasional rooster's crow.

Evelyn pauses beside me, and I feel her tension. She's

been quiet since we landed, lost in thought. But before either of us can move, Mia spots us and bounds over, her dreads bouncing. She throws her arms around Evelyn, and they hold each other for a long moment.

"You came," Mia whispers, and I hear the layers of meaning in those two words.

"Of course I came, honey." Evelyn sniffs and wipes at her eyes.

A goat wanders past our feet, seemingly at home among the restaurant tables. Two dogs doze beneath a nearby chair, and several chickens scratch in the dirt under another table.

Donald stands as we approach. He's wearing loose linen pants and one of his signature Hawaiian shirts, his feet bare in leather sandals. He looks healthy and happy.

Evelyn greets him, and their hug surprises me. She holds on longer than necessary, and I recognize the weight of unspoken judgments in that embrace. Her father doesn't know about all the times she dismissed his happiness as a midlife crisis, all the cynical thoughts she had about Candy, all the ways she refused to understand his choices. The extended hug is her silent apology for doubts he never knew she harbored, for criticisms she kept to herself.

"You look wonderful, princess," he tells her, and she does. The past months have changed her in subtle ways. Her smile comes easier, her shoulders carry less tension, her laugh is more frequent and real. She's amazing.

Candy jumps up to hug Evelyn next, completely at ease in this humble setting. She's wearing a plain knee-length dress, her hair pulled back in a messy bun, and she looks genuinely happy to see us. A chicken pecks at her bare feet, but she doesn't seem to notice.

"I'm so glad you came too," Mia says to me, and she

pulls me into a hug. She shoots me a wink as she steps back and rubs my shoulder.

"Indeed. Val, what a lovely surprise!" Donald chips in. "You two must have become good friends."

Evelyn and I exchange glances. We haven't discussed how or when to tell them about us, and Mia clearly hasn't told them either. I can see Evelyn wrestling with the moment, but before she can speak, a server appears with plates of food, and Donald gestures for us to sit.

"Dinner first," he says to me with a smile. "Don't worry about your luggage. The staff will take it upstairs." He lowers his voice and grins. "Food before you see the room. It's...let's say it's authentic, critters and all. We didn't want Evelyn to run off before we'd shared a meal hence the impromptu sit-down. There aren't any other hotels nearby, but this is wonderfully charming in its own rustic way, and the staff is incredibly friendly."

Evelyn, who has heard the comment, laughs as she settles into a chair. "Trust me, Dad, I've slept under worse circumstances and survived without a concierge or minibar. Though I do still appreciate a good coffee in the morning."

"You mean when you got stranded?" Candy asks. "Mia told me. That must have been terrifying!"

"I wouldn't say terrifying. It was an interesting experience."

Candy points to the bar. "Well, one thing is guaranteed here and that's good coffee."

"Yes, the Vietnamese coffee is incredible," Mia chimes in. "It's like rocket fuel, but in the best possible way."

The server returns with more dishes—bowls of fragrant soup, plates of fresh herbs, grilled meats, rice, spring rolls, summer rolls, and a salad.

"You'll love the food," Mia says. "Everything's so fresh. And wait until you try the street food tomorrow."

"I'm excited," Evelyn says, and I hear the sincerity in her voice. "How are things going at the orphanage?"

"It's good, Mom. It's emotionally draining at times but really rewarding, and the kids are so sweet. I'm going to stay longer, if I'm able to extend my visa. I'm hoping for a year."

Evelyn frowns. "A year is a long time."

"Yeah. There's a little girl there, three years old, and she's been clinging to me. It breaks my heart and I honestly don't think I can leave her. I've..." Mia hesitates. "I know I'm not supposed to but I've become emotionally attached to her over the past two months. I want you to meet her."

"Oh, honey." Evelyn regards her daughter. "Of course I'd love to meet her, but...I mean, you're not thinking of..."

Mia remains silent, avoiding her gaze.

"Mia, you're such a wonderful, kind soul, but you know you can't save the whole world. You know that, right?" Evelyn presses on.

"I know." Mia nervously fiddles with her chopsticks. "But if I can save one. Make one life better..." She holds up a hand when Evelyn is about to interrupt. "Look. I know what you're going to say, and you're right. I don't have my shit together. I don't have a home or a partner, I travel all the time, and I know nothing about being a mother. But I'd be lying if I said I wasn't considering adopting her. I've thought of little else lately. It's a lengthy and complex process, but I think I can do this, Mom."

I half expect Evelyn to protest, but she doesn't. She just stares at her daughter like she's the most beautiful creature in the whole world. "Mia, being a mother is privilege and a blessing," she says softly. "And if anyone would make a great mother, it's you." She swallows hard and takes Mia's hand. "Just think about it, okay? Take your time, and if it's what you want, you have my full support."

"Really?" Mia stares at Evelyn. She clearly didn't expect this reaction.

"Yes..." Evelyn shifts her gaze to me for a beat as if her words are not just directed at Mia. "I'm here for you."

I feel my heart swell, and although I want to pull her into my arms, I restrain myself as Donald and Candy have no idea what's going on between us. I don't know if I want kids. I'm pretty sure I don't, but I also know that comes from a place of fear and who knows if I'll change my mind? Either way, Evelyn's support means everything.

"Thank you, Mom. I thought you'd try to talk me out of it," Mia says.

Evelyn tilts her head from side to side, considering this. "I've learned a lot lately. I've learned that love comes in many forms and it sneaks up on you when you least expect it. Some things are meant to be, however unconventional."

"That's beautifully said, princess," Donald agrees. "Mia told us about the little girl yesterday when we arrived, and I've been lying awake all night. Not with worry but because I'm so proud of my granddaughter."

"He was so excited, he couldn't stop talking about it," Candy adds. "And I'm here for you too, of course. Anything you need."

"What's her name?" I ask.

"Mai," Mia says. "It's an anagram of my name. That's cute, right?"

I'm close to choking up listening to this loving conversation. Somewhere in that orphanage, one very lucky little girl has no idea she'll become a Rothschild. Yes, she'll be wealthy, but most importantly, she'll be very, very loved. "You're amazing, Mia," I say. "And incredibly brave."

Mia smiles and her gaze drifts, momentarily unfocused, seeing beyond the restaurant—probably picturing Mai, imagining a future no one could have anticipated two months ago. Life can change in a heartbeat; we all know it. "Thank you. I love you all so much," she says, then straightens herself, gesturing to the food and to me and Evelyn. She's diverting the conversation as if she's worried her mother might change her mind. "Let's eat before it gets cold. You two must be hungry after the long journey."

"We're just glad to be here," I say, certain I'm speaking for us both. Evelyn, who was nervous about telling her father about our relationship, has visibly relaxed beside me, a genuine smile plastered all over her face.

"Yes, it's wonderful that you could join us, Val." Donald passes me a bowl of phở that smells incredible. "You must be busy with your new project on Ibiza. Mia told me."

"Oh, I'm busy enough," I say. "But I don't need to be on site. My team is dealing with it and I check in with them a few times a day. And Evelyn's in talks about a potential acquisition in the Caymans, so we'll probably need to hunt down a coffee shop with reliable Wi-Fi tomorrow. But that's the beauty of it—we get to work and travel together."

Evelyn's hand finds mine under the table, and I give it a squeeze. She takes a deep breath, and I know what's coming.

"Actually, Dad," she starts, "Val and I..." She pauses, and I see Mia grin through a mouthful. "We're together."

The words hang in the humid air for a moment. Donald's chopsticks pause halfway to his mouth, and Candy's eyes widen.

"Together?" he repeats. "As in..."

"As in together," Evelyn confirms. "We've been seeing each other since Mallorca."

Donald sets down his chopsticks and glances between us. He looks confused more than anything. "You're serious..."

"Yes." Evelyn turns to me and meets my eyes with a smile. She's blushing and it's adorable.

Donald leans back in his chair, running a hand through his silver hair. "How did I not know this about you?" he asks. "All these years..." He looks at Mia. "Did you know?"

"Only because I walked in on them." Mia chuckles. "I'm not entirely sure Mom would have told me otherwise." She shoots Evelyn a look that's part amusement, part lingering reproach.

"Oh, my God! This is amazing!" Candy practically bounces in her seat, her enthusiasm cutting through the tension. "We have so much to celebrate! I knew there was something brewing in Mallorca. Didn't I say that, Donald?"

Donald frowns and nods. "Yes, you did, sweet pea. And I told you that was a ridiculous assumption." He turns to us and studies me, then Evelyn, like he's trying to spot signs of gayness or whatever proof it is he's looking for. He dabs his mouth with a napkin and clears his throat. "Needless to say, I'm happy for you both. Love is all I ever wanted for you, Evelyn. I just... It's just unexpected."

"I understand. Much like how I felt when you first told me about Candy." Evelyn smiles at Candy. "No offense."

The irony isn't lost on anyone at the table. Donald looks at his daughter, then lets out a short laugh. "I suppose you're right," he says, picking up his chopsticks again.

"I knew how you felt about me," Candy says. "When your father and I got together." She stirs her soup, pausing. "But I figured words wouldn't mean much. I could have told you my intentions were sincere, tried to convince you that I genuinely love your father, but you wouldn't have believed me. So I decided to let time do the work—to let you see for yourself how happy we are together."

Something shifts in Evelyn's face as the words sink in. I can see her reassessing Candy, noting the wisdom in her approach, the dignity beneath the bubbly exterior. The moment stretches.

"I'm sorry," Evelyn says finally. "You're right. I judged you unfairly."

Candy shakes her head. "Don't be sorry. Just pass the spring rolls—they're getting cold."

A ripple of laughter breaks across the table. Evelyn laughs along, the sound infectious and genuine. Candy isn't the overexcited, social-media-obsessed woman everyone assumed her to be. There's a quiet strength there, a well of patience and emotional intelligence that has gone unnoticed.

"So what's the plan?" Candy asks, helping herself to a spring roll. "New York and San Francisco are quite far apart."

"We haven't figured that out yet," Evelyn admits, glancing at me. "For now, we're taking each day as it comes."

"And cherishing every moment," I add, wrapping an arm around her. "We'll work out the logistics eventually, but it's not a concern to me. I'll do anything to be with the woman I love." I pause, realizing what I've just said—that I've spoken aloud the feeling I've carried in my heart for a while. I turn to Evelyn and brace myself, hoping it's not too soon. "It's true, you know. I love you."

Evelyn's eyes fill with tears, and I see everything in them—our short past, our present, our future. "I love you too," she whispers, her voice thick with emotion.

The words land like a gentle earthquake, shifting everything inside me. My heart doesn't just race—it explodes. It's as if every moment we've shared suddenly crystallizes into something more tangible. It's not just a declaration of love. It's a promise, and when she smiles, I cup her cheeks, the blurry vision from my own tears taking in her gorgeous face.

Donald sniffs, breaking the moment, and he gets up to hug us both from behind. His arms envelop us, pulling us close in a prolonged embrace that speaks volumes more than words. His body trembles, not just a fleeting quiver but a sustained shaky squeeze. Happy tears trace slow paths down his cheeks, warm and unashamed, landing on my shoulder. He holds us for several heartbeats longer, communicating everything he cannot articulate.

When he releases us, he takes a moment to kiss Evelyn's cheek before settling back next to Candy, letting out a long breath and a chuckle. "Forgive me for my outburst," he says. "I seem to have gotten a little sentimental. I blame Candy. She made me human again," he jokes, his eyes still glistening and his smile wide.

"Yes, my robot father's mechanics are broken and it's all your fault," Evelyn agrees, equally trying to lighten the mood. She shoots Candy a sweet look. "I never thought I'd say this, but thank you."

"Aww..." Candy leans in close to Donald and kisses his temple. "I love love," she says with a swoony sigh. "Look at us. The most dysfunctional family on paper, yet we couldn't be happier." She turns her attention to me and grins mischievously. "Speaking of dysfunctional... Val, are you ready to be a grandmother at twenty-eight?"

"Oh, I can beat you on that," I say with a smirk.

"Fair game." Candy humorously rolls her eyes. "Just say it."

I lean in and point at her. "Are you ready to be a great-grandmother at twenty-eight?"

Laugher breaks out again and I sit back, taking Evelyn's hand. Sure, I'm rubbing it in, but we need to be able to talk and laugh about these things. The world will judge us, no doubt, but in the end, we *are* family, imperfect and unexpected, bound not by blood alone but by something far more powerful: understanding, support, and love that stretches beyond the boundaries we once thought defined us.

The night cradles us in its humid embrace. Somewhere between the tangled electrical wires, the roosters' calls, and the noise of sizzling woks, we exist—not as perfect beings, but as travelers mapping entirely new territories of the heart. We are a constellation of improbabilities, connected by threads more intricate than blood, more enduring than conventional understanding—a family stitched together by moments of raw vulnerability and the quiet courage of choosing each other. And together, we are more than we were.

Afterword

I hope you've loved reading The Turning Tides of Us as much as I've loved writing it. If you've enjoyed this book, would you consider rating it and reviewing it? Reviews are very important to authors and I'd be really grateful!

Sign up to my monthly newsletter and get a free novella: https://BookHip.com/XQMDKJW

About the Author

Lise Gold is an author of lesbian romance. Her romantic attitude, enthusiasm for travel and love for feel good stories form the heartland of her writing. Born in London to a Norwegian mother and English father, and growing up between the UK, Norway, Zambia and the Netherlands, she feels at home pretty much everywhere and has an unending curiosity for new destinations. She goes by 'write what you know' and is often found in exotic locations doing research or getting inspired for her next novel.

Working as a designer for fifteen years and singing semi-professionally, Lise has always been a creative at heart. Her novels are the result of a quest for a new passion after resigning from her design job in 2018.

When not writing from her kitchen table, Lise can be found cooking, at the gym or singing her heart out some-where, preferably country or blues. She lives in London with her dogs El Comandante and Bubba.

Also by Lise Gold

Lily's Fire

Beyond the Skyline

The Cruise

French Summer

Fireflies

Northern Lights

Southern Roots

Eastern Nights

Western Shores

Northern Vows

Living

The Scent of Rome

Blue

The Next Life

In The Mirror

Christmas In Heaven

Welcome to Paradise

After Sunset

Paradise Pride

Cupid Is A Cat

Members Only

Along The Mystic River

In Dreams

Chance Encounters

Songbirds of Sedona

Red Rock Ranch

Mistletoe Motel

Under the pen name Madeleine Taylor

The Good Girl

Online

Masquerade

Santa's Favorite

Spanish translations by Rocío T. Fernández

Verano Francés

Vivir

Nada Más Que Azul

Luciérnagas

Solo Para Socios

German translations by Iris Pilzer

Members Only: Nur für Mitglieder

Hindi translations

Zindagi